Falling Embers

THE TATTERED & TORN SERIES

CATHERINE COWLES

Editor: Susan Barnes
Copy Editor: Chelle Olson
Proofreading: Julie Deaton and Janice Owen
Paperback Formatting: Stacey Blake, Champagne Book Design
Cover Design: Hang Le
Cover Photography: Michaela Mangum

Dedication

For Laura & Willow.

The Love Chain is one of the greatest gifts this writing world has brought me. Thank you for the never-ending laughter in good times and bad, encouragement that means I never feel alone, and love that moves mountains. Oh, and for brainstorming the titles for this series with me until you were probably ready to pull out your hair.

Love you both to the moon and back.

Falling Embers

Prologue

Hadley

PAST

"Hads, you know there's no way she's going to let you go."

I leaned back against my bed and cradled the phone against my ear. "I think I can convince her."

Jenna was silent for a moment before speaking. "I know you've got megapowers of persuasion, but your mom is on another level."

I didn't need my best friend to tell me that. I lived with my mother's overprotectiveness every day. No, *overprotective* wasn't the right word. It was paranoia.

"I'm going to go talk to her now. I'll call you back when I'm done."

"Okay." Doubt dripped from Jenna's tone. She'd watched me go down this road too many times before.

But I wouldn't let her doubt get to me. I was holding on to hope. I pushed to standing and started for the door. I paused as I pulled it open, listening. I could hear voices wafting up from downstairs and moved in that direction.

"It sounds like a herd of elephants is invading," my dad called as I pounded down the stairs.

"Just one daughter," I told him, rounding the corner.

He had a baseball game on mute as my mom worked on hand-stitching a quilt.

"Where's Shiloh?" I asked.

Mom's jaw tightened, and I knew I'd already made a misstep. I shouldn't have asked. My dad gave me a smile that didn't reach his eyes. The kind I'd seen far too many times during the past eight years. "She needed some air, I think. She's in the barn with the horses."

My sister practically lived out there these days. And every time she ran off, a muscle in my mom's cheek fluttered, or her knuckles bleached white—as they were now.

I didn't know what to say. Not when we were already starting here. Instead, I shuffled from foot to foot, rethinking my approach.

Dad patted the couch cushion next to him. "Take a seat and tell us what you're working through in that big brain of yours."

His words had my mom lifting her gaze from her stitching and eyeing me carefully. I swallowed as I sat, my throat seeming to catch on the movement. I tucked a leg under me. "I wanted to ask you something."

"Go ahead," Dad said.

I toyed with a loose thread on the couch cushion. "Jenna is going to a party at Toby Jacob's house tonight. I know you're not crazy about parties, but I really want to go. I promise I won't drink anything but sealed bottled water. You can breathalyze me if you want. And I'll text you every thirty minutes, so you know I'm okay. I'll stay with Jenna the whole time."

Mom's knuckles lost even more color. "Hadley—"

"Are his parents going to be home?" Dad cut her off.

"Um, no. But they know he's having the party. They're in Portland this weekend."

My mom tossed her stitching onto the coffee table. "I can't believe the Jacobs would be that irresponsible. Letting a bunch of kids run wild in their home while they're away. Drinking. Probably drugs. Anything could happen."

"Now, Julia," my father began, but Mom cut him off with a glare.

"Anything, Gabe. Absolutely *anything* could happen."

"But not to me. I'll be so careful. I promise."

Mom's gaze shot to me. "You might be careful, but you could still get hurt because of someone else's reckless decision. I won't risk it."

"Please, Mom," I whispered. "Everyone in my class will be there. I don't want to be the freak anymore."

She stiffened. "You are not a freak simply because your parents want to make sure you're safe."

But I was. Everyone whispered. The girl whose sister had been kidnapped. The girl whose parents practically kept her locked in a bubble. The girl who never got invited to anything anymore because people had given up. Jenna was my only friend, but I could feel even that relationship waning. It was too hard for her.

I looked at both my parents. "I only have one friend because no one wants to put up with the insanity it takes. I have no life. It's pathetic."

"Hadley," Dad warned. "You're not pathetic. And you have a wonderful life. You ride horses, we go to the lake, go on hikes. That would be a pretty good life to some people."

"But what about the life *I* want? To go to a party. God, maybe even on a date. To ride the bus to away games like everyone else. But, no. All of those things are too dangerous."

"Stop it." My mom's voice lashed out like a whip. "How can you be so selfish? You know what we went through with your sister."

"Newsflash, Shiloh's fine. It's awful what happened to her, but it was eight years ago. Please don't steal my life because of it."

"Go to your room, right now," my mother barked.

I turned on my heel and ran. But not upstairs. I went out the front door. The house walls felt too claustrophobic, my parents bearing down, everything closing in around me. I tried to suck in air as the door slammed behind me. But I couldn't seem to get my lungs to obey.

I started towards the paddocks as tears streamed down my cheeks, and I willed my lungs to cooperate. As I rounded the corner of the barn, I collided with a solid form.

Hands encircled my arms to steady me. "Shit, Hads. Sorry, I didn't see you."

I tried to get out my own apology, but no words came. The fact that I was struggling to find my voice only made it harder to breathe.

"Hads? What's wrong?" There was a slight panic to Calder's voice. "Want me to get your mom and dad? Hayes?"

I shook my head quickly, but the movement was jerky. I didn't want my older brother, and I certainly didn't want my parents.

"Okay. I won't get them, but I need you to slow your breathing, okay? You're going to pass out."

He would know the facts about that. While my two older brothers had gone to college, Calder had only had eyes for the fire department. He'd done both fire school and EMT training but opted to focus on being a firefighter.

He guided me towards a bale of hay and eased me down onto it. "I'm going to count. Just follow me. In for one, two, three. Out for one, two, three."

My lungs burned as I struggled to hold the inhale and exhale for his counts. Then he upped the count to five. Then eight. Then back down to five again. I couldn't figure out the rhyme or reason for the pattern, but the burn slowly receded, and it no longer felt as if my rib cage was crushing my lungs.

"Thank you," I croaked.

Calder's dark eyes searched my face as he stayed crouched in front of me. "What brought this on?"

I stared down at my boots, thankful the darkness would hide the worst of my splotchy face. "Fight with Mom and Dad."

"About?"

"Having a life. What else?"

Calder pushed up and leaned against the fence. "You know they went through a lot when Shiloh was kidnapped. It's hard for them to loosen the reins now that you're all home and safe."

"It's been eight years. Am I really supposed to give up everything because of it? I have no one because there isn't a soul who's willing to put up with my parents. And, sometimes, it's just too much. I just want a little normal. I want to be able to breathe. To feel *alive*. Just once."

He stared at me for a few moments and then pulled out his phone, tapping a couple of buttons. "Hey, Gabe, it's Calder." Pause. "I've got Hads with me."

I stiffened at that. If he told my dad where I was right now, I'd knee him in the nuts.

"Yeah. Listen, can I take her to blow off some steam for a bit? I'll be with her the whole time." Calder chuckled. "No, I think I'm a little old for high school parties. I'm just gonna take her for a drive." Silence. "I'll call if we'll be later than ten-thirty."

He hung up and then slid his phone into his pocket. "Let's go."

I scowled at him. "You know you were in high school three years ago. It's not like you're forty."

"True enough. I'm still not taking you to that pipsqueak Toby's party."

"Fine," I grumbled but pushed off the bale of hay.

Calder beeped the locks on his SUV. "Hop in."

I climbed into the passenger seat and waited as he started the engine. "Where are we going?"

"You'll see."

We were both quiet for a bit as he drove. The darkened fields and forests blurred until it almost looked like a painting.

"They love you. You know that, right? It's where all of this comes from."

"I know." A fire lit along my sternum, a potent mixture of guilt and the desire for more. For a life. For freedom. "Sometimes, I feel like I'm going to crawl out of my skin. Like I'm drowning and burning up all at the same time. Just once, I want it to be okay for me to be whoever I want."

His gaze flicked to me for a brief moment before returning to the road. "Sometimes, it's worth it to stand your ground and fight for that."

"Like being a firefighter?"

His mouth curved, but I saw a hint of pain behind his eyes. "My dad was never crazy about the idea, but I knew it would make me happy." He paused, his hands tightening on the wheel. "You should fight for your happiness, Hads. Even if it ruffles feathers."

I looked out the window as the mountain drew nearer. "I don't think I've really had a chance to find out what makes me happy."

Calder turned off the two-lane highway. "Let's see if we can't find you some of those things."

I searched the stretch of road in front of us. "I thought this was closed for the Fourth." It led to the top of the peak, where they set off the fireworks each year.

"Good thing I know the code to the lock." He slowed the SUV to a stop and hopped out. Heading to the gate, he punched in a code on the lockbox and opened it. He hurried back to drive us through and then locked the gate behind us.

Silence reigned again as Calder guided his SUV up the winding, paved road until we reached the overlook. It was a beautiful spot, looking out over the valley below. The stars felt as if they were close enough to touch.

Calder shut off the engine and turned to face me. "You want to feel alive?"

"Yes." I wanted it more than anything. No more of this half-life I was living. If almost losing Shiloh had taught me anything, it was that nothing was guaranteed. I wanted to live every moment to its fullest.

"Let's go."

We climbed out of the SUV, and Calder rounded to the back, raising the hatch. Two bikes and helmets were back there. I recognized one as belonging to Hayes.

"Are you guys going mountain biking?"

"Tomorrow. But I don't think Hayes will mind if you borrow his tonight. I just need to lower the seat." Calder had me stand next to the bike as he pulled out tools and made some adjustments. Then, he motioned for me to climb on. "How's that feel?"

"Good, I think."

"Okay." He picked up a helmet and put it on me, adjusting the straps.

My breath hitched as the rough pads of his fingers grazed my skin. Every time he got close to me, my heart took up acrobatics in my chest. But this was more.

Calder jostled the helmet. "Feel secure?"

I cleared my throat, ignoring the heat I felt in my cheeks. "Yup."

"Okay." He flicked on a light at the front of my bike. It was a lot brighter than I expected, illuminating at least twenty feet or more in front of me.

Calder pulled on a helmet and climbed onto his bike. "Want to fly?"

"Fly?"

"You wanted to feel alive. There's nothing like taking a bike down a mountain."

My heart rate picked up speed. We were going to take these bikes down that windy road in full dark?

He looked me in the eyes. "Remember, you're in control. Check your brakes before you pick up too much speed."

"Okay."

"I'm going to follow behind you, so if you get scared, just stop."

"I'm not scared." I was terrified. But I wouldn't let Calder know that.

"There's no shame in fear. It's how you tackle it that counts."

I met his gaze. "Let's go."

He grinned. "Lead the way, Little Daredevil."

I guided my bike towards the start of the road. Giving myself a few good peddles, I checked my brakes as Calder had instructed. They were nice and strong.

I gave a few more rotations, and the bike picked up speed. The wind made my hair whip out behind me, and my adrenaline cranked up a notch.

"That's it," Calder called.

I grinned into the night and went faster. I leaned into one turn after the other. It was as if I were made for this. My body instinctively knew what to do.

The wind stung my eyes and cheeks, but I didn't care. My heart pounded in my chest, but for once, it wasn't because I was angry at having to sit yet something else out. It was because I was alive and truly living.

The light from the stars blurred overhead as I went even faster. The trees beside me lost their shape. I was flying.

For the first time in forever, I felt completely free.

Chapter Two

Calder

Blood roared in my ears. I'd watched the whole thing as if it were happening in slow motion. It was the speed at which the biker approached the drop that had concerned me at first. I was sure I'd have to call the paramedics after a crash. And then the person had launched themselves into the air, flipping before landing hard.

When they'd taken off their helmet, and I'd seen those white-blond locks, all the air had left my lungs. I'd moved before considering the wisdom of it. "I asked you a question," I growled.

Hadley met my stare, not looking away. "I don't answer to you."

The roaring in my ears intensified.

"Dude, maybe you need to take a breather."

I took in the boy-man next to Hadley. Toby Jacob hadn't changed a bit. He'd stirred up trouble all through high school, and it seemed he was still doing it today. I thought he worked part time at a bike shop in town and lived above it. I took a few steps forward. "Don't tell me to take a breather, *dude*."

"What's your problem?" Hadley huffed.

"My problem? Oh, I don't know. Maybe you tearing down th

trail like your ass was on fire and then launching yourself into the air. You could've broken your neck."

Saying the words aloud had my rib cage tightening around my lungs, making it hard to suck in air. The girls would've been devastated if something had happened to Hadley. As strained as things had become between Hadley and me, she'd never let it affect her relationship with Birdie and Sage. But she put that in jeopardy by doing stuff like this.

"Newsflash, Officer Safety, I know what I'm doing, and I wear protective gear."

The other man-boy next to Hadley snickered. His name was Josh, but his friends called him something idiotic I couldn't remember.

My jaw ticked at Hadley's less-than-affectionate nickname. "None of that shit protects you from a broken neck."

Hadley strode forward and shoved me towards the parking lot, away from her so-called friends. "For your information, I wear a neck brace. And I practice a trick in a foam pit dozens of times before I try it on land."

I took in the woman in front of me. My gaze traveled over her face. Those piercing, ice-blue eyes. Her pale skin now flushed pink around her cheeks. "When did you start all of this?"

We'd done our share of riding over the years, even pulled some tricks on mountain bike trails, but nothing like this.

She looked out to the forest beyond us. "It's been years. You just didn't care to know about it."

That cut more than it should've. "If you hadn't noticed, I've been a little busy. I have two daughters who count on me."

That blue heat flared as she turned her gaze back to me. "Don't you dare put this on Birdie and Sage."

Hell. She was right. That wasn't fair. "I don't want you to end up hurt."

"And I don't want to play it safe." Hadley's eyes pleaded with me. Begged for understanding. For a little bit of that thing we'd once shared.

But I couldn't give it to her. Not anymore. "You don't know what it's like to almost lose the people you love most in the world. I do. That's what will kill you. Not taking up a normal sport that won't get you paralyzed."

Hadley looked as if I'd slapped her, but I couldn't let her hurt sink in. Instead, I stalked towards my truck, climbed in, and slammed the door. The roaring in my ears didn't let up even as I pulled out of the parking lot and headed out onto the dirt road that led to Wolf Gap.

I checked my odometer as I pulled onto the two-lane highway and eased off the accelerator a bit. I cracked my neck in an attempt to relieve a little of the pressure that'd settled there. I hated fighting with Hadley. Everything about it felt wrong, but it seemed it was all we were capable of anymore.

I slowed my speed even more as the highway brought me downtown. I could've made the rest of the drive with my eyes closed. I liked that kind of familiarity. It was reassuring, somehow. I'd never understand how my parents left this community behind, even for sunshine and sandy beaches. Even now, they rarely left Tampa to visit.

I shoved down the flicker of annoyance. I'd tried more than once to get them to have a better relationship with their granddaughters, but nothing I said seemed to penetrate. Luckily, the girls had the Eastons. I'd spent so much time at Hayes' house growing up that it shouldn't have surprised me that Julia and Gabe had stepped in for Birdie and Sage in such a massive way. But it did. They were the grandparents the girls deserved.

I turned off Aspen Street, leaving behind the shops with the Old West façades and lampposts that had recently been decorated for spring with hanging pots of flowers. As I did, the mountains came into full view. I'd never get tired of the sight. Those epic peaks and the lake that lay at their base were just a few of the many reasons I felt grateful to raise my girls here.

Wolf Gap was a town where people looked out for their neighbors and did anything to help if someone was down on their luck.

Most residents didn't even bother locking their doors. I didn't have to worry about the girls playing in the front yard or even walking to school themselves someday.

I pulled into the driveway of our gray two-story. The front porch had sold me on the place. I could picture watching the girls playing in the yard from that very spot as they grew up. Birdie and Sage must've heard my truck because the screen door banged against the frame. I took a long breath, rolling my shoulders back. I wouldn't let any of the stresses of my day leak into my time with my daughters.

I climbed out of my truck and started up the steps to the front yard. Birdie hit me on the fly, her arms wrapping around me. "I thought you weren't coming home till later. That's what Addie said."

"I decided to bail on my run." More like Hadley had stolen that plan out from under me. She might be free to put her life at risk, but I didn't have to watch.

"Yay!" she cheered.

Sage smiled up at me as I ruffled her hair. "Hey, Daddy."

"Hey, Buttercup. How was your day?"

She pressed into my side. "Good. Addie showed me how to press flowers into a book."

"That sounds like fun." I started towards the house, one arm wrapped around Sage as Birdie skipped around us, chattering about their trip to the park.

I looked up at Addie, waiting on the front porch. "Thanks so much for watching them again."

"I'm happy to." Her voice was soft, and she took a step back as I approached. I knew it was instinct, born of the situation she'd only recently removed herself from, but it still had my jaw tightening.

She shuffled her feet, looking down. "I made some chicken white bean chili. It's cooling on the stove."

My stomach rumbled at the mention. "Appreciate that. Make sure you take some home with you."

"Oh, I don't need—"

"Addie. Please. Take some home for dinner."

Her fingers braided into some sort of intricate knot in front of her. "Okay. Thank you."

"Do you want a ride home?" It was still light out, but I didn't want Addie worrying about running into her father or what that run-in might lead to.

"I'll walk. I could use the fresh air. Do you want me to pick up the girls from school tomorrow again?"

"That would be great." It had been a godsend, having an extra set of hands. One of our neighbor's college-aged daughters stayed with Birdie and Sage when I pulled an overnight shift at the firehouse, but we'd been desperate for after-school help for the past few months after our regular sitter had moved to Portland.

Hayes' fiancée, Everly, had suggested that her cousin might be a good fit. And she had been. Something about her quiet spirit had been especially good for Sage. And Birdie loved Addie's cooking.

Addie smiled at Sage and Birdie. "See you guys tomorrow."

"Will we bake cookies?" Birdie asked hopefully.

"I was thinking peanut butter chocolate."

"Yes!" Birdie cheered.

Sage ducked forward and gave Addie a quick hug. "See you tomorrow."

Addie waved and headed out the front door.

"Hey, Dad?"

"Yeah, Birds."

"Will Hads come over to bake with us, too? We haven't seen her in *forever*."

I stiffened. It hadn't been forever. It had been two days. "I'm sure she'll stop by soon." Guilt pricked at my skin. Hadley hadn't deserved my anger earlier. She'd just scared the hell out of me with that stunt she'd pulled.

"She said we'd have a sleepover and watch *Annie*," Sage added. "She said it was her favorite movie growing up."

A memory slammed into me of Hadley standing on the couch in the Eastons' living room, belting out *Tomorrow* at the top of her lungs. She'd been nowhere near on key, but that hadn't stopped her. Hadley had always lived her life unapologetically, pretty much from the moment she could walk. She never let anyone squash that spirit.

And I didn't want to do that now, but I didn't want her to be reckless, either. Yet, whenever I tried to explain that to her, it never came out right.

I looked at my daughters, mirror images of each other with dark hair and amber eyes. "What? Is your old man chopped liver?" I went for Sage's sides, tickling her. "Are you too cool for me already?" I dove for Birdie next.

"Daaaaad!" she yelled, grabbing a pillow from the couch and hitting me with it.

"You know what that means…"

The girls froze.

"War!" I shouted.

Everyone grabbed a pillow, and chaos ensued. But their shrieks of delight were worth every single feather of the dozens I'd have to pick up later. It meant that my girls were safe. Happy. And I would do everything in my power to keep them that way. Even if I'd failed before.

Chapter Three

Hadley

AS I PULLED INTO AN EMPTY SPOT AT THE FIRE STATION, my phone buzzed in my cupholder. I swiped it up, reading the text.

Toby: *Video is live, and people are freaking! I hear those sponsorship dollars calling…*

Me: *Your money-hungry nature is really showing.*

Toby: *What can I say? I'm a capitalist at heart. But, seriously, check it out.*

Me: *I will. Thanks for editing and uploading.*

Toby: *Always.*

I exited out of my messages and switched over to the app we used. *Voyeur* had been steadily growing in popularity, and I wouldn't be surprised if it reached a YouTube level, eventually. But I liked it better. It was more homegrown, less professional-studio-production quality. Just people posting videos of things they were good at.

Some were more like instructional how-tos. Others were day-in-the-life kinds of things. My videos were a mixture. Some like the one Toby had put up today were highly edited, set to music, and cut in a way that made it look more like an amateur action film. But, sometimes, I went for a simpler approach. I'd taken my GoPro when I hiked a section of the Pacific Crest Trail alone. I'd revealed pieces of my soul in that video, almost like a diary. Something about the anonymity made it so I was completely free to be myself and encourage others to do the same.

I pulled up the latest video on my account and pressed play. I'd give it to Toby: he always made me look like way more of a badass than I actually was. The way he spliced cuts of video together. The music he chose. It was all perfect. I held my breath as I watched the drop down and then the flip.

I could still feel the rush—that moment of complete weight-lessness. Watching the landing made my lower back twinge. Not even my brutal ice bath last night had completely relieved the pain.

Toby had more than earned his percentage of any sponsorship dollars that came in on this one. I scrolled down to the comments. I grinned at some familiar screen names leaving a trail of excited emojis and vows to try the trick themselves. There were the usual trolls, too. I snickered at BMXgrl21, who suggested that I might have gained some weight because I wasn't catching air the way I used to. There would always be haters, and I would always mute that noise.

A knock sounded at my window, and I jumped. Calder's face appeared. I quickly locked my phone and shoved it into my bag.

"Hey," I greeted as I climbed out of my SUV. I scanned his face, looking for any clues as to what I might be in for. With Calder, I never knew anymore. Sometimes, I'd get a glimpse at that bond we used to share, but more often than not, I ended up with foe and not friend.

"Hey." He twirled his keys around his finger. "You and Jones on duty?"

He knew we were. Calder had moved up to lieutenant a few years ago and was now shadowing our captain in hopes of taking over for him when he retired next year. That meant he helped oversee all of the schedules for not just the firefighters but also EMTs like Jones and me.

"Yup."

Calder's key-swinging stopped, and his hand fisted around them. "That's all you're going to say?"

"What else did you want me to say?"

"Yell at me. Call me a prick."

I arched a brow. "A prick, huh?"

His lips twitched. "I thought it was a good start."

I looked up at the man who had once been my closest friend. The person who had understood me better than anyone. It would've been easier if I'd thought he was a prick. But I knew why he was how he was now. I knew that it came from wounds that would likely never heal. I still couldn't give him what he wanted.

I couldn't take up knitting as a hobby and feel happy and fulfilled. I understood why he'd backed away from biking and the climbing we used to do together. I understood why he didn't want me doing any of it, either. But I couldn't change who I was. And where did that leave us? With some sort of tenuous tightrope to walk.

"I'll let you off the hook if you take kitchen duty for me. I'm supposed to be cleaning up after Mac."

Calder groaned. "That's mean."

Mac was by far our best cook, but he was also the messiest. Pulling cleanup duty after him, meant hours in the kitchen.

"But if you do it, I won't even call you a prick."

"Fair enough." He started for the station, inclining his head for me to follow. "You going to dinner at your parents' on Sunday?"

Now it was my turn to groan. I had two voicemails and three unreturned texts from my mom. "I'm on duty."

Calder was quiet as we walked inside. "I think if you showed up every week, she might get off your case a bit."

"She has no reason to be on my case in the first place." I sucked in a breath, air hissing through my teeth. "Sorry, I'm not trying to bite your head off."

He caught my elbow, bringing me to a stop. "Are things getting worse?"

The heat of Calder's hand seeped into my skin, even through my uniform jacket. "She's been on edge ever since things happened with Everly."

When someone had kidnapped my brother's fiancée last year, it had brought back memories of Shiloh's kidnapping for all of us. But we'd all made it through. Everly was safe, and so was Shiloh. I was empathetic to what my mom was going through but I couldn't take her trying to control me anymore.

Calder dropped his hold on my arm. "Understandable."

"I know it's understandable. And I feel for her. But I'm also not going to let her micromanage my life because it'll make her feel better."

Calder's lips pressed into a firm line. "I know Hayes had a talk with her, but I can try—"

"No," I cut him off. "She'll just blame me for turning you against her."

"She wouldn't."

I raised my brows. "Really?"

He gave me a sheepish grin. "Or she might."

I scoffed, but before I could get out a response, the siren sounded. We immediately started moving as dispatch relayed a call—car accident off one of the back roads outside of town.

Captain Murray appeared in the hallway as the rest of the squad hurried to don their gear. "You coming with?" Calder asked.

Cap jerked his chin. "Sounds like a bad one. I want to be there."

If he didn't come along, Calder would be in charge. But one of the things I admired most about Calder was that this kind of thing was never a power play for him. He would always accept all the help he could get.

Calder nodded in assent and then jogged towards the garage. I followed behind, catching sight of Jones just as he climbed behind the wheel. I hoisted myself up into the cab.

"You ready to rock and roll, Easton?"

I held my hand out for a knuckle bump. "You know it."

It was always a thrill when the sirens went off. Even though it meant that something bad had happened, it also meant that we had the opportunity to help.

Jones flicked on our lights and sirens. We were usually out the bay doors before the two fire engines, but if we were headed to the scene of a blaze, we'd have to wait for backup. Something like a car accident, it depended. If there was no immediate danger, we could proceed and treat casualties. I hoped that was the case today.

I grabbed the bar above my head as Jones took a tight turn. He shot me a wink and a grin as he straightened us out.

"You enjoy that far too much."

"Is it really a crime to love your job?"

"If it kills me, then yes, it is."

He chuckled. "You never want me to have any fun."

"Greg would be pissed if you got dead on my watch."

Jones' eyes alit at his husband's name. "True enough. He wants to know if you want to come over for a barbeque on our next day off."

"I'd love that. I'll bring the beer."

"I know better than to ask you to bring something you cooked."

"Hey," I griped. "I might not be a skilled chef, but I am an *excellent* baker."

"True enough. You can bring that sugar berry thing you made last year."

"A pavlova?"

"That's the one. Shit, that was good."

I chuckled. "Sugar was always the way to your heart."

My laughter died on my lips as Jones pulled the rig up to where two vehicles had collided on the side of the road, one hanging precariously over the side of the ravine. It looked as if the only thing keeping it from falling was a short tree stump caught on the undercarriage of the luxury sedan. A strong gust of wind could send it tumbling.

We hopped out of the ambulance and grabbed our gear bags from the back. "This doesn't look good," I muttered.

A woman emerged from the SUV, holding her head.

"Ma'am, are you all right?" Jones asked.

"I-I think so. There was a deer. It came out of nowhere."

Jones took her elbow. "I'll help you."

I could just make out a man slumped over the wheel of the sedan, moaning. "Sir, are you all right?"

He made another sound, but no intelligent words emerged. I approached the side of the ravine, trying to get a better look. And that was when I smelled it. Gas.

Sirens sounded as the first truck pulled up to the scene. Firefighters spilled out of it.

"What do we have?" Cap called.

"Male, conscious but not lucid. And I smell gas."

"Fall back so we can assess."

I gritted my teeth but did as ordered. I watched as Calder and Mac moved forward, trying to get a better look at the vehicle.

"Sir, can you hear me?" Calder asked.

The man made another unintelligible sound.

"I need you to unlock the door."

Mac made his way around to the other side. "We need to stabilize the vehicle, and we need to move quick. The gas is spreading."

I stood on tiptoe, trying to get a better view. If the gas was spreading, we were running out of time. There was no way to know if the crash had created damage that might spark a blaze, and the man's car was still running.

"Cap," I called. "There's an open window I can fit through. I can turn off the vehicle and unlock the door."

"No," Calder barked. "There's gas, and we don't know the condition of the vehicle."

Cap was quiet for a moment and then nodded at me. "Move quick."

"She doesn't have gear," Calder argued.

"I'll be fine." I was already moving. "Get me a harness."

One of the probationary officers tossed me one. "Here."

I worked as quickly as possible, slipping the harness in place and checking each buckle. Then I hooked a carabiner to it. I looked up and met Calder's stormy expression. "Trust me." It was a plea. I needed him on my team. Would've given anything to feel that again.

His eyes flashed. "It's not about trusting you. It's about the possibility of that car going over."

"I can do this."

He ran a hand through his hair. "I'm your belay."

"Good." I'd feel better knowing that Calder was the one tethering me to the earth.

He hooked up his harness, and Mac moved in as his secondary. Then, I headed to the most stable side of the vehicle.

"Just get it unlocked," Cap called. "I don't want you throwing the vehicle off-balance."

"Okay." I eased over the side of the ravine. "Tension."

The rope pulled taut, and I leaned against it. Calder and I had done this dance dozens of times, only it was typically on a rock face for fun, not to rescue someone from a car.

I curved myself in through the window, doing my best not to touch anything. The vehicle groaned, and I froze.

"Hads, you need to get out of there."

I reached out, fingers stretching. "Almost got it."

Calder let a stream of curses fly.

My fingers stretched, and I hit the unlock button. "Done." I arced back out of the car, but as I did, my rope caught on a twisted branch on the side of the ravine. "Shit."

"What is it?" Calder barked.

"Give me a second." As I surveyed the root snagging my rope, two other firefighters pulled open the driver's side door and cut the man free.

"We got him," one of them called. "Pull us up."

The vehicle tottered on its balancing point.

"Hadley..." Calder gritted out.

"I'm stuck on an old tree root or something." It had me pinned down good, too. They could give me more slack, but I didn't think they could pull me up. "Try bringing me up."

The rope strained, and the root made a snapping sound but didn't quite break free.

"We need more hands," Calder shouted.

The vehicle slid down a foot, the back end crashing into my left side. My ribs screamed in protest, and my heart ricocheted around in my chest.

McNally leaned over the side of the ravine. "Hads, you okay?"

"Yeah," I wheezed. "But they can't get me up like this."

The car made another groaning sound as metal bent and creaked.

Calder appeared next to McNally. He was still holding my belay, but I knew he had countless guys behind him, backing him up. His face had gone completely white. "Climb over and get out of the line of fire of the car."

"I can't," I said through clenched teeth. My gaze jumped around, looking for options. I caught sight of a small indentation in the rock face.

Metal screeched, and the vehicle dropped another two inches.

"Hadley!" Calder shouted.

"I'm okay." But I wouldn't be for much longer. "Give me some slack."

Calder's jaw turned to granite. "Are you crazy? That'll just put you more in the path of the car."

I met his gaze, begging. "Trust me."

That muscle in his cheek ticked, but he called out, "Slack!"

They let me down a few more feet just as more snapping sounded. I pushed myself flush against the cliff face, into the tiny divot I'd seen. The car careened over me, the whole world going silent for a moment. Then a crash sounded, followed by the whoosh of an explosion.

I lifted my head, seeing Calder's panicked expression. "I'm okay. Really. I just need to climb up and untangle myself."

As others in the crew aimed hoses at the blaze below, I climbed up to where the car had been, using all those skills Calder had taught me years ago. I curved one hand around the tree root for balance as I used my other to untangle the rope.

"Okay, pull me up, boys."

I was moving so fast, my feet could barely keep up. And then Calder pulled me into his arms. I landed against his chest with an oomph, ignoring the screaming pain in my ribs. His heart thudded against my cheek as he held me close.

"You're okay." He said the words over and over like a chant. As if he'd seen me die and come back to life before his very eyes.

"I'm okay."

Calder's entire body shuddered. Then he released me and stormed away.

I watched him as he disappeared behind one of the trucks. What the hell had just happened?

Chapter Four

Calder

THE SMELL OF BURNED RUBBER FILLED THE AIR AS WE PILED out of the truck. "Shit," McNally said as he adjusted his helmet. "That's bad."

I moved towards the edge of the ravine, and my entire world stopped. The vehicle at the bottom was familiar. Too familiar. The station wagon I saw in my driveway every day when I got off work and every morning when I left again.

Hands grabbed hold of my arms, jerking me back. It was the only thing that made me realize I'd already been charging over the edge, my girls' names on my lips.

I jerked awake, sitting up in bed. Sweat dotted my forehead, and the sheets, now damp, clung to me. I muttered a curse as I swung my legs over the side of the bed.

I should've known the nightmares would come back after today. The scene had been too familiar. I stared down at my hands. They trembled as if I'd been right back there. I tightened them into fists, my nails digging into my palms.

I pushed to my feet, heading for the hall. Everything was quiet. Still. I eased open the door to the bedroom at the end of the hall. Birdie lay sprawled diagonally on her twin bed, hair everywhere and face pressed into her pillow. I watched as strands fluttered as she breathed deeply, a little snore escaping.

Sage was twisted into a sort of pretzel shape, her arms covering her head. Her chest rose and fell. I counted the breaths. In and out. Up to fifty and then back down. She was fine. Breathing. Heart beating. Alive.

My hand tightened on the door handle, anger lighting through me so fiercely, I had to back away, worried I'd take the knob right off. I closed the door as quietly as possible and retreated into the hallway.

I had to get it out. This rage would eat me alive. Fury at what had almost been taken from me.

I quickly changed into gym shorts, ignoring the sheets that would need to go in the wash. I picked up a pair of socks and sneakers and carried them downstairs. Opening the door to the garage, I went inside. I left the door ajar just enough so I'd be able to hear the girls if they called out. Then I sat on my weight bench and put on my socks and shoes.

Climbing onto the treadmill, I forced myself to start at an easy jog, even though I wanted to go straight for a punishing pace. After a few minutes of a warmup, I clicked up the speed and incline.

The steady pounding of my feet was the only music I needed. Each hit against the track released a little more of the rage I kept buried deep. Fury at my ex, who had almost taken my girls from me. But more at myself. For not paying close enough attention. For not seeing the truth.

I pushed harder, the burn in my lungs a welcome relief. I turned the speed higher. The whir of the machine kicked up.

I kept going longer than I should've, but my usual outlet wasn't working like it used to. After the accident, I'd needed these runs as much as I needed air. I'd ask Hayes or Hadley, sometimes even Shiloh, to sit with the twins as I took off to beat miles of pavement. Once they were home from the hospital, I'd purchased this treadmill, and it had been my only escape from the images and screams that haunted me.

It had worked for years. But the past nine months or so, I'd needed to push myself harder and farther to get even a fraction of the release I used to. It pissed me the hell off. I didn't need much, but I needed this.

Hadley's face flashed in my mind. She didn't show fear often, but I'd seen it today. A flash across her beautiful face as the panic set in at her lack of options. I'd almost sent myself hurdling over the cliff after her without a harness.

My heart hammered my ribs, and it wasn't because the run brought it out in me. It was the fear setting in at the truth. I'd almost lost her today. It didn't matter that I'd kept her at arm's length for the past four years. It didn't matter that I hadn't let myself come to terms with just how much I cared for my Little Daredevil. I knew the truth now.

If something happened to Hadley, I'd never be the same. And I would've wasted precious time pushing her away.

"Make me a bear, Dad," Birdie urged.

"One bear, coming up. What about you, Buttercup?"

Sage took her time before answering. "A flower, please."

I whisked the pancake batter, smoothing out all of the lumps. "You got it."

The doorbell rang, and Birdie hopped off her stool at the kitchen bar. "I'll get it."

I grabbed her by the back of her sweatshirt, lifting her into the air. "Not so fast."

She giggled as she made a swimming motion. "I'm nine. I can answer the door."

"Not if you don't know who it is, you can't."

Birdie rolled her eyes. Nine going on sixteen. "I'll ask first."

"Okay." I set her down, and she charged forward.

"Who's there?"

"I'll give you three guesses," Hadley called through the door.

Birdie threw open the door and launched herself at Hadley. "I was hoping it was you!"

Hadley caught her with an oomph and a wince. "Funny, I was hoping it was *you*."

"You know I live here."

"True, but you could've had other plans, and then I would've been sad that you weren't home."

"We're always home on Saturday mornings. Right, Dad? It's pancake time."

Hadley's expression went from gleeful to wary as she met my gaze. "Hey."

I hated that I'd put that guardedness there. "Want to come in and have some pancakes?"

"Sure." Hadley set Birdie down and made her way inside.

Sage appeared then. "I thought I heard your voice."

"Hey, Goose."

Sage moved to her with ease, folding into her arms. "Missed you."

Hadley pressed a kiss to the top of her head. "Missed you more."

"Nuh-uh."

"I did so. But what I want to know is if you missed me enough to share your pancakes with me."

Sage beamed up at her and nodded, but Birdie made an exaggerated thinking face, tapping a finger against her lips. "I'm not sure…"

Hadley clutched her chest. "You wound me."

"Okay, you can have some," Birdie acquiesced.

"Thank you." She looked up at me. "I'd offer to help, but…"

"We know you'd just end up burning something?" I finished for her.

"Bingo." Hadley grinned at me, but it quickly slipped from her face as soon as she realized what she was doing. She turned her attention to the girls, talking about what activities they'd done with Addie this week and whether they wanted to go to the park after breakfast.

I refocused on the pancakes, making sure everyone had as many as they could possibly want, but sliced some strawberries for the girls to consume, as well. Hadley kept her distance from me throughout breakfast, remaining zeroed in on Birdie and Sage.

When we'd finished, and the dishes were in the dishwasher, she clapped her hands. "Ready to go?" Birdie cheered, and Sage ran for her sweatshirt. Hadley turned to me. "I can take them if you have stuff you need to get done."

The hopeful lilt to her words grated against my skin. "No, I'll go."

"Okay." She started towards the door and out of it, linking arms with Birdie.

I locked up as Sage waited for me. She eyed me carefully. "Are you and Hads in a fight?"

I almost fumbled my keys. "No, why would you ask that?"

Sage shrugged and headed down the path with me to the side-walk. "She was looking at you funny at breakfast. Like she was waiting for you to yell at her."

Hell. Sage had always been so observant, wise beyond her years, but this wasn't something I could explain to her. I couldn't even explain it to myself. "We had a hard day at work yesterday." It wasn't a lie, but it wasn't the whole truth, either.

Sage's steps faltered. "Did someone die?"

I pulled her in close to me, wrapping an arm around her shoulders as we walked. "No. Everyone will be okay. But there was a minute where I was scared for Hads."

"You don't like it when you're scared."

"No, I don't." I did everything I could to mitigate as much worry as possible. It was why I worked my ass off, hoping to move into a more administrative role at work. It was why the girls had memorized an emergency plan when they were six. It was why I'd given up chasing those adrenaline highs with Hadley.

Sage hooked a finger into my belt loop. "Everyone's scared sometimes."

"I know, Buttercup."

We were quiet for the rest of the walk, Hadley and Birdie almost a block ahead of us. I liked these silent moments with my daughter. Sometimes, she filled it with unexpected revelations like she had earlier. Other times, we simply were.

"Hurry up, Sage!" Birdie called from the monkey bars.

Sage tipped her face up to mine and grinned. "I'm gonna beat her this time."

"Have fun."

She tore off, launching herself up to catch one of the rungs. She and Birdie counted off how many bars they could get without falling.

I came to a stop next to Hadley. I had the urge to bump her shoulder with mine like I used to whenever she was quiet. More, I wanted to pull her into my arms and tell her I was sorry. To vow to fix what had gone so wrong between us.

"Thanks for coming by this morning."

Hadley rocked back on her heels, not taking her eyes off Birdie and Sage. "I love them."

"I know you do."

Hadley had been there every step of the way. When I found out that Jackie was pregnant. When Birdie and Sage were born. She'd babysat so many times I'd lost track. And she'd been at the hospital every day after the accident. After me, Hadley was the greatest constant in the girls' lives.

"I'm sorry I was a prick again," I whispered.

"Maybe, instead of apologizing, try not to pull that shit. I already get it from Hayes and my parents. I don't need it from you, too."

"Easier said than done."

Hadley looked up at me, the wind whipping her hair around her face. "Why?"

"Because I don't know what I'd do if I lost you."

Chapter Five

Hadley

BECAUSE I DON'T KNOW WHAT I'D DO IF I LOST YOU. Calder's words had replayed themselves over and over in my mind all week. I knew the accident had marked him. That things had been different after that day. But seeing the *why* so clearly now changed things. It didn't make it hurt any less, but I understood.

I stared at the fire station in the morning light, willing myself to get out of my SUV and walk inside. Things had been different between Calder and me since that day at the park. As if we were both treading a bit more carefully around each other.

It felt good to know that he cared. That he didn't want to keep hurting me the way he had been. But I hated it at the same time. I missed the ease we used to have with each other, the total comfort and peace.

Maybe that would come again someday, but I wasn't sure. Not when neither of us was willing to bend our positions. I couldn't give up the air I got from riding or climbing, and Calder couldn't magically erase the trauma that made him hate it. My only hope was to be a little better at hiding that from him.

Mr. Gibbs scowled at Calder. "I don't want to make a donation. I want to thank the woman who saved my life."

"And you have," I cut in. "I appreciate your gratitude, and I promise that the gift isn't necessary."

A muscle in his cheek ticked. "I'll speak with the captain. He'll make an exception for me." And with that, he turned on his heel and left.

The tension between my shoulder blades eased a fraction as Mr. Gibbs disappeared, but I couldn't seem to shake it altogether. Warm hands landed on my arms, turning me around. "You okay?"

Calder's eyes bored into mine, and I fought the urge to take a step back. "I'm fine."

"I heard he's a new real estate developer in town. I don't think he's used to hearing the word *no*." He scowled over my shoulder, his hands dropping away.

I missed the warmth of that simple touch immediately. "I'm sure Cap will find a way to smooth it over."

Calder's gaze came back to me. "Tell me if he bothers you again?"

"What are you going to do, beat him up?"

The corner of his mouth kicked up. "I don't think it'll get that far."

"He doesn't exactly strike me as the fighting type."

"More like he'd throw a lawyer at the problem."

I chuckled. "Can you imagine bringing that before a judge? '*Your honor, she won't let me give her a gift.*'"

"It'd be an interesting case." Calder sobered. "But, seriously, promise me you'll tell me if he hassles you."

"I promise."

"Good." Calder wrapped an arm around my shoulders, guiding me back to the counter. "Now, let's finish our breakfast."

I couldn't breathe. My lungs refused to cooperate. It had been so long since I'd felt this kind of warmth from Calder. I wanted to sink into it and never come out. But I knew that would be a mistake. Because it could break my heart all over again.

Chapter Six

Hadley

I SAT IN MY SUV AND STARED AT THE RANCH HOUSE. THIS property had been in my dad's family for generations. The house itself was full of history. I couldn't count the number of nights I'd spent on the porch swing outside, staring at the stars.

There were a million beautiful memories contained in those walls. And a million more hard ones. But now, every time I walked inside, it was charged. As if I had to don armor before I could cross the threshold.

I had no choice tonight. And if I waited another few minutes, I'd be late. Everyone else was already here. Everly and Hayes. Shiloh. Addie. My parents. Calder, Birdie, and Sage. I was the only one waiting on the outside.

No matter how hard I tried, I couldn't seem to find my way to that inner circle. Part of me wanted to be there more than anything, and another rebelled at the very idea.

Instead of trying to explore the whys of that, I grabbed my bag and hopped out of my SUV. As I headed towards the steps, Hayes appeared from the shadows of the porch.

"I was starting to wonder if you'd turn around and leave."

"Just catching my breath after a long day."

I climbed the first few steps, taking in my brother's face. "Everything okay?"

"Just small-town politics."

It wasn't a job I'd want. I'd be horrible at trying to soothe tempers and getting people to see reason. "Better you than me."

He snorted. "You'd end up in lockup on day one."

I gave Hayes an elbow to the gut. "Hey, now."

He wrapped an arm around my neck and pulled me in so he could give me a noogie.

"I'm gonna tell Everly that you're picking on me."

Hayes released me with a little shove. "That's not playing fair."

"Nope. But it's smart."

He pulled open the door for me. "Vicious."

"Damn straight, and don't you forget it."

"Hadley!" Birdie yelled as she caught sight of me.

I lost a lungful of air as she wrapped her arms around me. "Are you taller since last week?"

She giggled. "I dunno. Maybe. If I'm taller, you think Dad will get me a skateboard?"

I glanced at Calder, whose gaze was zeroed in on me and his daughter. Skateboards or anything that reminded Calder of our past daredevil antics was likely a no-go zone. But that didn't mean Birdie should let him off the hook. "I don't know, Birds. You should ask him."

She grinned up at me. "I'm gonna ask on the drive home."

"Good luck," I whispered.

Everly rose from the couch, crossing to give me a quick hug. "So good to see you."

"You, too. I've been meaning to come out to the sanctuary and see the new critters you got, but life has been crazy."

"You're welcome anytime, but there's no rush. We're getting two alpacas tomorrow."

"Really?"

Everly had created the most amazing home for abused and neglected animals, or those who simply needed a place to live because their owners could no longer care for them.

"I'm going to ask Birdie and Sage to help me name them," she said.

"They'll love that."

"And they're good at it, too. I can't imagine Petunia the pig having any other name."

My mom bustled around the corner. "Oh, good, you're finally here."

I stiffened. "I was told six."

She checked her watch. "It's ten after."

Hayes wrapped an arm around my shoulders. "I held her up on the porch for a little catch-up."

Mom made a humming sound in the back of her throat and then headed for the kitchen where Addie was chopping vegetables.

"I don't know why she even wants me here," I muttered.

Hayes pulled me in closer. "She loves you."

I didn't doubt that. But while she might love me, she didn't like me very much. The knowledge burned, but I shoved the hurt aside.

I moved into the living area where most of our group had gathered. Shiloh was perched on the hearth, giving Hayes' dog, Koda, a rubdown. Sage was curled up in an armchair, engrossed in a book. And Calder and Dad were talking about one of Dad's new horses.

I bent and whispered in Sage's ear. "Hey, Goose."

She tipped her head back so she could look up at me. "Hey."

"Whatcha reading?"

Sage turned the book around so I could see as I sat on the ottoman in front of her chair. "It's about wildflowers. Addie's helping me make a book of pressed ones, but I need to know the right names to write down for each one."

"Wow. That's pretty cool. How many do you have so far?"

I pushed down the flicker of jealousy and focused on the little girl in front of me, who clearly loved the activity.

"Almost ten."

I widened my eyes. "Really? Where are you finding them?"

"In the field behind the park, mostly. Addie said there are more in the mountains, but she doesn't have a car, so we can't go up there."

Sage's words punched me right in the gut, guilt sliding through me at my earlier jealousy. Addie didn't have a car, and she likely didn't even have a driver's license. I doubted her controlling father would've allowed it.

"I'll talk with Addie. Maybe we can plan a time for me to take you guys up to the mountains and we can all go on a hike."

Sage straightened in her chair. "Really?"

"Really."

She shot up, leaving her book on the chair and pulling me towards the kitchen. "Addie! Hadley said she'll take us to the mountains to look for wildflowers."

Addie wiped her hands on a kitchen towel and met my gaze. "I don't want you to go to any trouble."

I sent her a warm smile. "It's no trouble at all. I'd love to go with you and the girls."

She twisted the towel, running it through her fingers. "I'd like that."

"Don't be cancelling on them, now," my mom cut in as she took a baking dish from the oven.

I ignored her and kept my gaze on Addie. "When you know what days you'll be watching Birdie and Sage, just let me know, and I'll check my work schedule."

Addie glanced from my mother back to me. "Okay. Thanks, Hadley."

I left Sage and Addie chatting and moved away from the kitchen and my mother. If she kept at it, I wouldn't be responsible for my actions.

A hand snaked out and tugged me towards a tall form. "Is my baby girl ignoring me?"

I wrapped my arms around my dad's waist, inhaling his comforting, woodsy scent. "Never."

"That's what I like to hear. How are you?" He released me but kept hold of my shoulders as he surveyed my face.

"Good. Busy. Same ol', same ol'."

"Heard you guys caught a touch-and-go call last week."

I caught Calder's gaze over my dad's shoulder, and a muscle in his cheek ticked.

"It was fine," I assured Dad. "Nothing to worry about."

He squeezed my shoulders. "Can't tell a father not to worry."

"We're ready to eat," Mom called as she strode towards the massive table with a platter of chicken.

I grabbed the salad from the bar and carried it over, choosing the seat farthest away from the chair my mom always used. Hayes and Everly sat opposite me with Birdie to my right. As the chair to the left of me slid back, I looked up to meet dark eyes.

Calder bumped my shoulder with his as he sat. "Hey."

"Hey."

How long had it been since Calder had opted to sit next to me at a family dinner if other seats were available? I honestly couldn't remember the last time.

Sage filed in, taking the chair on Calder's other side, and Addie took the seat next to that. Shiloh, Mom, and Dad filled in the rest. Dad cleared his throat as he sat. "Love having all of you at the table." He shot Mom a grin. "Thank you for preparing this feast."

"You're on duty next week," she shot back.

"Fair enough. Now, let's chow down."

Dinner went by in a din of at least three separate conversations at all times. That was how I liked it. The attention couldn't be focused on me that way.

We made it all the way past dessert to clearing the table

before Mom started in again. "Hadley, will you be here next week?"

"I'm on the roster to work."

Mom's fingers tightened on the stack of plates she held, her knuckles bleaching white. "I'm sure Calder could arrange for someone to switch with you."

"It's not just me. It's my partner's schedule, as well."

"Jones will understand."

"Mom, I can't make it to dinner every week. I'll come when I can."

She let out an exasperated sigh. "I really don't think it's asking too much for one dinner a week."

I met her gaze dead-on. "Then why didn't you say anything two weeks ago when Hayes missed? Or the week before when Shiloh was gone?"

My mom stiffened, setting the stack of plates down with a clatter. "Hayes had a callout—"

"So his job is more important than mine?" I was done with her crap. She treated each of my siblings differently than she treated me, and I could never figure out why.

"Hayes doesn't have someone who can cover for him."

"Bullshit."

"Hadley! You will not use that language. Especially in front of Birdie and Sage."

The twins glanced at each other, their eyes wide, and Addie ushered them out of the main living area towards the family room at the other end of the house.

"I'm done with this, Mom."

"Done with what? Your family?"

"Your double standard when it comes to me."

Dad stepped between us. "Okay, I think that's enough. Let's everyone take a breath."

I looked him in the eyes. "You see it. You have to."

"He does not," Mom cut in. "Because it doesn't exist. I don't think it's unreasonable to ask you to show up *on time* for one thing a week."

It didn't matter that she didn't care if Shiloh would take off for a week at a time, escaping into the mountains to silence her demons. Or that Hayes would get calls in the middle of family dinners. That Beckett rarely came home between his medical missions all over the world. All of those were acceptable to her.

I never would be.

I waited to see if Dad would say anything, but he was silent. That was the final straw. I didn't bother saying another word. No one would hear it anyway. I grabbed my purse and started towards the door.

"Hadley," my brother called.

I ignored him and went right outside, hurrying down the steps. I was a dozen feet from my SUV when an arm grabbed my elbow. I whirled, ripping my arm from my assailant's grip. "What?!"

Calder held up both hands. "Whoa there, slugger."

"I'm not going back in there."

"Neither would I."

I rocked back on my heels. Usually, he pled my mother's case. Tonight, he moved forward and wrapped me in a hug.

I was stunned motionless for a moment, but then I relaxed into Calder's chest, my fingers fisting in his flannel shirt. Tears stung the backs of my eyes, but I refused to let them fall.

"I'm sorry, Hads," he whispered into my hair.

"Why does she hate me so much?"

"She doesn't. But she struggles with how strong you are. How well you know your own mind and won't bend to anyone."

"I can't keep doing this."

His lips ghosted across my temple. "I know. Maybe you both need a little bit of a break."

We were silent for a bit, simply standing there in the moonlight. Calder didn't let me go, and I held firmly to his shirt. I was scared to even breathe too deeply, that it might ruin this moment. But I was scared to lean into it, too. Terrified to trust he would be there for me when I needed him.

That thought had me unclenching my hold on his flannel and stepping back. I couldn't meet his gaze. "Thank you."

"Hadley," he whispered, his voice rough.

"I'll see you on Wednesday." I turned and walked towards my SUV. I didn't look back at him as I went.

But as I drove away, I couldn't resist looking in the rearview mirror. Calder stood there, illuminated by the moonlight. His hands were shoved into his pockets, and he looked so damn forlorn. I kept driving anyway. Because if I leaned into Calder and he wasn't there? The last shreds of my heart would be torn apart.

Chapter Seven

Calder

I STOOD THERE WATCHING AS THE TAILLIGHTS FADED INTO the night. Hell. I could feel the hurt pouring off Hadley in waves. The bone-deep sorrow carved into her marrow. And there didn't seem to be anything I could do about it.

I gave a piece of gravel a healthy kick and turned back to the house. Hayes opened the front door as I climbed the steps. He extended a beer to me. "Figured we could all use one of these."

I grunted in ascent. I needed something a hell of a lot stronger than beer.

Hayes headed towards a grouping of rockers on the front porch and eased down into one. I followed, taking the one next to him. We were silent as we stared out into the dark fields. The deep purple of the sky was crystal-clear tonight, making the stars almost look fake; they shone so brightly.

There was a tug in the vicinity of my chest. What I should've done was jump into Hadley's SUV and found a mountain to tear down. I should've helped her forget all about the hurt her mother had heaped onto her.

Even just thinking about it made my hand tremble. The result of want battling with fear and responsibility.

I set it on the bed, staring at my fingerprints in the dust. Had it really been that long since I'd looked at the contents? Long enough that dust piled on the surface?

I grabbed a t-shirt from my hamper and wiped off the surface, then tossed it back in with the dirty clothes. I reached out for the lid, but my fingers stalled as they grasped it. I forced myself to flip open the top.

Photos and mementos from what felt like a different lifetime were piled inside. The image on top had my back teeth grinding together. Jackie in a white dress. Me in my best suit. Hayes at my side. A friend whose name I couldn't remember at hers. Jackie's belly swollen under her dress.

She'd been seven months pregnant when we went to City Hall and promised our lives to one another. To love, honor, and cherish had been a part of those vows. It had been a lie. I hadn't been in love with Jackie. She'd been a one-night stand after blowing off some steam with the guys from the station.

I'd thought that I could grow to love her. That if she birthed my babies, there was no way I wouldn't fall. And in that moment, when Jackie had given me the two greatest gifts of my life, I'd seen the possibility.

But that spark of hope had been doused eventually. In lies and betrayal. In deceit and destruction.

I shuffled through the stack of photos with her face, flipping them upside down on my bed so I didn't have to look at them for longer than necessary. I slowed as I reached what I was looking for—a ticket stub for a BMX competition in Portland. Hayes, Hadley, and me, grinning at the camera, arms wrapped around each other, dirt smeared on our clothes.

The photos came one after the other. Memories slammed into me along with the images. I swore I could almost feel the rush that accompanied them. The feeling of freedom.

My fingers stilled on a photo of Hadley. It was the one I was looking for. The picture had been taken a few years after the girls were born. Mud covered Hadley from head to toe. She'd taken a spill off her bike and landed in what had turned into almost a marsh after a good rain.

I could still feel the way my heart had stopped in that moment. Hadley had sailed over her handlebars but had somehow managed to tuck and roll, coating herself entirely in mud. She'd come up laughing as I'd rushed over to her.

That laugh. I hadn't heard it since that day. The uninhibited and free one. The joy that always hit me right in the rib cage and twisted.

Once I'd known she was unharmed, I'd snapped the photo with my phone. Hadley looked so damn beautiful. Somehow managing to appear wise beyond her nineteen years and yet full of an innocent joy at the same time. So determined to live every moment to its fullest.

Hadley and those moments where we'd silenced the world to race the wind had kept me going when I felt a ten-ton weight on my shoulders. She and that rush of adrenaline had kept me sane. Until it had all come crashing down around me.

The accident had happened one week later. Months afterwards, when I'd found this picture on my phone, I couldn't resist printing it out. I'd needed the reminder. Until it had become too much temptation, and I'd had to lock it all away.

The memories. And everything I felt for Hadley Easton.

Chapter Eight

Hadley

MY FINGERS CURVED INTO ROCK AS I HOISTED MYSELF up to another plateau. This mountainside fell off into a sheer rock face in one section, disappearing into a lake below. It was hell making it out here. You had to take an ATV or come on horseback, but the views were breathtaking.

The trek and destination were almost always empty. You'd run into a hiker or backpacker occasionally, but they were few and far between. The wind and the call of the birds were your only company.

It was exactly what I'd needed after last night. To feel the burn in my muscles and hear nothing but my breathing and nature around me. Calla had offered to make the climb with me, but I'd told her to stay with Toby and Jinx below. I wanted my solitude.

But with that came my mother's words, taunting me. Not just the ones from last night but also from the last seventeen years— ever since Shiloh had gone missing.

That night had stolen my mischievous, adventurous mother, who used to take us at insane speeds on horseback or let us trek out alone to the creek on our property. Someone who needed to control every last detail of our lives had taken her place. And when I pushed back on that…it wasn't pretty.

I searched for another handhold to make the final part of the climb. But as I did, I heard her voice louder. *Irresponsible. Foolish. Cruel.*

I shoved the echo from my mind and hooked my fingers around one rock, then placed my foot on another. She didn't get that real estate in my mind. I pushed up, scrambling over to the flat outcropping. My chest heaved as I took in the view around me.

Land went on forever. Fields and forests. Streams and mountains. I was so small in comparison. Just a little speck in the vastness of it all. Somehow, that was comforting. My problems might seem big to me, but not when you looked at all this.

I sat down, leaning against the side of the cliff and letting my breaths even out as I took it all in. I'd never get tired of these landscapes. Despite the many places I'd traveled to in the world, this would always be home. I'd thought about moving a million times, but I could never pull the trigger because I couldn't imagine leaving this behind.

The wind rippled a field of grasses below, almost making it look like water. And that same breeze lifted a scent of pine to my nose. It had a pang lighting along my sternum. There was only one person I wished was with me right now, and it was the one who would never come—not anymore.

I swore I could still feel Calder's arms around me. Last night, as I'd tossed and turned, I could still smell hints of his familiar cologne. It was a beautiful kind of torture to have glimpses of the man who would never be mine—not in friendship or anything more.

I shoved those thoughts from my mind too and pushed to my feet. Peeking over the edge, I waved to my friends below. Toby gave me a salute in return, and Jinx sent his drone into the air. That was my cue that they were ready.

I surveyed the water below. The lake didn't show any signs of the breeze affecting it. The surface looked like perfect sea glass.

These waters were untainted by civilization, crystal-clear and almost turquoise.

Calla had swum out to do a depth check for me and make sure there weren't any unexpected rocks. We were good to go.

I took a long, slow breath and stepped back from the edge. I twisted my shoes in the dirt and rock, getting a feel for the ground.

I didn't give myself time to think, I simply started moving. In three strides, I was flying. My body tucked into one flip and then another before straightening out. There was nothing but me and the air around me. I was free.

My feet stung as they broke the surface of the water. The temperature stole my breath. I had to fight against my body's urge to panic as I kicked towards the surface. When my head broke into the sunlight, I sucked in air.

Jinx hooted and hollered from the shore. I flipped to my back, floating and staring up at the sun. The water was so cold it hurt, but I didn't care. It made me feel alive.

I let myself drift towards the shore, soaking in those tendrils of adrenaline and peace. But they were already fading. I reached deeper for them, trying to hold on, but I couldn't quite grasp them.

I rolled to my stomach, my back teeth grinding together as I swam towards my friends. It wasn't enough. Not after yesterday. But it was as good as I was going to get.

Calla held out a towel to me. "That was amazing."

"Thanks." I grabbed the terrycloth and wrapped it around my shoulders. "I can't believe you didn't complain about the water. It almost froze my brain."

"It wasn't too bad."

I shook my head. "Not too bad? I'm a wimp compared to you."

She smiled and ducked her head.

Toby wrapped an arm around my shoulders, pulling me into his side and giving me a little shake. "People are going to love it. They're still losing their minds over the bike trick. This will just take it to the next level."

Jinx set his drone back in its case. "Did you tell her about the sponsorship offer?"

"I totally forgot."

"What offer?"

We all made a decent chunk of change from the sponsorships that came in for the videos. *Voyeur* didn't run ads on the streams, but companies asked people to use their gear or have their other products in the videos. I made more than a comfortable living from the money I earned from that alone, but I loved being an EMT and wouldn't leave it behind for anything.

Toby released me but held onto my shoulders. "Brace yourself."

I rolled my eyes and looked at Calla for commiseration. Toby always made a production out of everything. "Do you need me to do a drum roll?"

"That would be appreciated."

I shrugged out of his hold. "Out with it already."

He gave a mock pout. "You never let me have any fun."

Jinx smacked him upside the head. "One of these days, she's gonna hit you."

"All right, all right. It's Sport-ade."

My jaw fell open. "Seriously?"

"Fifty Gs. We just have to show you drinking one of their drinks at some point in your video. And they want to talk about long-term sponsorship."

I pulled my towel tighter around me. If they kept up that kind of money for each video, we would set a record this year. "Did you send the offer to Angela?"

"I wanted to wait until I told you."

"Send it. If the contract looks good, we are going to need to celebrate."

Jinx rubbed his hands together. "Hells, yeah. I've been eyeing this new bike, and I'm pulling the trigger if this goes through."

Toby shot me a cocky grin as he crossed his arms over his chest. "Go ahead. You can admit it."

"Admit what?"

"Don't make me say, '*I told you so.*'"

I groaned. Toby had been the one to suggest this channel in the first place, trying to convince me that I could make real money on the platform. "You don't need anything else going to your big head."

He moved fast, lifting me into his arms and starting for the water. "What were you saying?"

"Don't you dare. I will cut you out of this deal and put pink hair dye in your shampoo."

"You talk a big game, but I know you'd never."

I gave his side a hard pinch.

"Ow! Hell, woman."

I twisted the skin. "Set me down on land, or I'll go for your nipple next."

"Shit!" Toby practically tossed me on the grassy shore. "That was uncalled for."

I gave him my best innocent smile. "Who, me? I'd *never* do something like that."

Jinx wrapped an arm around Toby's shoulders. "You should know by now that there's a lot of badass in that tiny package."

"Damn straight," I muttered.

"How could I forget?" Toby moved out of Jinx's hold and dropped to one knee, taking my hand. "Please, dear badass maiden, forgive me."

I swallowed down my chuckle and looked at Calla. "Has he been playing those weird role-playing games again lately?"

She snickered. "Probably. He's always playing something."

"Hey, now," Toby griped. "It's no fair, two against one."

I tugged my hand free of his grasp. "That's what you get for being an idiot."

"Rude," he grumbled.

Jinx bent to pick up his drone case. "Come on, you crazy kids. We need to get moving so we don't lose the light."

"I just need to change out of these wet clothes." I grabbed my pack and unzipped it, hunting for what I needed.

"Want me to hold the towel for you?" Calla asked.

"Sure. Thanks." For a while, it had only been me, Jinx, and Toby. They'd both seen me in several states of undress, and I honestly couldn't find it in me to care. But it was nice to have another girl around.

We rounded a side of the rock face that made a natural little alcove, and Calla held up the towel while I awkwardly peeled off my bathing suit and shorts.

Calla was quiet. That wasn't unusual for her, but this one felt heavier somehow.

"Everything okay?"

She nodded, biting her lip. "Just thinking. Next time, I want to jump, too."

I pulled on a tank over my sports bra. "I bet Toby and Jinx could come up with a cool concept for a video of a double jump."

Calla's mouth curved. "I bet so, too."

"You should do a practice or two before the actual jump. We can come out together if you want."

"Really? That'd be awesome."

"Just name the time." I pulled on dry socks and slipped my feet into the boots I'd worn on the hike to the cliffs. "All set."

Calla dropped the towel and folded it neatly into a square. "Here you go."

"Thanks." I shoved it into my pack and put the bag on. I moved out of the alcove and started down the path to the little beach but almost collided with someone as I rounded a corner.

Hands caught my shoulders, steadying me.

"Sorry," I apologized, but my words cut off as I looked up at the familiar face. "Mr. Gibbs." I hadn't seen him since he'd appeared at the station, trying to give me those thank-you gifts.

He dropped his hold on me, scowling. "I told you to call me Evan."

I fought the urge to roll my eyes. Talk about a man used to getting his way. "All right. Out for a hike?" He was dressed in ritzy hiking gear that looked as if it had never been worn before.

"I heard this was a good spot. I'm glad I ran into you. I've been meaning to stop by the fire station again."

I stiffened, preparing myself for him to try and foist the gift on me again.

"I'm sorry if I put you in a tough spot with the gift. I didn't mean to do that. How about I take you out to dinner as a thank you instead?"

My feet shuffled in the dirt. "I appreciate that offer—and the gratitude—but I can't."

A muscle in Evan's cheek flickered. "There's a rule against that, too?"

It wasn't expressly forbidden to date someone you had been on a call for. Wolf Gap was simply too small a town for something like that. But it wasn't a good idea. That was my personal rule.

Evan was good-looking, with sandy brown hair and broad shoulders. He was older than me for sure, likely in his late-thirties. And he had some of that douchebag air that was a no-go zone for me. But it wasn't any of those things that made up my mind.

Every single time I dated someone, it ended in disaster. I was forever comparing them to the one person I'd wanted for almost as long as I could remember. The one with dark hair and even darker eyes which seemed to see straight to the depths of my soul. Because of Calder, the answer to a man like Evan would always be no.

"I'm not really interested in dating right now." It was true enough. I just hoped one day a man would come along with the power to make me forget all about Calder Cruz.

Chapter Nine

Hadley

I PIPED THE ICING ONTO THE CUPCAKES IN A SWIRL OF COLOR, finishing with a flourish.

Everly moved closer to the counter, surveying my work. "That looks amazing."

"I never would've thought to put those colors together," Addie said softly. "They look beautiful. Birdie and Sage will love them."

I gave her a smile even though it made my insides hurt. She was everything I wasn't—graceful, reserved, quietly beautiful. I had a feeling she was exactly what Calder was looking for. And when he finally opened his eyes, he'd be lost to me forever.

But none of that was Addie's fault. I pushed the tray of cupcakes towards her. "A slumber party needs cupcakes. Want to put the sprinkles on?"

She took in the array of decoration options on my counter. "I don't want to screw anything up."

"They're unicorn cupcakes with every color under the sun in them. It would be impossible to screw them up."

"Okay…" Addie examined each jar before picking one and delicately dusting some pink sugar on one of the treats.

Everly squeezed my arm and mouthed *thank you.*

My phone buzzed in my pocket.

Toby: *Video's rendering. Should be done in a couple hours. You look badass!*

Me: *Thanks for weaving your magic. Just shoot it over when you're done.*

I moved from my texts to my email, scanning to see if Angela had sent the completed contracts for the Sport-ade deal. There wasn't anything from her, but another message caught my eye. The subject line read: *liar.*

I clicked on it.

You think you're so special. You're not. I bet you bought every last follower. You're nothing but smoke and mirrors, and one day people will find out. I'll make sure of it.

A chill skittered down my spine, but I shook it off. It was probably some weirdly jealous teen. The message didn't exactly scream maturity.

A hand landed on my shoulder. "Hey, you okay?" Everly asked.

I forced a smile. "Sorry, just work stuff." I motioned for her to follow me. "Why don't you help me with the sleeping bags and air mattresses?"

"Sure." She followed me into the garage. "I really appreciate you including Addie and me."

"Of course. How's she doing?"

It had been less than a year since Everly and Hayes had helped Addie break free of her controlling father, and I knew the transition hadn't exactly been easy.

Everly glanced back towards the kitchen as we stepped into the open garage, and I could see the worry for her cousin etched into her face. "I'm honestly not sure. I thought by now she'd have opened up to me. But I'm lucky if I can get her to have one or two meals with me a week. I want to help, to make sure she has whatever support she needs, but everything I do seems to be the wrong thing."

I pulled Everly into a quick hug. "All you can do is be there when she's ready." Ev had already done everything she could for

Addie, setting her up in Hayes' old house and helping her get the babysitting job with Birdie and Sage.

"I can be as patient as the day is long with animals, but it's harder with people."

I chuckled. "I can't be patient with anything, so you've got me beat."

Everly scanned the storage boxes in my garage. "What am I looking for?"

"It's over here." I grabbed a box labeled *camping gear* and another with no label at all. "Can you get three sleeping bags out of that box? I'll get three air mattresses."

"Is Shiloh not coming?"

I shook my head. My sister wasn't big on group activities, especially ones where she was at risk of ending up the focus of attention and didn't have an easy out.

Everly nodded as if she understood every reason for Shiloh's absence. And maybe she did. Shy had seemed to flourish as she helped Everly start up her animal sanctuary. She still helped out a couple of afternoons a week.

The sound of tires on my gravel drive had me looking up. Calder's familiar SUV appeared in the distance, and I started towards it. He'd barely put the vehicle in park before the girls were climbing out and running towards me.

I grabbed them both up in a hug. "I missed you guys."

Birdie giggled. "We saw you a few days ago."

"Too long."

Sage smiled up at me. "I agree."

Everly waved at the twins, and they shouted hellos.

I released them both and bent to whisper. "Guess what?"

"What?" they asked, copying my hushed tone.

"Addie's in the kitchen decorating cupcakes."

They both took off like a shot, and I couldn't help but laugh.

"I'll get these inside," Everly called, disappearing into the house.

I turned to face Calder. "Hey."

The corner of his mouth kicked up. "I'm guessing there's some form of sugar inside?"

"Cupcakes."

"You always did make the best."

The wistfulness in his tone hit me squarely in the chest and twisted. How many times had I made him cupcakes? Too many to count. But it had been years. Four to be precise.

"You're welcome to come in and have one." It was an olive branch. A piece of hope. That maybe we could slowly find our way to a new normal. One where we were friends. Even though my heart would always long for more.

"I'll take one to go. Wouldn't want to interrupt girls' night."

"It's definitely no boys allowed."

Calder chuckled, his familiar deep laugh sending vibrations over my skin. "I promise not to invade." The humor fell away from his expression. "How are you doing? I've been worried about you."

We'd seen each other during shifts at work and when I'd come to take the twins to the park, but I'd been careful to make sure we were never alone. He saw too much. Knew all my scars. And I couldn't handle his searching gaze.

"I'm fine. Just been busy."

"Hurtling down mountains?"

I stiffened at his words. There was no bite to them, but there didn't need to be. They were an accusation, nonetheless. "If I was, are you going to chew me out for it?"

Flickers of anger sparked to life in my gut. Not simply at his judgment but at what he'd taken from me: my partner in crime.

"I just want you to be safe."

I met Calder's stare. "I'm not going to stop living to exist in some sort of bubble that's acceptable to you and my mom. You used to understand that."

Those dark eyes of his blazed, turning almost amber in the early evening light. "I made a lot of mistakes back then…"

I took an involuntary step back as if he'd slapped me. He might as well have. That would've hurt less. "That's what I am to you? A mistake?"

"What? No. That's not how I meant it—"

"You sure about that? You've made it pretty clear how much you don't want me around these past four years."

Every millimeter of distance Calder had put between us had been a carefully placed slice of a blade.

"I had to." The words were guttural as if torn from his throat.

"Why?" It was the one question I'd always wanted to know the answer to but was too afraid to ask.

"You make me want things I can't have."

I sucked in a sharp breath, and then my breathing halted altogether. His statement could mean a million different things. I let my silence do the prodding, begging him to explain.

Calder ran a hand through his hair, tugging on the ends. "You don't think I miss it? I loved those adventures. Letting the world burn around us and disappearing into whatever piece of sky we were chasing that day. But when we did that, people I love got hurt. Those girls are my number one priority, I don't have the luxury to be reckless like that anymore."

I couldn't believe what I was hearing. A part of me had always guessed that Calder wasn't willing to have any sort of risky hobby when he was the only parent to his girls. But the other piece…it made no sense.

"Calder, Jackie wasn't in that accident because you went mountain biking and rock-climbing. She was in that accident because she was sick and selfish."

His gaze cut to me, rage filling it. "I left her alone to go take off on some adventure with you. Too many times to count. I gave her the space to get back into that poison and it almost cost me everything. Now, I'm all Birdie and Sage have."

I couldn't seem to get air into my lungs. The ugly stew of guilt and blame and anger pouring out of Calder was like a cloud of thick, black smoke. It would kill us before the flames ever would.

"You blame me." It was the one thing he wouldn't say. Because I had been the one to ask him to go with me all those times. Sure, he occasionally had, too. But I'd needed it more than he did, drowning in the pressure from my family to be someone I never had a shot of being.

"Fuck!" Calder spun, kicking a piece of gravel. "No, I don't. I blame myself, and I sure as hell blame Jackie. But I don't blame you."

I stayed quiet. I didn't believe him. No wonder he'd pushed me away. It all made a hell of a lot more sense now.

Calder turned back around, moving in close. "Hadley."

I didn't say a word. His revelations were still spinning around in my head, eating away at what was left of my heart.

His hands came up, framing my face. Those rough palms that I always wished I could feel on my skin were there now. And I felt nothing.

"Hads."

Everything hurt.

"Little Daredevil."

I jerked at his words, pulling out of his grasp. "No. You don't get to call me that."

He hadn't used that nickname since he'd all but disappeared from my life. He didn't get to pull it out now. This time, I would be the one walking away.

And Calder could see how it felt.

Chapter Ten

Calder

HERE I WAS, WATCHING HADLEY STORM AWAY *AGAIN*. BUT it was my own damn fault. The nickname had been a step too far. Something I didn't have a right to anymore. That killed.

I stood there for a long moment. Watching the house and hoping Hadley would appear. She didn't.

Finally, I turned and headed back to my SUV. I felt a painful tug in my chest as I climbed behind the wheel, my body telling me just how wrong it was to drive away. But I didn't have a choice. Hads wouldn't hear me now even if I could force her to talk to me.

The leather on my steering wheel creaked, and I made myself loosen my grip. I didn't blame Hadley. That wasn't what I had meant at all. I shifted in my seat as I made the turn towards town. But I could see how she might think I did.

I blamed Jackie, and I blamed myself. Hadley had been my escape back then. When my marriage was a disaster, and everything felt as if it were falling apart, I'd needed her. Her friendship and that hit of adrenaline that reminded me that my life wasn't over. That I had so much to live for.

I couldn't help but wonder if all of my time away had allowed

Jackie's addiction to fester. Had I simply not wanted to see the signs? We'd been like two ships passing in the night by that point. Even though we lived in the same house, we'd been more like separated parents sharing custody, passing the girls off to one another as we went. I'd taken to sleeping in the guest room, and she hadn't argued.

The fields and ranch lands around Hadley's home slowly turned to neighborhoods as I made my way to town. My fingers drummed against the wheel, my muscles feeling twitchy. Too much memory lane and the look of hurt on Hadley's face. No, of *betrayal*. And I'd put it there.

I needed a run. Since the girls were gone for the night, I could do it outside. I'd run until I no longer felt Hadley's pull. Until the temptation to ask her to chase the stars with me wasn't quite so strong. It might take hours, but I'd get there.

I turned off the main drag and made my way towards home. By the time I reached my street, my skin felt too tight for my body. The itchiness distracted me, didn't let me see that someone was sitting on my front steps.

I'd climbed out of my SUV and headed up the front walk when she stood. My steps didn't falter, they halted altogether. Her auburn hair and the tilt of her head had a memory crashing into me.

The fire truck pulled to the side of the road, engines blaring. We poured out of the vehicle, one after the other, searching for the car. A passing motorist had called it in but had said they couldn't reach the station wagon to see if everyone was okay.

"It's down there," a woman called. "Oh, God. It's awful."

We hurried to the edge of the ravine. It wasn't especially deep, but the slope was nasty.

Everything in me froze when I caught sight of the car. How many maroon station wagons were there in Wolf Gap? There was only one I'd ever recalled catching sight of, and that was the one parked in my driveway every night.

I made some sort of strangled sound and started over the edge. It wasn't logical. All I could think was that I had to get to my girls.

Mac caught hold of my arm, pulling me back. "You can't, Cruz. We have to do this safe."

"Get off me!" I bellowed.

Mac's grip didn't loosen, and I moved to take a swing at him. Anything to get free. Anything to get to Birdie and Sage.

McNally cursed and grabbed my other arm. "Calm the hell down. What's gotten into you?"

Mac met his gaze over my shoulder. "That's his wife's car."

The next few minutes, hours, and days were patchy when it came to my memories. Some were as vivid as if they'd happened two minutes ago. Others, I'd lost altogether.

But I'd never forget that Jackie had been laughing as they'd brought her up the side of the ravine on a stretcher. Laughing, even though blood trickled from her hairline. Laughing because she was high as a kite. Nothing would stop that laughter. Not even the fact that she'd almost killed our daughters.

And now, she was standing on my front steps.

"Calder," she said softly.

"What the hell are you doing here?" I could've had the girls with me. Nine times out of ten, I did. Birdie and Sage barely remembered their mother. I'd done my best to explain what had happened in a way that was truthful but didn't do unnecessary damage.

They had glimpses of memories of being in the hospital. Especially Sage, who had been there for almost a month. And they knew that it was their mother who had put them there. I'd had to explain why she was gone. Equating prison to a time-out for a four-year-old was a challenge.

They almost never asked about her. When they did, it was usually around Mother's Day. Schools lacked some serious empathy when it came to kids in single-parent households. It had always been Hadley or Julia who had stepped in to attend the school events that required a mother. Not even my mom, who had already taken off for Florida with my dad to live the cushy retirement life.

Jackie toyed with the zipper on her purse. "I came to talk to you."

I took stock of the woman in front of me. I knew she was beautiful, at least to the average passerby. Long, auburn hair curled around her shoulders. She had curves for days and startling green eyes. But nothing in me stirred.

"Why?"

She swallowed. "I want to see Birdie and Sage."

I was silent, but my blood turned to hot lava. How dare she? After the accident, I had filed for sole legal and physical custody with zero visitation. The courts had granted my request. For all intents and purposes, Birdie and Sage were my daughters and mine alone.

"No."

It was only one word, but it was all I needed.

Jackie looked up at me, her eyes wide and pleading. "I'm sober, Calder. I have been for a long time. I want to see my daughters, to be in their lives again."

I noticed she didn't put a number on her sobriety. *A long time* to her could've been two weeks.

"You lost your right to see them a long time ago."

Tears filled Jackie's eyes. "You'll never know how sorry I am for what I did. But I'm trying to make it right."

I had never been able to tell when Jackie's tears were real or fake. They'd often been a tool in her arsenal to get what she wanted, but right now, they seemed authentic. "The best thing you can do is leave them alone. They're happy. *Safe.* Loved. You coming back around will only confuse them. When they're older, I can give them the option of getting in touch with you. You can give your phone number and email to my lawyer."

I didn't even want her contact information. Wanted nothing to do with this woman who had almost cost me everything.

"Calder, please. I don't want to miss out on their lives."

"You already have. And that was your choice."

Jackie's grip on her purse strap tightened. "Let me prove to you that I've changed. I moved back. I'm just staying at the motel for now, but I got a job at the resort, waitressing. I'm saving up for an apartment."

Hell, no. This wasn't happening. Wolf Gap was too small. I couldn't shield the girls from Jackie forever. Eventually, we'd run into her. Worse, they could run into her when they weren't with me. It could've already happened. If she'd secured a job, Jackie had likely been in town for a few weeks, at least.

"Don't do this. Don't make their lives harder. Don't cause them pain."

Her jaw hardened, that familiar stubborn streak flaring to life. "I know it won't be easy at first, but it'll be worth it in the end. I have a right to see my girls."

"You have no rights. None. You lost them when you sent your car over a cliff and almost killed those girls. Sage barely made it. You pull this, and I'll do whatever I have to. Get a restraining order and have you arrested. Don't think I won't."

"Calder," she whispered. "Don't do this. Think about what we used to have."

"What we used to have was only a pile of lies." I'd thought I could love Jackie someday. There were moments I'd almost felt it. But it had never been real, and I wouldn't expose Birdie and Sage to the same thing. "Leave."

Jackie turned, laying a folded-up piece of paper on the steps. "That's my cell phone number. Call me when you're ready to talk."

I hoped she didn't hold her breath because it would be a cold day in hell before I ever called her.

Chapter Eleven

Hadley

"**A**LL RIGHT. I'M READY TO ROCK AND ROLL," TOBY SAID as he lifted his camera.

I bit back the flicker of annoyance as I adjusted the helmet on my head. I'd wanted a solo skate session today. Just me and the half-pipe I'd had built in the old barn on my property. But Toby had pushed, saying he needed some new content for the channel.

I loved our projects, but sometimes I wanted to ride or skate just for the sheer joy of it, not for likes or comments or sponsorship deals. But Toby and Jinx counted on me. They both had other part-time gigs, but the channel had become more and more a part of their monthly revenue. Since I gave them a percentage of the cut each month, the more videos we put up, the better they did.

I closed my eyes and took a deep breath. There was no room for these kinds of negative emotions dogging me when I was about to pull tricks. I needed to focus. I had to drown out Toby and the pressure I felt there. Calder and our encounter yesterday. The three missed calls I had on my phone from my mom. All of it had to be silenced.

I found my freedom in those moments of nothingness. In the blissful quiet where I ceased to exist. Weightless and flying.

I opened my eyes and tipped over the edge of the half-pipe. I lost myself in that nothingness and the rush of the wind whipping my face. I didn't plan my moves, simply executed whatever felt right in the moment. From one to the next, my speed and freedom built until I was truly flying.

I didn't stop until I was struggling to catch my breath and my muscles ached. I came to a halt on one of the decks and grabbed the bar I'd put in place on the side. My chest heaved as my heart rattled against my ribs.

"Hells, yeah!" Toby called from below.

His voice shook me out of those last tendrils of freedom swirling around me. I bit the inside of my cheek to keep from biting his head off. I picked up my skateboard and climbed down the ladder.

"That was badass. Kinda beautiful, too. That sounds goofy, but it was."

I forced a smile at my friend. "Thanks, Tobs."

He was quiet for a minute as he took me in. "You okay? You've been off lately. Not as jazzed about what we're doing." Color leached from his face. "You're not thinking of quitting, are you?"

"Not quitting, but I might need to step back a little. I've just got a lot going on."

He eased down on the bench by the half-pipe. "Your mom?"

I used the back of the bench to balance as I started to stretch. "Her and a million other things."

"Things seemed a little strained with you and Calder this morning."

Toby had arrived with bagels and coffee when the girls were packing up from our sleepover and had witnessed my awkward handoff with Calder.

I blew out a breath and sat on the floor, taking up another stretch. "It's complicated."

"You still love him?"

I stilled but kept my focus on reaching my hands towards my

shoe. One night after my falling-out with Calder, I'd had a little too much tequila and spilled my guts to Toby and Jinx. Thankfully, neither of them had mentioned my admission again. Until now.

"There will always be a piece of me that loves him. I'm not someone who can turn something like that off."

Toby was quiet again for a minute. "You deserve better. Someone who appreciates you for who you are and doesn't try to force you to be someone you're not."

His words hurt. Because a part of that was true. Calder had been the one to give me the gift of finding my freedom, but he had also been the one who tried to take it away. Who'd told me to stop being so reckless. I didn't know what to do with that juxtaposition.

"I wouldn't have tried to change you."

"Toby…" I said his name softly, the single word trailing off at the end. I didn't know what else to say.

"I know you don't feel that way about me, and I'm not trying to put pressure on you. I'm happy with Calla. I just want you to know that you deserve someone who loves you for you."

Toby had made a move on me once. About a year after my friendship with Calder had dissolved. I'd let him down as gently as I could, but it had been awkward between us for a couple of months.

"I'll find the right person one day. I won't settle until I do."

Toby kicked my shoe with his. "That's what I like to hear."

My phone rang from its spot on the bench, and I leaned forward to pick it up. Hayes' name flashed on the screen. "Hey, Bubby."

"Hey, Hads. I need a favor."

It had to be important if he wasn't giving me a hard time for using my childhood nickname for him. "Name it."

"Can you watch Birdie and Sage tonight?"

"Sure. What time?"

"Can you be there at seven-thirty? I need to take Calder out for a beer."

I toyed with one of my shoelaces. "Is everything okay?"

"Jackie's back in town."

I stiffened, my muscles locking. "You've got to be kidding me."

"Nope, showed up at his house yesterday."

Guilt pricked at my skin for giving Calder the cold shoulder this morning. "I'll be there at seven-thirty. Let me know if he needs anything else, will you?"

"You got it. Thanks, Hads."

I hung up and stared at my phone. This was a recipe for disaster.

"One more story?" Birdie pleaded from her bed.

I drilled a finger into her side. "I already gave you three."

"She just doesn't want to go to sleep," Sage mumbled.

"Not true," Birdie argued. "I like reading."

I chuckled. "Well, we're all booked out for the night. It's time to get some sleep. I bet your dad has big Sunday plans for you."

Sage nodded. "We're going on a hike."

"See? You need to rest up so you can kick his butt on the trails."

"Fine," Birdie muttered.

I pushed to my feet and headed for the door, flicking off the light, leaving only the glow of the girls' nightlight. "I'll be downstairs if you need me. Love you."

"Love you, too," they chorused.

I headed down the stairs and towards the kitchen. I wasn't hungry exactly, but I needed a distraction. My mind had been reeling since Hayes and Calder had left. Calder had barely met my gaze when I showed up to watch Birdie and Sage, and there'd been a slump to his shoulders that had me worried.

I opened the door to the pantry and surveyed the shelves. None of the chips looked appealing right now, but I paused when I saw a box of popcorn. That should do the trick.

I put it in the microwave and set the timer. Within seconds, the kernels were popping. When they slowed, I pulled it out, cursing softly when the steam burned my fingers. I set it on the counter and opened a cabinet to grab a large bowl. More carefully this time, I picked up the bag and opened it, spilling the contents into the container.

I tossed the bag into the trash and moved to the living room. Settling on the large, overstuffed sofa, I grabbed the remote and began channel surfing. Nothing kept my attention for more than five minutes, but I finally forced myself to settle on a rerun of *Matlock*.

One episode turned into two, and I demolished the entire bowl of popcorn. After pizza and ice cream with Birdie and Sage, I started to feel a little ill. My phone buzzed on the cushion next to me.

Unknown Number: *Stop trying to steal things that don't belong to you.*

My heart rate picked up a fraction. The phone number wasn't from an area code I recognized. I copied it into the internet browser on my phone and searched. It showed up as coming from Minneapolis, but the number wasn't listed.

I toggled back over to the text message and stared at it. Unease slid through me. It sounded similar to the email I'd received.

Unknown Number: *It's a bad idea to ignore me. You need to learn your lesson.*

I blocked the number. But how the heck had they gotten my phone number, to begin with? The address the email had been sent to was public, listed on my website and the *Voyeur* channel. Anyone could find it. But my phone number? That was private. I didn't have it listed anywhere. I didn't even have social media accounts under my real name.

I nibbled on the corner of my thumbnail as I stared at the screen. The thought of going to my sheriff brother flickered through my mind, but I immediately shoved that aside. He'd surely spill the beans to my parents, and they would try to force me to move home.

None of my family or anyone outside of Toby, Jinx, and Calla knew about this other life I lived. That was how I liked it. Then none of them could try to convince me that I needed to stop.

The front door rattled, and I jumped to my feet. "Hello?"

"It's me," Hayes called. "Can you open up? I can't find Calder's keys."

I hurried over and pulled open the door. My eyes widened. Calder was glassy-eyed and leaning against Hayes. I didn't think I'd ever seen the man drunk. I knew he and Hayes had tied one on when they went camping right after Calder's divorce, but that was all I'd ever even heard about Calder being intoxicated.

My gaze flicked to my brother. "Is he okay?"

Hayes grunted as he tried to get Calder inside. "He's feeling just fine. But he's heavier than the last time I had to do this."

"You calling me fat?" Calder slurred.

"Oh, boy," I muttered. "Let me help you get him upstairs."

"Hey, Little Daredevil." Calder sniffed my hair as I ducked under his other arm to help balance him. "You smell nice."

Hayes chuckled. "Anyone would smell nice compared to you, booze breath."

"Hey, now. I had a mint."

"There's not a mint in the world strong enough for what you're rocking."

Hayes and I slowly moved Calder up the stairs and maneuvered him to his bedroom. Calder flopped back on the mattress with an oomph.

Hayes bent and picked up one of his feet. "I'll get your boots, but if you think I'm getting you out of your jeans, you have another thing coming."

"I don't want you copping a feel."

I couldn't hold in my giggle.

Calder put a hand to his head. "The room's spinning."

"I'll bet it is," Hayes said as the boot gave way.

"Hayes," I whispered. "I don't think we should leave him alone tonight. What if he gets sick?"

Hayes grimaced as he pulled Calder's second boot free. "You're probably right. Hell, I have a seven a.m. breakfast meeting. I didn't need this tonight."

"I can stay." The words were out before I considered how wise they were. "I don't work until tomorrow night."

He eyed me. "You sure?"

"Positive."

A snore came from the bed.

My brows lifted. "Did he just fall asleep half off the bed?"

"I'm pretty sure he did."

"Here, I'll help you get him actually on the bed."

We each picked up a leg and swung him so that Calder was at least completely on the mattress. His snores stuttered but didn't stop.

Hayes shook his head. "You sure you got this?"

"I'm sure. Go home to your fiancée."

"All right. I'll lock the door on my way out. Text me if you need me."

I moved to Calder's dresser and snagged an extra set of house keys. "Here's a key for the deadbolt."

"Thanks." He pulled me into a quick hug. "Love you, Hads."

"Love you, too, Bubby."

He pinched my side. "Quit with that nickname."

I gave him an evil grin and ducked out of his hold. "Never."

Hayes waved me off and headed for the stairs. I listened to his footfalls and then to the door opening, closing, and the deadbolt latching.

I stared at the man snoring away, his mouth half-open. Even in his ridiculous state, he was beautiful. I forced my gaze away from his face. "You might be sleeping in jeans, but I am not."

I riffled through his dresser until I found a t-shirt and some sweatpants with a drawstring. I'd swim in them, but at least I could tie the string tight. I went to the bathroom and changed. When I got out, Calder had turned onto his side, facing the opposite side of the bed. It was a better position in case he got sick in the night, but I really hoped he didn't.

I moved slowly towards the bed. Calder, Hayes, and I had gone camping together a number of times when we were younger. We'd shared a single tent, but that was as close as I'd ever come to sharing a bed with Calder.

I grabbed a blanket from the overstuffed chair in the corner and eased onto the bed. Crawling under the covers felt like taking it a step too far. I laid back on the pillows and pulled the blanket up around me.

Calder stirred, his eyes opening. "Little Daredevil."

"Hi."

"Hi." His gaze bored into me as if he could see every scar and still-bleeding wound. "I'm sorry."

"For what?"

"Hurting you. You're the last person I'd ever want to hurt." He was quiet for a moment, his eyes falling closed. "You were my air."

Chapter Twelve

Calder

THE FIRST THING I FELT WAS WHAT SEEMED LIKE A MINI jackhammer on the inside of my skull. The second was that my mouth was as dry as the Sahara. But the third had me freezing.

It was warmth. So much warmth pressed against my front. I was curled around a petite form, and my body wasn't mad about it. It felt right. As if we were two puzzle pieces that fit perfectly.

I searched my mind, flipping through a series of memories and reaching for the last concrete one. Hayes and me at the Wolf Gap Bar & Grill. The whiskey I'd opted for instead of beer.

Hayes knew better than to let me take some random woman home when I had the girls. Hell.

I slowly peeled my eyes open. The light streaming in from the window hurt, and I had to blink a few times before my vision focused. When it finally did, my heart gave a healthy spasm against my ribs.

Hair so blond it almost looked white cascaded around slender shoulders. A face relaxed in sleep but so damn beautiful it almost hurt to look at. Pink cheeks and bow lips. And my body pressed

How the hell had Hadley ended up in my bed? My body gave a small jerk as my mind finally caught up with the reality of the situation. Hadley was in my bed.

As I scrambled back, Hadley startled awake. "Wha—? Are you okay? Are you sick?"

I looked back at her as the drumbeat in my head intensified. "What are you doing here? Did we? We didn't, right?"

Pain lanced across Hadley's features. "Nothing happened. I just stayed with you to make sure you didn't choke on your own vomit. Trust me, I'm well aware that you find me repulsive."

I blinked a few times. The last thing I found Hadley was repulsive. Her beauty was a living and breathing thing that wove around a person. Not just the physical that heated your blood and made you question your sanity. No, it was more than that. She had a beauty burned into her, and it manifested in the most surprising ways. In how she connected with others. In the fact that she could make the most ordinary of experiences extraordinary. In how she lived every moment to the fullest.

"I don't find you repulsive."

Hadley scoffed. "Okay, fine. Now that I know you're not going to stop breathing, I'm going to go before the girls wake up."

She swung her legs over the side of the bed and started to get up, but I caught her arm, pulling her back to the bed. "Don't go."

Her eyes flared and her jaw hardened. "Why? I don't need to be reminded of all the reasons you would freak out by finding me in your bed."

"I don't want you to go." The single sentence was beyond lacking. But it was also the truth. I never wanted Hadley to go. It was playing with fire, having her so close, but I couldn't help myself. "Stay and let me take you and the girls to breakfast. It's the least I can do to thank you."

Hadley's gaze swept over my face, searching for something. The truth, maybe? I didn't look away.

"I wasn't disgusted to find you in my bed. I just—I don't remember much about last night and that freaked me out." If Hadley was in my bed, I wanted to remember every second.

She sighed, her shoulders slumping a bit. "I'd probably be freaked, too. But you know what? You deserved it. You were drunk as a skunk last night. And you snore. Loud."

The side of my mouth kicked up. "Maybe it's *you* who snores."

"Trust me. You passed out while Hayes was still taking off your boots."

I winced. "Sorry about that."

Hadley toyed with the edge of the blanket. "Are you okay?"

"No." The fact that Jackie could be around any corner had me more on edge than ever. Later today, I'd have to sit down with the girls and explain everything, ripping their world apart yet again. "It's so damn selfish."

"Her coming back?"

I nodded, sitting up against the pillows. "If she loved them, she'd stay away."

"I'm not sure it's that simple."

My gaze narrowed on Hadley.

She held up a hand to stop anything I might say. "Trust me, I am not a Jackie fan. I think she used you from day one, and the fact that she put Birdie and Sage at risk makes me want to bitch-slap her into next week, but I also can't imagine the guilt she has to live with. If I had that kind of weight, I'd want to do whatever I could to make things right."

I reached out, my fingers lacing with Hadley's. I needed that point of contact. Something to ground me. "That's you. Because you have this amazing heart. You're always trying to make people feel seen and understood."

I'd seen it a million times with Birdie and Sage. Sometimes, people in the twins' lives treated them exactly the same. But not Hadley. She met each girl exactly where they were. She celebrated their interests and strengths and helped them not be embarrassed by their weaknesses.

Hadley looked down at our interlocked fingers. "I never want anyone to feel like they should be anyone but who they are."

Pain flared in my chest. I'd made Hadley feel as if she should change who she was. I'd given her that wound every time I accused her of being irresponsible or reckless. Every time I told her not to do something. "I'm sorry."

Her gaze jumped to me. "For what?"

"Trying to get you to dial back what you needed. It's not because I thought that what you were doing was bad." My fingers tightened around hers. "It's because I couldn't bear it if I lost you. I came so close to losing my girls. I saw a glimpse of what might happen if you lost the people most important to you. I wouldn't be able to take it, Hads. I need you safe and whole."

She blinked rapidly at me. "Why didn't you just explain that? I wouldn't have stopped, but at least we could've talked about it."

"I was drowning. All of a sudden, I was a single parent. Sage was still recovering from the accident. I had to work. There were meals and laundry and a million other things. And all I saw was danger everywhere. All the ways someone could get hurt. How I might lose someone. I was just trying to stanch the bleeding."

Hadley leaned forward, her head resting on my sternum. "I'm sorry. So sorry you felt that way. But I don't know where we go from here. I can't stop doing what I love to help your demons. I'd be miserable, and it would weigh down our friendship."

I glided a hand down her hair, letting my fingers tangle in the strands. It was the softest thing I'd ever felt. "We take it one step at a time. I'll try not to ask you to stop things."

Hadley sat up, looking into my eyes. "And I'll try to

understand where you're coming from when you're an over-bearing ass."

I barked out a laugh. "Sounds like a deal. Shake on it?"

I held out a hand, and Hadley took it.

"Deal." She bounded off the bed. "Now, feed me."

That, I could do. Our problems weren't magically gone. We had so many things to weed through and untangle. But I wasn't walking away from Hadley like I had before. Doing that had left me only half-alive. Walking through life but not really living it. That had to change. And Hadley was a part of that.

Chapter Thirteen

Hadley

I SHOT CALDER A GRIN AS HE RUBBED AT HIS TEMPLES. The clatter and noise of families and friends as they ate wasn't exactly a great environment for someone with the hangover from hell, but it had been Calder's idea to go to The Cowboy Inn. It was the most popular breakfast spot in town for tourists and locals alike.

Our waitress poured coffee into Calder's mug.

"Thank you, Angie. You're a godsend."

She winked at him. "Rough night?"

"Something like that."

"Daddy went out with Hayes last night," Birdie added helpfully.

"It's all becoming clear." Angie reached over and filled my mug. "Do you know what you want, or do you need a minute?"

"Waffles with whipped cream and strawberries," Birdie immediately called out.

"All right, sugar, we got waffles coming up. What about you, Sage?"

Sage ducked her head, focusing on the pictures on the menu. "May I please have the scramble and a side of cheese grits?"

"Yes, you most certainly may. And what about you two?"

he had my back. He normally would've taken my mother's side on this kind of thing.

He scrubbed a hand over his stubbled jaw as he tossed his credit card on top of our receipt. "I didn't realize how bad it had gotten."

Calder hadn't realized because up until a few weeks ago, he'd been mostly keeping his distance from me.

Angie grabbed the check and card. "Be right back."

Calder nodded and then turned his focus back to me. "That's not true. I think I chose not to see it. Things were easier that way."

"I get it. I wish I could ignore it."

He reached over and squeezed my hand. "I'm sorry that I added to it. I was wrong."

Warmth spread up my arm as Calder held on a few beats before letting go.

"I'll have your back from now on."

"Thanks." The single word came out in a croak, and I cleared my throat. "But I think I need to keep my distance from her for right now. It's too hard. Hurts too much."

"Hadley," Calder whispered.

"It's okay. I mean, it sucks, but I have to take care of myself first."

Angie dropped the card and receipt back on the table. "There you go, chickadees. Thanks for coming in."

I forced a smile. "Thanks for taking such good care of us."

"Always." She gave us a wave and headed to another table as Calder signed the slip of paper.

"Thanks for breakfast."

"Thanks for taking care of my drunk ass last night. I'm pretty sure I owe you more than breakfast, but we'll start there."

I grinned as I stood. "I could think up some manual labor at my house to make us even."

"You're cruel, woman."

"In this case, I'm going to take that as a compliment."

As we headed towards the doors, a guy in his mid-twenties

stepped into our path. "Hey, I'm sorry to interrupt, but are you The Little Daredevil?"

I froze. The only time someone had recognized me from my channel was when I'd gone snowboarding up on Mount Hood. And it had only happened once.

Calder stiffened next to me. *Shit, shit, shit.* I forced a smile. "Sorry, I don't know what you're talking about."

The guy pulled out his phone where he had a photo of me from my solo trek along the PCT. "You look just like her."

Calder bent forward, his eyes narrowing on the image. "Who is she?"

"She's this totally badass extreme sports girl. She's got over half a million followers on *Voyeur.*" He shrugged. "They say everyone has a doppelgänger."

"I guess she's mine."

"No doubt."

The man returned to his table of friends, and I walked stiffly towards the door. Once we were outside, Calder grabbed my elbow and tugged me into a small alcove next to the building. "What the hell was that?"

It felt as if the walls were closing in around me. I'd built this outlet for myself and me alone. No one in my real life was supposed to know about any of it. "Mistaken identity, I guess."

"That's what you're really going with, Little Daredevil?"

I winced and looked up at Calder. "Please don't tell anyone."

"Don't tell anyone what?"

"I have a channel on this platform. Toby and Jinx make these videos of different tricks and upload them there."

"What, like some sort of social media?"

I nodded. "It's a photo and video streaming site. Some people just share their lives. Others teach people how to do things. Mostly, it's watching people who excel at something. Everything from video games to cooking to sports."

"And half a million people follow you there?"

My teeth pressed into my bottom lip. "It's closer to a million now."

Calder's jaw slackened. "And you just do it for fun?"

"Mostly. The site pays out some because people purchase subscriptions. And you can get sponsorship deals."

"So, you're making money doing this."

I was making more than I would ever make as an EMT, but I wasn't ready to share that tidbit with Calder. "Yeah."

He scrubbed a hand over his face. "And your name is The Little Daredevil?"

It was too much. Even tucked away in this little alcove, I felt exposed. That this one tiny fact would tell Calder everything. That I'd never stopped loving him. That I'd never let go. But I refused to be ashamed about it. Instead, I looked him straight in the eyes.

"Yes."

Chapter Fourteen

Calder

I BLINKED MY EYES A FEW TIMES AS I STARED AT MY LAPTOP screen. Juggling the spreadsheet of work schedules had pressure building at my temples. I reached for the bottle of eye drops on my nightstand and tipped my head back. The cool liquid helped, but it would only give me relief for so long.

I refocused on the screen, moving people around so that everyone could get the days off they needed. It was one of my least favorite parts of the job, this kind of admin minutia. But it was a necessary evil, and I'd only be doing more of it if I took over for Cap.

A heaviness took root in my gut. The same sensation I'd felt for the past couple of months whenever I thought about taking on that role. It would be safer for sure, but a lot of it would be boring as hell.

The letters and numbers on my screen started to blur, and I finally exited out of the program altogether. I'd have time before my shift tomorrow to finish it. I moved to shut the laptop and then paused.

Instead of putting the device away and getting some

much-needed sleep, I opened an internet browser. I typed in *The Little Daredevil*.

The first thing that popped up was a website with the name. I clicked on it. A series of still images traveled across the screen. Hadley mid-air after a mountain bike jump. Rappelling down a cliff. Doing a trick on her skateboard.

I hit the menu button and there was an option for videos. When I clicked that, it took me to a site called *Voyeur*. I grimaced at the name. They might as well have called it Stalkers-R-Us. An endless sea of videos cascaded over the screen. How long had she been doing this?

I scrolled and scrolled until I reached the end. I hit the very first video and checked the date. It couldn't have been more than a month after our falling-out. I toggled over to play.

Music and voices filled the speakers. I recognized Toby's voice cheering Hadley on as she took her place at the top of a half-pipe. But she was completely focused on something else altogether. In a zone where no one around her existed.

That look wasn't one she'd worn with me. I'd always been allowed into the bubble she created for herself on our adventures. Our energy fed off each other's, creating something new. Something better.

Hadley tipped over the edge. I'd never been one for skateboarding, but even with little knowledge of the sport, I could tell that she had skill. Not enough to be a professional, maybe, but more than enough to give me a heart attack.

As Hadley picked up speed, her board swung past the lip of the half-pipe as she grabbed the edge with her hand. I held my breath as she continued to skate back and forth. I didn't think I took in air until the video ended with whoops and hollers.

I scrolled to one a few months later of Hadley snowboarding. The editing on this one was more advanced. Someone had cut it between three camera angles. One that came from Hadley's POV, another clearly shot by another snowboarder, and a third that must have been from a drone. I had to admit that the effect was pretty amazing. I got sucked in, leaning closer to my screen, watching as she launched into trick after trick.

I moved farther along and came to one titled *Peace on the PCT.* I clicked on it. This one didn't have a bunch of fancy camera work. It was mainly a single point of view. More subdued instrumental music played over the video of some breathtaking sights.

I remembered when Hadley had hiked this section of the PCT completely alone. Of course, she hadn't told anyone what she was doing until she was already gone. She'd scheduled an email to Hayes that told him her route and where she'd be checking in with approximate dates.

Hayes and his parents had been livid, and I hadn't been far behind. But I'd used it as a reminder, just another reason why Hadley and I could never be. I didn't think that type of reckless disregard was something I could have in my life in any real way. Now, I could see that Hadley had been desperate for freedom and peace, to silence the noise we'd all been throwing at her.

Soon, the landscapes switched to Hadley's face. Even streaked with dirt, she was breathtaking. Immersive beauty pouring out of her. She gave the camera a small smile.

"I thought it might be fun to do a daily check-in. A journal, of sorts." She looked off into the distance. "Day one is in the books. It was rough, I won't lie. Not the physical stuff, although I'm sure my muscles will be aching tomorrow. It's the mental that gets you as you're walking away from civilization, knowing you'll be mostly alone for weeks."

Hadley picked up a stone and flipped it back and forth between her fingers. "I don't know why the idea of being alone is so scary. I feel alone every day of my life. My family loves me, but they don't get me. The person I cared most about in this world decided he could walk away from me without a second glance."

My breath seized in my lungs. I couldn't breathe, couldn't move as I watched the screen.

"I know what it's like to be alone. Yet, somehow, walking away from that first parking lot was still terrifying. Maybe this is my chance to make peace with aloneness, perhaps even become friends with it."

She shot a sad smile at the camera. "I'll let you know how it goes."

The music came back up as Hadley's face faded away. And then there was a black screen and silence. Nothing at all. But I could still see the pain etched onto her features as she spoke. I'd known that Hadley needed me, and I'd left her anyway. That made me lower than dirt.

I scrolled to the top to exit out when something caught my eye. It was a one-line comment. *"What a slut."*

My scrolling halted. It was on a semi-recent video. One of her cliff jumping, from the looks of it. I expanded the window of comments. There were hundreds of them, maybe thousands. Most of them were kind.

That was killer!

I'm going cliff diving next week. Totally trying this!

There were lots of comments that consisted only of emojis and little image graphics.

But there were ugly ones, too.

Talk about a show-off.

I heard she buys her followers.

She's always with those two guys. I bet she's screwing both of them.

Someone needs to take her down a peg.

My hand moved to my phone before I could even think about how late it was.

Hadley's groggy voice came across the line. "What's wrong?"

"I'm looking at one of your videos on *Voyeur*."

She was quiet for a second as the sheets rustled. "Are you calling to yell at me?"

"I'm calling to ask what the hell is with these disgusting comments on your videos."

Hadley sighed. "They're just trolls. Ignore them. I do."

My gaze swept over the screen, and my hand tightened around

the phone. "There's one here that says you deserve to break your neck." And there was another from a guy who described exactly what he'd do to her if he got her alone. "Some of this stuff is sick."

"My team tries to report it. A lot of times, the site will take the comments down. Sometimes, even block the users. But it's hard to keep up with it all."

I zoomed in on the user profile pictures. Most of them weren't actual photos. They were little cartoon drawings—cruel and jealous bastards hiding behind a keyboard.

"Do they contact you anywhere else?"

She was quiet.

"Hadley…"

"I've gotten some emails. A couple of texts."

I pushed off the bed and paced to the door, then back to the bed. "This isn't normal. And why do you have your phone number listed?"

"I don't."

I froze. "Someone texted you on a number that's unlisted."

"I blocked them and haven't heard anything since."

"We need to tell Hayes." I had half a mind to do it right now and make him go out to her house. Hadley lived alone with no neighbors within sight of her property. It was how she liked it, but it also meant that no one could help if she needed it.

"Calder, no. No one in my family knows that I do this, and that's how it's staying."

"This is your life we're talking about—"

"No, this is a bunch of jerks hiding behind their phones. No one is going to hurt me. They just want to knock me down a few pegs."

I gripped the back of my neck, squeezing hard. "You haven't received anything in the mail? No weird visits from people you don't know?"

"Nothing, I promise."

I blew out a harsh breath. "I won't tell Hayes on one condition."

Hadley groaned. "What?"

"You tell me immediately if something happens, even if you think it's nothing."

She was quiet again.

"Hadley..."

"Fine. Now, can I go back to sleep? If I have dark circles tomorrow, I'm coming for you."

The corners of my mouth curved. "Sorry I woke you."

"You owe me all the coffee I want tomorrow."

"Deal."

"Goodnight, Calder."

"Goodnight, Little Daredevil."

She hung up, and I stared at my phone. All I wanted was Hadley here, to know she was safe. But I didn't want her down the hall in the guest room. I wanted that warmth next to me, surrounding me. When I looked at my bed, all I saw was the empty space that should've been hers.

Chapter Fifteen

Hadley

THE TINY BELL JINGLED AS I PUSHED OPEN THE DOOR TO the coffee shop. The Bean & Tea Leaf always did steady business, but since my shift didn't start until ten a.m. today, I thankfully missed the worst of the pre-work rush. The quaint shop had mismatched tables and chairs that made the space feel homey and inviting.

Calla sat hunched over a laptop in one of the corners, clearly on a break from her shift and oblivious to the world around her. I moved to the register, my gaze traveling over the array of chalkboards above. "Morning, Aaron."

"Morning, Hadley. You want the usual?"

"That, and I'll take a black coffee and two of your breakfast burritos."

Jones would owe me big for picking up his favorite breakfast, but I wanted to stay in my partner's good graces, and I wasn't above bribery.

"It'll be just a few minutes. You want your latte while you wait?"

"That'd be great." I handed him my insulated travel mug to fill.

Aaron whipped it up in a flash and handed over the caffeinated goodness. I needed it. After Calder's late-night call, I'd struggled to get back to sleep, tossing and turning, unable to get comfortable. I inhaled the rich aroma. "If you weren't already taken, I'd try to marry you for the coffee alone."

Aaron chuckled. "If you weren't half my age and I hadn't met my Lucy, I just might take you up on that."

"Tell her I said she caught a good one."

"I'll do that. Be just a few more minutes for those burritos."

"No rush."

I moved towards Calla at her corner table. She was still intently focused on her computer screen, headphones on. I crouched so my face was just above the top of the laptop, and she jolted, hand flying to her chest and headphones popping free.

"Hadley, you scared the crud out of me."

I grinned. "Isn't that what friends are for?"

"Friends are for heart attacks?"

"Well, when you put it like that…"

Calla shook her head. "I'm gonna get you back for that one."

"I'd expect nothing less. What were you so focused on?"

Pink rose to the apples of her cheeks. "I'm taking an online class in video editing."

"Really? That's great."

"I thought I might be able to help Toby out, and maybe we could start a company. He's so talented. He should do more than just edit your videos."

I tried not to take her words as an insult, I knew it wasn't how she'd intended them, and Toby *was* crazy talented. Maybe if he had other clients, there wouldn't be so much pressure on me to do video after video. He'd texted yesterday, already wanting to know what the plan was for the next one.

"I think that's a great idea."

Calla's brows rose a fraction. "Really? I wasn't sure if you'd be upset…"

"Not at all. He should expand. I'm sure you guys could get all kinds of gigs around here."

"I think you're right. I'm already working on our website."

I took a sip of my latte. "If you're good at that kind of thing, you might even think about offering to build people's websites and create video content for them."

"That's a great idea." Calla typed out something on her computer. "I'm just writing that down."

The bell over the door sounded, and I glanced up to see Evan Gibbs striding in. His gaze swept over me in a way that had me fighting a shiver.

"Why is that guy suddenly everywhere?" Calla whispered.

"Small town," I muttered. They were a blessing and a curse. You got a solid, tightly knit community, but it was hard to escape the people you wanted to avoid.

"Hadley," Aaron called.

"I gotta head out. Let me know if you need any help with the new business. I can give you guys an endorsement if you want."

"That would be great. Thanks, Hads."

I gave Calla a little wave and moved to the counter to pick up my burritos and Jones' coffee. Evan stared at me the whole time, not saying a word.

"Thanks, Aaron," I said, already turning to leave. I hurried out and tried to shake the creepy-crawly feeling.

Calder set a cup on the coffee table in front of me before easing down beside me on the couch. "This is cup one."

I grinned at him. "Good to see you making up for disrupting my beauty sleep."

"I do what I can." He was quiet for a moment, gaze sweeping over my face. "Any other issues?"

I rolled my eyes. "I promised I'd tell you if there were."

"Just checking."

"It's the internet. It brings out the gross and evil in people."

Calder leaned back into the couch's pillows, turning his body so that he was facing me. "So, why do you do it then?"

I glanced around the lounge room. Only McNally was nearby, and he was focused on some sports show doing a breakdown of last night's baseball game. "There are good people, too. I've had little girls message me and tell me that I gave them the courage to take up a sport they never would've otherwise. A woman who decided to hike the PCT after her divorce because she saw my series on it. I can connect with people all over the world and share what we love."

I picked at a piece of lint on my uniform pants. "I needed to feel a little less alone. Like I had a community. My channel gave me that." At least, it had when it was small. Now, it almost seemed like its own monster.

Calder reached out and squeezed my thigh just above my knee. "I'm sorry you felt alone. Even sorrier that I played a role in it."

I swallowed against the burn in my throat. I had forgiven Calder a long time ago. I'd had to if I wanted to stay in Birdie's and Sage's lives. But just because I'd forgiven, didn't mean I'd forgotten. That kind of pain carved itself into your bones.

"Have you heard any more from Jackie?"

It was a cowardly move. But I couldn't go where the current conversation was headed.

Calder released his hold on my leg, sinking back farther into the pillows. "Nothing yet. But I had a conversation with the girls last night and let them know she was in town."

"How'd they take it?"

"How you'd expect. Birdie stormed off and slammed her bedroom door. Sage got really quiet."

"I hate that they have to go through this."

Calder's jaw worked back and forth. "Me, too. Jackie has always had a selfish streak."

One that Calder had constantly looked past. There might've been issues in their marriage, but there clearly had been passion, too. The proprietary way Jackie had latched onto Calder any time another woman came near told me that she had something to fight for.

Calder toyed with a zipper on one of the couch's throw pillows. "I'll have to talk to her at some point. I'm just not sure I'm ready for it."

"I'm sorry."

"Not your fault."

"Doesn't mean I can't be sorry that you're going through it."

An alarm cut through the air, and lights above flashed red. "Structure fire." More tones sounded. "Structure fire."

We were on our feet in a flash. Calder pulled out his phone, skimming the readout. "Burn pile. Jumped to the house."

"Shit, man," McNally said as we all hurried towards the bays. "It's too late in the season to be burning."

The weather had already turned warm. The last thing anyone needed was a forest fire.

Calder yelled out the address to Mac, Jones, and Wilson. "Gear up."

I hurried to our rig as Jones climbed behind the wheel. The bay doors were already sliding open, and the alert lights outside were on.

Jones started her up. "Ready to rock and roll?"

"You know it."

In seconds, we were pulling out and speeding towards the scene, sirens blaring. The fire trucks were hot on our heels.

I caught sight of the smoke before we even turned on to the residence's road. "Hell, this isn't good."

"No, it's not."

Jones pulled the ambulance to the shoulder, leaving lots of room for the fire rigs as the house came into view. It was almost entirely engulfed. A man was crumpled on the front lawn, clutching his chest.

I grabbed my gear bag and jumped out, running towards him. "Sir, tell me what hurts."

"My-my wife, she's inside. She was taking a nap. Wasn't feeling well. I gotta go get her."

"Sir, the firefighters are here. They're going to help."

"Please, my wife."

My fingers moved to check his pulse; it was way too high. "The best thing you can do for your wife right now is to help yourself."

Wilson hopped from one of the fire trucks, yelling over to me as she went for one of the hoses. "Anyone inside?"

"One adult female," I called. "Where's the bedroom?" I asked the man.

"T-top floor, in the back."

Jones rushed over with the oxygen tank and secured the mask over the man's face.

Calder was barking orders at his crew. The building made a groaning sound, and Calder cursed. "Mac? It's you and me."

My heart gave a healthy lurch in my chest as flames licked out of an upstairs window. I wanted Calder to give the job to someone else. Anyone else. But that wasn't the kind of man Calder was. He would never ask someone to face danger instead of him.

His gaze flashed to me quickly, something unreadable in his expression. And then he disappeared into the smoke and ash.

Chapter Sixteen

Calder

THE SMOKE WAS THICK AS I MOVED CAUTIOUSLY UP THE stairs, testing each one before I put my weight on it. The heat of the fire was in the walls themselves, a silent warning that we were running out of time.

Finally, I hit the landing, Mac on my heels. "Let's move."

The door to the back bedroom was open, and a moan filtered through the air. I hurried forward towards a small form on the bed. Just as I reached her, an explosion sounded from next door.

"Backdraft," Mac called. "Let's get her and go."

I pulled the comforter around the woman and picked her up in my arms. "You lead the way," I called to Mac.

"Let's dance."

Flames flew out of the room in front of us, and I knew we had no choice but to move as quickly as possible past them. "Go, go, go!"

Mac picked up to a jog, and I followed. Even though the woman in my arms was light compared to some, the combination of her, my gear, and the heat made my muscles burn. I turned my back to the flames, shielding the woman as much as possible.

We made it to the stairs, but they groaned as we rushed down them. Running for the door, we made it through just as another explosion sounded from upstairs. The bedroom we'd just been in, I realized.

Hadley rushed forward with a gurney, and I laid the woman on it. She began to cough as I did, and I knew that was a good sign. Hadley worked swiftly and gently, getting the woman on oxygen and starting an IV. She glanced up at me as I took my helmet off. "You injured?"

"All in one piece."

"Then stop that damn fire before someone else gets hurt."

The corner of my mouth kicked up. "Yes, ma'am."

I groaned as I stepped out of the shower. Everything hurt. I needed a massage, a whiskey, and to sleep for a solid twelve hours. It felt amazing.

This was the kind of hurt that assured you that you were alive, and it came with another high. One that would last for hours. Saving a life. Marty and Abel Griggs would both make a full recovery.

I toweled off and pulled on clothes from the clean pile I kept on hand at the station. Tossing my towel in the hamper, I headed out the door and down the hall. I passed the captain's closed door just before I walked outside. He hadn't been at the blaze today. He'd been stuck at some county meeting.

I paused in my walk to my SUV. Was that what I really wanted for my future? Endless meetings, schmoozing, and rarely getting to be on the scene? I thought about today. The rush of getting inside, of getting Marty out. The tears in her husband's eyes as he thanked me.

I loved that part of my job, and I wasn't sure I was ready to give it up.

"You look like you're thinking awfully hard."

I blinked a few times, bringing Hadley into focus. "I don't know if I want to be captain."

"I never understood why you said you wanted that in the first place. You were born to be a lieutenant."

"Born to be, huh?"

She sighed as if I were an idiot, and the truth was plain as day. "You're an amazing firefighter. Today was the perfect example of that. But you're also a great leader. People want to follow you. You're the perfect go-between for the crew and the brass. You should stay exactly where you are."

"How can you be so sure of that?"

"Because I know *you*."

She did. Better than anyone. Even Hayes. He and I had a brotherhood that would never be broken. But Hadley and I shared an understanding that ran deeper than friendship. It was one of the soul. And I'd pissed all over that. I wasn't sure how in the world I could make something like that right.

"You do know me." I glanced back at the building. "I still have to think about it. Captain would mean a salary increase, less risk, more regular hours."

"You have a more-than-comfortable life. The girls are used to the pattern you have now. They have plenty of people who love them to spend time with."

I didn't look away from Hadley. "And the risk?"

She looked towards the park across the street from the station. "That's something you'll have to make your peace with if you want a life that makes you happy."

"You're probably right there." I knew she was. I just wasn't sure I had it in me to face the demons I needed to in hopes of making that peace.

Hadley's phone dinged, and she pulled it out of her pocket. "It's Shiloh. I told her I'd go with her to look at a colt she's thinking of buying."

"You guys have fun."

She shoved her phone back into her pocket. "See you tomorrow?"

"See you tomorrow." I watched as she walked to her SUV and climbed behind the wheel. Then I forced myself to turn towards my own vehicle. What I really wanted was to tell her to come to my place, say that we'd take the girls for Mexican and watch a movie. But I didn't have the right to ask for that.

"Calder." Jackie straightened from where she leaned against a tree in front of my SUV.

"What are you doing here?"

"We need to talk, and I didn't want to drop by the house in case the girls were there."

"You didn't seem to care much about that the other day."

Jackie toyed with the keys in her hands. "I'm trying to do this the right way."

"The right way is for you to leave."

She met my gaze, pleading. "I can't do that. I'm sorry, Calder. I know I messed up. I'm trying to make things right."

I ran a hand through my hair, tugging on the ends of the strands. I glanced at Hadley's SUV, but she was focused on her phone.

"Are you and Hadley seeing each other?"

I stiffened at Jackie's question. "That's none of your damn business."

"I think I have a right to know who's in my daughters' lives. She was always hanging around when we were married, just waiting for her shot."

I moved in closer to Jackie. "If you think attacking Hadley will get you what you want, you're dead fucking wrong. She was there for the girls when you destroyed them. She was there for me. She picked up the pieces, and you should be kissing her feet for doing it."

Jackie's back went ramrod straight. "I'm glad you guys had help." Her words barely escaped through gritted teeth. "And I will keep apologizing until I'm blue in the face. I'm not giving up, Calder. I need you to give me a second chance."

I fell back a step, studying the woman in front of me. "You need the girls to give you a second chance, or you need *me* to?"

"All of you. I want my family back."

I searched Jackie's eyes for any signs that she was high. Glassiness. The size of her pupils. I saw nothing that made me think she was currently under the influence, but it was either that or the woman was delusional. "If I saw that you had your act together and the girls were older and wanted to see their mom, I'd consider supervised visits. But we will never, ever be a *family* again. We were never one to begin with."

"That's not true. Remember our first Christmas after Birdie and Sage were born? We were still in that tiny apartment, but we made a big to-do of it, decorating the tree and giving the girls presents, even though they had no idea what was going on."

"You can't paint over an entire history with a handful of happy memories. It's not happening, Jackie. Get that through your head."

The stubborn set of her jaw told me that this wasn't over. "You'll remember all the good times. You'll see that it can be even better now."

"Get out of here before I call the sheriff."

"I'll give you time. But I'm not going anywhere, Calder."

Chapter Seventeen

Hadley

I couldn't tear my eyes away from what I was seeing—Jackie and Calder with only inches separating them. I couldn't see his face, but hers was gentle as she looked at him. All doe eyes and meticulously curled auburn hair. Meanwhile, I sat in my SUV, smelling like smoke and my hair in a rat's nest bun.

He moved in even closer. God, I was an idiot. It took only seconds for her to get those hooks into him again. Maybe the truth was the hooks had never left. Jackie's hold on Calder was something I could never figure out how to break. Maybe because he cared about her more than he thought.

I closed my eyes as tears burned. I would never learn my lesson. Not when it came to my mom, and not when it came to Calder. I'd keep hoping for a different outcome, unable to see the truth for what it was.

I searched back through my memories, sifting through the happy ones and going for the one I needed to look at. I'd spent the past four years trying to bury it, forget that it had ever happened. But it was time I reminded myself.

My socked feet hit the final step as I descended the stairs. "Girls are on their way to dreamland, and it only took four books this time."

Calder didn't look up from where he sat on the couch. He simply stared at some papers on the coffee table, his gaze unfocused.

I moved farther into the living room. "You okay?"

He took a sip of an amber liquid. "The divorce is final."

I stilled, not moving forward or retreating. Calder had wanted this since the moment he'd found out that his wife had driven his daughters high as a kite, not a care in the world that she could've killed them. But it had taken almost a year to get here. The custody case had been quicker, judges moving swiftly to remove all of Jackie's parental rights.

I eased down next to him on the couch. "That's good, right?"

My stomach churned at the idea that he might be having second thoughts. That he missed Jackie.

Calder chuckled, the sound darker than I'd heard from him before, and took a sip of whatever was in his glass. "Nothing about this last fucked-up year is good, Hadley. But at least I'm free."

I wanted freedom for Calder. That feeling we always chased. But he'd rejected any of my suggestions for finding it together. No mountain biking or rock-climbing. No snowboarding or anything else. There was always an excuse or a brush-off, and each rejection ate away at another little piece of me.

I knew he needed time to settle in to this new normal and get his feet back under him. But I missed my best friend. He was sitting inches away from me, and it felt like a million miles.

It was more than that. As I studied Calder's face, the thick scruff on his jaw, those dark eyes that I could get lost in for days, I knew it was more.

I'd loved Calder Cruz from the moment he'd taught me how to fly. Racing down a mountain and giving me the release I'd so desperately needed. He'd been my understanding and safe space.

I couldn't lose that. I'd fight to the death for it. Calder was slowly disappearing before my eyes. Existing but no longer living, other than to take care of Birdie and Sage. I had to show him there was more. For both of us.

I leaned forward, plucking the glass from his hand and taking a sip. I couldn't help the cough that followed. "What is that? Jet fuel?"

The corner of Calder's mouth kicked up in that way that always sent flutters through me. "It's whiskey. A little more of an acquired taste."

I set the glass down on the table. "Who would want to acquire a taste for burning your throat alive?"

"Me, apparently."

"Masochist."

He shrugged. "Maybe."

I was so close now. I could feel the heat of Calder's body seeping into mine. Those dark eyes glowed with a hint of amber in their depths tonight. A hue that I wanted to see burn hotter.

My heart hammered against my ribs, sending little tremors through me. I pressed my hands into the cushions of the couch so they wouldn't shake. Then I closed that last bit of distance.

Calder was stunned at first. My lips met his, and he didn't move. I was about to pull away, cheeks already heating with mortification, when he leaned into the kiss.

His hand came up, sliding along the curves of my jaw and neck. His tongue slipped between my lips, teasing and toying.

My palm landed on his chest, bunching his t-shirt and pulling him closer. All I could think was that I needed more.

Calder lifted me so that I could straddle him, his movements desperate and hungry. A different kind of tremor swept through me as his hardness pressed against my core. I let out a little moan as I searched for more of that contact.

A cell phone rang out from somewhere. I was so lost in the haze that was Calder that I barely heard it. But Calder froze.

He moved so fast the world spun around me. I was off his lap and back on the other side of the couch as Calder paced.

He ran a hand through his hair, tugging on the strands. "Shit. That shouldn't have happened. I'm sorry. I was just…in a bad headspace. Been drinking."

All the heat had left me the moment Calder had thrown me off him, but it was coming back. It wasn't from desire now. It was from anger. I pushed to my feet. "Bullshit."

Calder stopped mid-stride and turned in my direction. "Excuse me?"

"Bullshit. You want me. Don't blame what just happened on two sips of whiskey or anything else. It's a slap in the face."

"Hadley, I'm not trying to hurt you—"

"You've been hurting me for months! Disappearing right in front of me. Taking away my best friend. The man I'm in love with."

Calder stiffened. "You don't love me. It's just a crush. You're young—"

"Shut up! I might be twenty, but I know my own mind. I know that I've been slowly and steadily falling in love with you since you showed me I could touch the stars. I've fallen in love with you, watching you care for those two precious girls. I've fallen in love with your bravery every time you run into a fire instead of away. I've fallen in love with how you make me feel seen in a way I've never experienced before. So don't tell me I don't love you."

Calder's chest rose and fell, his breaths ragged. "I don't love you back. I don't have that in me."

"You've loved me every time you raced down a mountain with me. You've loved me every time you held me when I was falling apart."

His jaw clenched, teeth grinding together. "That's friendship. You're my best friend's little sister. Of course, I care about you. But you're making this into something it's not."

A slap in the face would've hurt less. "That's what I am to you? Your best friend's little sister? That's all?"

"Yes."

"I don't believe you."

Calder's eyes darkened. "I don't look at you that way. You're too young, immature. You're proving it by what you're pulling right now. Do you think I need you laying this on me when I'm trying to put my life back together? Do you think I would bring someone

*else who's so reckless into my life in that way? Into my daughters'
lives? It'll never happen."*

*I staggered back a step. Immature. Reckless. They were words
that so often fell from my mother's mouth. Now, they were spilling
from Calder's.*

*The pain of that carved itself into my chest. But I didn't let my-
self look away from Calder's face. He must've seen the devastation
his words wrought because he took a step towards me. "Hadley—"*

*I stepped back. "No. I'm glad to know what you really think of
me. It's helpful."*

"I didn't—"

*I blocked out whatever else he said, moving towards the door.
Blood roared in my ears as I grabbed my bag and ran for my car.
But I couldn't stop the echoes of Calder's disdain running rampant
in my brain.*

It took me a few moments as the memory slipped away to realize that I was crying. I made no sound, but tears tracked down my
cheeks and fell off my chin. My hands shook as I wiped them away.

I reached for the glove compartment, pulling it open and grabbing some napkins I'd shoved in there. Why had I put myself in
this position again? One where Calder had all the power in the
world to hurt me. The shock of Calder wanting to be in my life a
little more had stunned me into letting him in. And I was already
paying the price.

I pulled into an open parking spot in front of the pizza parlor. I
didn't have it in me to cook tonight. Too much of a hellishly long
day. The fire, Calder and Jackie, and then going with Shiloh to
look at a horse she was thinking of buying. All I wanted was hot,
cheesy goodness, a steaming shower, and my bed.

Just as I was about to climb out of my SUV, my phone rang. I
answered it without thinking. "Hello?"

There was nothing at first.

"Hello?"

Then the breathing started. It was raspy. As if the person on the other line had a two-pack-a-day habit.

"Listen, I don't know who the hell you are, and quite frankly, I don't care. I have so much shit going on in my life, I don't need this. You think it's *cool* to try and scare someone like this? Get a life, you loser asshole!"

I jammed my finger against the screen as my chest heaved. My eyes burned with the desire to let tears fall, but I refused. I wouldn't give this jerk the power.

As I stared at my phone, notifications started going off. Texts. Emails. My *Voyeur* app. Dozens and dozens. My phone would barely finish dinging when another started.

I opened up my texts. All different numbers. All one-word or one-line texts. *Whore. Cunt. Die, bitch.* They kept coming one after the other. And I had no choice but to watch them.

Chapter Eighteen

Calder

I MADE MY WAY UP THE STREET TOWARDS DOUGH BOYS PIZZA, but my head was on a swivel, preparing for Jackie to jump out at any moment. I still hadn't been able to shake her words.

My gaze caught on a familiar SUV. Hadley was staring down at her phone, her eyes wide. A trickle of unease slid through me as I picked up my pace, heading for her vehicle.

I made it in seconds, pulling open her driver's side door. She let out a startled yelp.

"It's just me. What happened? What's wrong?"

Her phone kept dinging, one sound right after the other.

"What's going on with your phone?"

She didn't say a word, just handed me the device. It was open to her messages app. New texts popped up so quickly, I could barely read the words.

Slut.

Liar.

Trash.

Most of the messages were only a single word. Though some were longer. All of them were vile.

I switched the phone to silent and looked at Hadley, who had gone pale. "When did this start?"

"Just now."

"I'm going to call Hayes."

Hadley snatched her phone back from me. "No. I don't want him to know."

"Hadley," I gritted out. "This is serious."

"It's just some bug. I'll get my number changed, and it'll be fine."

I stared at her. It wasn't only that Hadley was pale. It looked as if she'd been crying earlier. Her eyes were red and swollen, cheeks a little puffy. "What's wrong?"

"You mean besides having a jerk-off harassing me?"

"Yes, besides that."

"Nothing. It's just been a long day. I want to get some pizza and go home."

The idea of her driving out to that house in the middle of no-where had panic setting in. "No."

"Excuse me?"

I cleared my throat. "Why don't you stay in the guest room to-night? The girls would love it. I'm just picking up pizza right now."

"I'm not staying at your house. I need to go home."

"If you want me to keep my mouth shut around Hayes, you'll stay with us tonight."

A little bit of color came back into Hadley's complexion as she climbed out of her SUV. "That's blackmail."

I shrugged. "It might be, but it's what I can live with."

She looked away from me, seeming to mull something over. "Fine. I'm too tired and hungry to argue with you."

"Good thing I ordered extra food."

Hadley beeped her locks and fell into step with me as I headed towards the pizza shop. "Who's with the girls?"

"Addie stayed late today."

Hadley's steps faltered just the slightest bit. "I don't want to interrupt."

"Interrupt what?"

"A date or whatever?"

I barked out a laugh, but it abruptly cut off. "Are you serious? You think I'm seeing Addie?" It wasn't that Addie wasn't beautiful—she was—but we didn't fit. Not like… I cut that thought right off.

"Seems like you two get along. It would probably be a good pairing. I know Mom's hoping you two get together."

"Julia thinks there's something between us?"

"She wants there to be."

I held open the door to the restaurant. "Well, then she doesn't know me very well."

⌇

Birdie patted her stomach. "That was so good."

Hadley licked her spoon clean in a move that had me forcing my gaze away. "Thanks for my extra sprinkles."

"I got your back," Birdie assured her.

Addie stood from the table and started gathering dishes.

"You don't have to clean up," I said.

"I'm happy to do it. Thanks again for dinner."

"You know you're welcome anytime." I stole a glance at Hadley, who studiously avoided my gaze. Shit. I needed to watch my words to Addie around Hadley. There was nothing there. I just wished Hads could see that.

Addie ducked her head and moved to the sink. Hadley stood to follow her but drilled a finger into Sage's side first. "Did you get enough to eat, Goose?"

Sage nodded. "Can I be excused to read my book?"

I ruffled her hair. "Of course. Birdie and I will help clean up since you helped me with breakfast."

"Aw, man," Birdie groaned.

I sent her a look. "You want pizza again?"

"Yeah…"

"Then let's go help Addie and Hadley."

Sage rose from the table and ran to give Addie a quick hug. "See you tomorrow?"

"We'll see if there are any new wildflowers in the park."

Sage beamed. "I'm going to try to finish the book tonight so I'll be ready."

I looked at Birdie. "Why don't you get all the napkins and put them in the dirty clothes basket in the laundry room? I'll get the rest of the dishes."

"All right." She sounded as if I'd just asked her to hug a cactus.

As Sage disappeared upstairs, I cleared the table and listened to Hadley and Addie in the kitchen.

"You rinse, and I'll load the dishwasher?" Hads asked.

"Sure."

"You have a real way with Sage."

"I think we're kindred spirits in a way," Addie said softly.

"I'm glad you found each other."

"Me, too."

I strode into the kitchen with a handful of glasses. "I think that's everything. What else can I do?"

Hadley stayed focused on loading the dishwasher. "I think we're good."

She'd been distant all through dinner, avoiding my gaze and focusing her questions on the girls or Addie. I couldn't figure out what misstep I'd made in the last few hours. Maybe threatening to go to Hayes?

Addie loaded the last of the glasses. "All done."

Hadley shut the dishwasher. "You should have Calder walk you home."

Addie shook her head. "I'm fine. It's just a couple of blocks."

"Addie—"

She gave Hadley's arm a quick squeeze. "I like to walk alone."

"Okay."

We wished Addie goodnight and watched as she disappeared down the street.

"You let her wander off on her own, but you blackmail me into sleeping over?"

I shook my head as I closed and locked the door. "She doesn't have someone harassing and threatening her."

"Her father hasn't exactly disappeared."

It was true. Addie's asshole of a father was still lurking around town, but he hadn't contacted Addie as far as I knew. "It's not the same."

"Whatever."

Birdie's footsteps thundered on the stairs. "I'm going to draw before bed."

I caught Hadley's elbow. "What's going on with you?"

She spun to face me. "Nothing. I just don't appreciate being essentially kidnapped."

I studied her, trying to see what it was she wasn't telling me. Hadley was annoyed with me for sure. But it was more than that. Hurt bubbled below the surface. "Did I do something today?"

She looked away towards the darkness outside the windows. "No. I just can't forget the past as easily as you can." With that, she disappeared up the stairs, too.

"Hell," I muttered, ambling towards the couch and sinking onto it. I didn't have the first idea how to heal the hurt I'd caused. The only thing I knew to do was to support Hadley in the here and now.

Part of that was keeping her safe. I pulled out my phone and scrolled through my contacts. I stopped on Mason Decker. I'd met the guy through an outreach program he'd started at his security company. He'd created these personal alarms that we could give out to anyone we came across on a call who might be feeling unsafe. All someone had to do was pull the little pin, and an ear-splitting alarm went off.

Mase had been distributing them all over the state of Oregon and had now taken the program nationally. But Wolf Gap had been one of his first stops, and Hayes and I had really hit it off with him. I tapped his name on my screen and waited. It rang four times before he answered.

"Hey, Calder. How are you?"

"Hanging in there. How about you?" I could hear kids shrieking in the background.

"It's barely controlled chaos over here, man."

"Exactly how you like it."

"That's the truth."

I leaned back against the couch cushions, sparing a glance up the stairs. "I'm sorry to bother you so late, but I have something I wanted to run by you."

"Don't apologize. Plus, you got me out of dish duty."

I chuckled. "Then I take back the apology."

The sound of kids playing faded away and the snick of a door closing sounded across the line. "Tell me what's going on."

"I have a friend. I think you met her briefly. Hadley Easton?"

"Hayes' little sister, right?"

"That's the one." I pushed to my feet, needing to move. "She's run into some trouble."

Mase was quiet for a moment. "There a reason you're calling me and not Hayes?"

I pulled open my back door, stepping out onto the deck. "Hayes doesn't know what's going on, and Hadley wants to keep it that way."

Mason let out a low whistle. "Sounds like a recipe for disaster."

"You're telling me." When Hayes found out that I'd kept this from him, he would lose it, but I couldn't betray Hadley's confidence like that. We'd never recover.

"Walk me through what's going on."

I did just that. From the video channel Hadley had started to the escalation in ugly comments and now the threats. As I spoke, I heard Mase typing on a keyboard occasionally.

"I think that's everything. I was hoping you might have some ideas for how to look into this."

There was a slight squeak as Mason must've leaned back in

his desk chair. "Some people at Halo can start the search, but you might want to get a P.I. on the case."

I knew Hadley would never agree to the private investigator. At least, not right now. "Start with what you can dig up. If you find something concrete, I might be able to convince her to loop Hayes in on this."

"From the little time I spent with her, Hadley doesn't strike me as the type to ask for help."

"Understatement of the century."

"How'd you find out what was going on, then?"

I knew what he was asking. Was there more to Hadley's and my relationship than simple friendship? Nothing about what was between us was simple, and it would never fit into the bounds of a category. It was more. Always would be.

"It was dumb luck," I muttered.

"And now you've got a whole lot on your shoulders."

The weight bearing down on me had the potential to make my knees buckle. No, it was more than that. If something happened to Hadley, I'd be crushed beyond recognition.

Chapter Nineteen

Hadley

I TIPTOED DOWN THE STAIRS, BAG SLUNG OVER MY SHOULDER. Just as my foot was about to hit the last step, a voice called out. "Going somewhere?"

Calder stood, leaning against the kitchen's entryway, wearing nothing but a low-slung pair of pajama pants. His tanned skin seemed to go on for miles, wrapping around a muscled chest.

I swallowed hard. "I didn't want to wake anyone up. I have to meet some friends."

Calder arched a brow. "Toby?"

"What do you have against Toby?"

"He's been trying to get you into trouble since you were teenagers."

"He's a friend who has been there for me since we were teen-agers," I gritted out.

"And what did he talk you into today?"

"He didn't talk me into *anything*. We're riding some trails." I was desperate for the release the ride would hopefully bring. After the past twenty-four hours, I felt as if I might crawl out of my skin.

Calder shifted his gaze towards the windows. "Please, be

My heart gave a healthy thud in my chest. This was the crux of it and would always be for Calder and me. Me needing to spread my wings, and him being terrified of the freefall.

"I'm always careful. Take every precaution I possibly can." My words held a silent plea. I'd be as safe as possible, but he had to let me fly. He was quiet, and I shifted on my feet, a hint of anger simmering low. "I told Birdie I'd give her another skateboard lesson this afternoon. That okay with you?"

"Sure. We can all go to the park."

I bit back my retort, telling him he could stay home. "Have you heard from Jackie?"

Calder's focus snapped back to me, assessing. "Yesterday, in the parking lot. But you already know that, don't you?"

I shrugged but heat rushed to my cheeks. "Looked intense. And cozy."

Calder muttered a curse and set his mug of coffee down on the counter with a clang. Then he was striding across the floor to me. He didn't stop until he was mere inches away, heat pouring off him in waves. "The last thing Jackie and I will ever be is cozy. She was asking about you, and it pissed me off. I was telling her to get out of my life. That's it."

I blinked a few times. There was no love lost between Jackie and me. When she and Calder were together, she'd always dropped snide comments about me being around. Yet she had no problem calling on me to babysit when she wanted to do something with her friends. "What did she want to know about me?"

Calder didn't look away. "If we were seeing each other."

"What did you say?" I couldn't help the question. What would Calder classify us as? Friends? Ex-friends? Family? Something else altogether?

"I told her it was none of her damn business. She doesn't have a right to know anything that's going on in my life."

"Okay," I whispered.

Calder's hands came up, framing my face. "There is nothing between Jackie and me. There never will be."

Air seemed to stall in my lungs. What was happening right now? Calder was close. Too close. It would only take inches, and his lips could be on mine. I jerked back. "That's your business. But for the sake of the girls, I'm glad that's your choice."

Calder scowled at my retreat.

"I'll see you this afternoon." I darted out the door before he had a chance to say another word and then practically ran to my SUV. It was cowardly, and I knew it. But I didn't trust myself around Calder. He would forever be my weakness, and there was nothing I could do to stop it. My only safety measure was distance.

I beeped my locks and climbed behind the wheel, starting her up. I didn't take a full breath until I was blocks away.

The drive to the trailhead went by in a blur. As I pulled into an open parking spot, I realized that I couldn't remember making a single turn, let alone stopping at a traffic light. I was lucky I hadn't caused a wreck.

I pushed open my door and climbed out of my SUV. I let my eyes fall closed for a moment, inhaling the fresh pine scent. It calmed the worst of my frayed edges. I hoped a long ride would ease the rest.

A whistle split the air, and I opened my eyes. Amusement lit Toby's features. "Whatcha doing?"

I scowled at him. "Mentally preparing for dealing with you."

Jinx let out a snorting laugh. "Maybe you should teach classes on that technique."

"You're both assholes, you know that, right?"

Calla slipped under Toby's arm and patted his chest. "I think you'll survive."

"Only if you kiss it better."

I turned back to my SUV as the two lovebirds made out. Pulling open my trunk, I moved to grab my bike.

"I'll help," Jinx said, coming up beside me.

"I think you know I can get my gear, but since you're probably trying to avoid your own private porn show, I'll let you help."

Jinx grinned down at me. "You're so kind."

I snorted. By the time my bike was out and checked over, Calla and Toby had come up for air.

"A-plus performance," Jinx shouted.

Calla's cheeks heated, and I smacked Jinx's stomach. "Don't be an ass."

"If they don't want me to comment on it, then they shouldn't be going at it against a tree."

I bit my lip to keep from laughing.

Toby sauntered over. "I brought the GoPros. Thought we might make a cool vid out of the ride."

His words had pressure forming behind my eyes. "Can't we just do this one for fun?"

"It'll be fun, but why not get some cash out of it, too?"

"Because I don't want to, all right?" My words had more of a snap to them than I'd intended. "Sorry."

Jinx leaned into me. "What's going on with you?"

I sighed and rested against my bumper. I needed to tell them. I was honestly surprised that Toby hadn't mentioned the uptick in troll comments on the channel page. "I've got a creeper who has been emailing and texting. A phone call, too."

Calla's mouth went slack. "But your phone number isn't on anything public."

"I know."

"Shit, Hads," Toby muttered. "Why didn't you say anything?"

"At first, I thought it was more troll stuff, but it's not. It's outright threats now."

"Have you talked to your brother?" Jinx asked.

I shook my head. "I don't want to get him involved."

"Smart," Toby said. "He'd freak."

No, he'd go nuclear. Then he'd probably lock me up in one of the jail cells at the sheriff's station and never let me out.

Calla nibbled on her bottom lip. "That is really scary. Maybe you should take a break from the videos. Give things a chance to calm down."

"I was thinking the same thing."

Toby straightened. "Seriously? You can't let an asshole like this win. If they know they can affect you, then they'll just keep doing it."

I squeezed the bridge of my nose, hoping to relieve the headache gathering there. "I don't know what I'm going to do, but for now, let's just pause."

"I don't think that's the right move," Toby argued.

Jinx slapped him on the shoulder. "It doesn't matter what you think. It's Hadley's face out there, so it's her choice."

Toby shrugged him off. "Whatever."

"I think what we all need right now is a ride. Let's burn off this negativity and remember why we do what we do," Jinx suggested.

"Yeah, sure." Toby headed for his bike, Calla on his heels.

I pulled Jinx into a quick hug. "Thanks, J."

"Always got your back, girl. You let me know if you want me to stay in your guest room for a bit."

Tears burned the backs of my eyes. "I think I'm okay, but thank you. You're the best."

"Don't I know it."

I snorted and gave him a shove. "Go get your wheels."

He gave me a mock salute and moved to his bike. We all made our way to the start of the trail.

"Why don't you lead the way?" I suggested to Toby. I wanted to give him something to soften the earlier blow. This wasn't enough, but it was something. The channel was Toby's whole world, and if anything screwed with that, he wasn't a happy camper. I had to hope that if Calla could convince him to start that business with her, things would get better.

"Only if you're ready to eat my dust." Toby pushed off and dropped down the incline.

Calla let out a little whoop and took off after him. I followed, and Jinx brought up the rear. We left enough space so we were safe and took switchback after switchback.

We freestyled on jumps and dips in the trail. That familiar taste of freedom lit inside me. I tuned out the world around me and focused only on the sensations. The wind whipping past my face. The sounds of tires crunching on gravel. The jarring of my bones as I landed each jump.

I loved every second of it, but I kept seeing Calder's face in my mind. The hurt as I pulled out of his grasp. The glow of amber in his dark eyes.

I gave myself a little shake and focused on the trail in front of me. Without warning, Calla slammed on her brakes with a little shriek. There wasn't time for me to stop, and unless I veered off the trail, I was going to hit her.

I jerked my handlebars to the left, trying to brake and also avoid colliding with any trees. But my tire hit a rock, and it was the perfect angle. I didn't have time to think. I was suddenly airborne.

I did my best to tuck into a flip to protect my neck but landed with a force that pushed all the air from my lungs.

"Hadley!" Jinx yelled.

I wanted to tell him that I was fine, but I couldn't form the words. Finally, I was able to suck in air. But the action hurt like hell.

"Are you okay?" He crouched down beside me as more footsteps sounded.

"Oh, God," Calla said. "I'm so sorry. This is all my fault."

"I'm okay," I wheezed.

Toby filled my vision. "Think you can sit up?"

I nodded. He grasped one hand and Jinx the other. "On three," I told them. "One, two, three."

I let out a whimper of pain as they got me in a sitting position. Jinx shot Toby a look. "There's no way you can bike out of here."

"Just give me a second. If I can't bike, I can walk."

Toby shook his head. "Maybe we could call the ranger's station—"

"You are not calling search and rescue because I have some scrapes and bruises."

Calla bit her lip. "I'm so sorry, Hadley. I saw a snake slither across the trail and panicked."

I bit back a less-than-kind retort. Calla still hadn't quite gotten used to living in the country and hated snakes more than anything. "Accidents happen. I'll be fine. After a hot bath and a truckful of ibuprofen." A million ice packs wouldn't hurt, either.

Chapter Twenty

Calder

BIRDIE RAN, SHRIEKING AROUND THE LIVING ROOM.
"Is there any reason for that kind of sound? Other than trying to make my ears bleed?" I asked my beloved daughter, who was two seconds away from making me pull my hair out.

"I'm excited, and I need to get my energy out," she yelled, still running. "Hadley said it's important my mind is centered when I skate."

"Why don't you do some laps around the backyard?"

"Good idea, Dad!" She charged out the back door.

Sage looked up from her book. This was a new one about edible plants and flowers. "Thank you. Geez, that was a lot."

I barked out a laugh and then dropped a kiss to her head. "You and me, kid, we gotta stick together if we have any hope of surviving Birdie."

"No kidding."

The doorbell rang, and I moved towards the entryway. "I got it."

I pulled open the door, and Hadley stood there, looking freshly showered, damp hair woven back into a braid. "Come in." I tugged her braid as she passed. "You leave your hair wet, you're going to catch a cold."

"That's a myth, and it's seventy-five degrees out." She tipped Sage's book as she moved towards the couch. "This one looks good."

"It is. Addie said there are all sorts of plants we can eat around here."

"Maybe we can find some when we go on our hike," Hadley suggested.

"That would be awesome."

I ruffled Sage's hair. "You want to change before we go to the park? You might be too warm in jeans."

She nodded and bounded out of the chair and up the stairs.

"Oh, to have energy like that again." Hadley winced as she eased onto the couch.

"What's wrong?"

Her face blanked. "Nothing."

I moved towards the couch. "The look on your face said otherwise."

"I took a little tumble on my ride today. Got a few bruises and scrapes. That's all."

"Where?" I bit out.

"Nowhere that's your concern."

"Hadley…"

"Just on my back."

I made a motion for her to stand. "Let me see."

"No."

"I just want to make sure you're okay."

"I am an EMT, Calder. I think I'd know if I was dying of internal bleeding."

My back teeth ground together. "That's not funny. And you couldn't possibly have been able to see and treat your entire back."

"Fine." She pushed to her feet and turned away from me, pulling up her shirt. "There, happy?"

Not in the slightest. There were angry gashes across her back, and the skin was already turning colors. She'd be black and blue for sure. "Come upstairs with me."

"Why?"

"Because you need bandages on some of those scrapes, and I have a first-aid kit in my bathroom."

"Calder, it's fine."

I fought the urge to throw her over my shoulder. "I'm not giving you crap for going in the first place. Can you just give me this?"

"Fine."

"I'm really starting to hate that word."

"Why? You're getting what you want."

I led Hadley up the stairs and towards my bedroom. "You would try a saint's patience."

"Thank you."

"It wasn't a compliment."

"Not to you, maybe."

I pointed to the bathroom. "Get in there, would you?"

She gave me a mock salute. "Sir, yes, sir."

"Such a smartass." I bent and opened the cabinet under one of the sinks, pulling out my first-aid kit.

Hadley let out a whistle. "Such a Boy Scout."

"Being prepared isn't a bad thing."

"No, it's not all bad."

I set the kit on the counter and pulled out some hydrogen peroxide and a cotton ball. "Lift your shirt again."

Hadley turned to face the mirror and lifted her tee. The angry gashes had to sting at the very least. I ghosted the cotton ball across the wounds, careful not to press too hard. "That hurt?"

"No," she whispered.

"Can you lift your shirt higher?"

Hadley grumbled something under her breath and met my gaze in the mirror. "Shield your eyes if you want to protect your virginal virtue."

I scoffed. Heat flared to life in Hadley's eyes, a mix of anger and frustration. She whipped her shirt over her head, leaving her in nothing but a pale pink, lacy bra. I wasn't blind. I knew that

Hadley had curves, that she was beautiful, but the sight in front of me had my mouth going dry. I fought the urge to lean in closer.

"Cat got your tongue?"

I scowled at Hadley through the mirror. "Took me by surprise, is all."

"Sure."

I returned my focus to her back, cleaning each scrape meticulously. "Hold your shirt to your chest."

"Too much boobage on display for you?"

I chuckled, the sound a little rougher than normal. "I need to unhook your bra. That might be too much boobage for *you*."

Hadley rolled her eyes but held her t-shirt to her chest, keeping her bra in place. I unhooked the little tines, letting it fall open. I cleaned the rest of the gashes and moved for the antibiotic ointment. As gently as possible, I spread it over the worst of her scrapes.

Hadley trembled slightly.

"Did that hurt?"

"No, I'm fine."

But her breathing was more shallow than usual, her gaze focused on the counter in front of her. Apparently, I wasn't the only one affected.

I ripped open two packs of gauze for the worst cuts. Carefully, I covered them and secured them in place with medical tape. When I finished, I let my hands skim lightly down her sides and gave her waist a squeeze. "How does that feel?"

Hadley's breath hitched. "Good. I mean, better."

My gaze locked with hers in the mirror, a million different things passing between us. Questions and pleas. Uncertainties and vows.

"Hadley?"

"Yes?"

"I don't find you repulsive."

Her words had haunted me since she'd carelessly tossed them out. "*Trust me, I'm well aware you find me repulsive.*" It killed me that she thought that. Especially when it couldn't be further from the truth.

Hadley's eyes widened a fraction in the mirror. "O-okay."

"Just remember that." I bent and kissed her bare shoulder, the skin so soft I wanted to trail my lips down the expanse of it. Instead, I straightened and got the hell out of there before one of my kids walked in.

Chapter Twenty-One

Hadley

"THANK YOU FOR COMING," HAYES said as he pulled open the front door to the ranch house.

I shouldn't have. Didn't truly know why I had. It had to be that dirty word: *hope*. Pulling me in with this image of what my family could be if we just worked out our differences. I gave my brother a quick hug. "I'm ten minutes early. Did you notice that?"

He let out a low chuckle. "Very impressive."

Shy appeared with Hayes' dog, Koda, on her heels. I gave her a shoulder bump. Hugs weren't my sister's thing—any physical affection, really. "You figure out when you'll get the colt?"

"Three weeks."

"Let me know when he gets here. I want to come see him."

The young horse Shy had picked out was a gorgeous chestnut with beautiful lines and plenty of spirit. Instead of Shiloh answering me, she simply nodded and moved towards the living room.

I glanced up at Hayes. "She doing okay?"

He scrubbed a hand over his face. "It's impossible to know

And that drove my brother crazy. I pinched his side. "Not your job to figure out if she is or isn't."

"Of course, it is." He wrapped an arm around my neck, pulling me in for a noogie. "Don't you know big brothers will *always* worry?"

I pinched his other side, this time harder. "Let me go, you big buffoon."

"Ouch! That hurt, you little witch."

"Music to a father's ears, his children battling it out just like the good ol' days."

I pushed out of Hayes' hold and went to hug my dad. "Control your son, would you?"

Hayes lifted his shirt to examine his side. "I'm pretty sure she broke the skin."

"Baby."

Dad barked out a laugh. "Man, am I glad I don't have to referee you two anymore."

Everly strolled up, patting Hayes' chest. "Don't worry, I'll protect you."

He pulled her into his arms. "Thank goodness. She's vicious."

"And proud of it."

"What's vicious mean?" Birdie asked as she popped into our circle.

"Mean," Hayes said at the exact same moment I said, "Strong."

Everly bit her lip to keep from laughing, but my dad let his laughter fly.

"You guys are weird sometimes," Birdie mumbled.

My dad bent down and ruffled Birdie's hair. "You are so right."

We moved into the living space where Addie and Sage were playing a game of checkers. As we entered, Addie looked up. "She's kicking my butt."

Sage grinned. "I kinda am."

The doors to the back deck were open, and Calder was standing at the grill. Our gazes locked, and I swore I still felt his hands skimming over my sides, the press of his lips against my shoulder.

I tore my focus away from Calder and settled in the kitchen. My mom was chopping vegetables for what looked like a salad. I took a deep breath and forced my feet to move in that direction. "Hey, Mom."

She looked up, almost startled by my greeting. "Hadley."

"Need any help?"

She opened her mouth, and I was sure the answer would be no, but then she paused. "Sure. Can you peel those carrots for me?"

"No problem." I moved to the sink and washed my hands before getting to work. "How was your week?"

"Good. Got some decent time in my garden, which always makes me happy."

My mom had a vegetable garden that would make even farmers jealous. Some of my best memories growing up were of helping her harvest for a meal or planning what we might cook based on what was available. "Did you grow these carrots?"

"That and some of the lettuce for the salad are from the garden. It's still too early for peppers and tomatoes, so those are from the store."

"They look great."

"Thanks, sweet pea."

The nickname burned something in my chest. I couldn't remember the last time she'd used it.

Mom dumped the lettuce she'd just chopped into the bowl. "How was your week?"

"Good. Same ol', same ol'. Work, a hike, a bike ride. I'm loving that the weather is warmer."

"Me, too. It's one of my favorite times of year."

I grinned down at my carrot as I peeled it. "You say that about every season."

"Oh, hush. I do not."

Dad moved in with a platter of chicken and kissed my mom. "You really do."

She swatted at him. "Two against one really isn't fair."

"The truth hurts," Dad said. "Just a couple more minutes on those steaks."

"We'll be ready to go," Mom assured him.

Calder appeared as my dad stepped away. Suddenly, the spacious kitchen felt tight, as if the walls were closing in. "Need an extra set of hands?"

I silently begged for my mom to say no. I'd been on edge since Calder's and my encounter in the bathroom. I'd been twitchy, my skin feeling too tight for my body. I'd tried long runs and even a couple of swims, but nothing seemed to help.

"Sure. Why don't you take that chicken to the table? And then you can help Hadley with the carrots."

I fought the urge to groan, but I was trapped. If I left now, Calder would hold all the power, and Mom would be pissed. So, I stayed and focused on my task.

It felt like mere seconds before heat was at my back. "Want me to peel or grate?"

"You can grate." My voice sounded husky, even to my own ears. Hell.

Calder picked up a grater and positioned himself so close to me, our arms brushed.

"Could you give me a little more space?"

Calder sent me a wicked grin. "Now, why would I want to do that?"

"Maybe because if you don't, I'm liable to impale you with this peeler."

"Eh, it doesn't look too sharp to me. I'll risk it."

"I could always pick up one of those knives from the butcher block…"

"Hadley!" my mom chided. "That's a little too much, don't you think?"

I scowled at Calder.

His grin only grew. "It's not my fault I'm her favorite."

Mom patted his shoulder. "You really are. You gave me grandbabies. You don't cause me to have heart attacks—"

"He's a freaking firefighter," I argued. "That doesn't give you a heart attack?"

"Calder knows how to handle himself."

I knew he did, but accidents could happen anyway. I shook my head and turned back to my peeling.

Dinner went by with its usual mixture of conversations. Calder sat next to me, bringing his chair in even closer to mine as dessert was served.

"What are you doing?" I hissed.

"Getting comfortable. Do you have a problem with that?"

Yes, I did. Because I had no idea what was running through Calder's mind, and the lingering touches were driving me mad. "I'm fighting the urge to stab you with my fork."

The corner of his mouth twitched. "Then you'll be the one who has to care for me. You're the EMT."

I growled at him. Full-on growled. I needed space. To feel like I could actually take a full breath. That I could think straight. None of that was possible with Calder so close.

I popped the last piece of brownie into my mouth. "I'm sorry to eat and run, but I have an early morning tomorrow." It was a lie, but I'd deceive the pope himself if it gave me some space from Calder right now. "Anyone else done? I'll clear plates."

A few people said they were, and I moved around the table, stacking plates and cutlery. As I bent over to take Hayes', my mom gasped. "Hadley! What in the world happened to your back?"

She lifted the back of my shirt, which I was sure revealed the purpling bruises there. I pulled out of her grasp. "I took a tumble when I was mountain biking. It's just some bruises, nothing serious."

"Did you go to a doctor?"

"No," I said through gritted teeth. "I'm an EMT. I would know if I were seriously injured."

Mom straightened in her chair. "You might be an EMT, but you're not a medical doctor. They have more training. Tests they can do. I want you to go first thing in the morning and get an x-ray."

"I'm fine. I'm not paying to see a doctor and have tests done that I don't need."

"I'll pay for it if money's the issue. If you would've gone to college like I suggested—"

"Mom, stop. I'm okay. But please don't do this." I was begging. I didn't care. I didn't have it in me with everything that was or wasn't going on with Calder to deal with my mother, too.

"Don't do what? Care about my daughter? How dare I?"

"Julia," my dad said softly. "She's taken worse spills than this. She'll be okay."

Mom's eyes hardened. "I know she has. So why for the love of all that's holy does she keep up with all of these reckless hobbies?"

I moved towards the kitchen, setting the plates in the sink. Raised voices sounded from the table, but I did my best to block them out as I moved towards the door. A hand caught my elbow, and I whirled.

Calder was right there. "Hey, it's just me."

"I can't—" I sucked in a sharp breath, doing my best to keep the tears at bay. "I can't do this right now. I need you to let me go."

"Hadley." My name on his lips was pained.

"Please," I whispered.

He released me, and I ran for the door.

Chapter Twenty-Two

Hadley

I PULLED THE BLANKET TIGHTER AROUND MYSELF AS I STARED out my windows at the dark fields that led to forests. Stars were starting to peek out in the purpling sky. I loved this property. The house that sat on it. It was peaceful with plenty of space to roam. I never felt fenced in.

But maybe it was time to consider letting it go. Selling and moving somewhere far enough away where weekly family dinners weren't a possibility. Beckett had opted for other continents altogether, but I would settle for another state. Maybe Montana or Colorado. I liked both of those places.

They weren't home, though. I'd get to leave my problems with my mom behind, but I'd also be leaving everyone else. Dad, Shiloh, Hayes, Birdie, Sage…Calder. The thought alone had pain lancing my chest.

I didn't think I could do it. Maybe that made me weak or co-dependent, but I didn't want to let go of the world I'd built here. A few stray tears escaped my eyes, cascading down my cheeks. They pissed me the hell off. I didn't want my mother to have this kind of power over me, but she did. With her disapproval and disdain

With the fact that I wouldn't ever be good enough. It hurt more than I wanted to admit.

A knock sounded on my front door. I didn't move. I didn't want to see anyone right now.

My doorbell rang. I still stayed right in my spot, staring out at my wide-open spaces.

This time, there was pounding. "If you don't open up, I'll break a window and let myself in," Calder yelled.

He would, too. I pushed to my feet, dropping my blanket onto the couch and starting for the door. The pounding picked up again. "I'm coming, don't break your damn hand."

I flipped the lock and pulled open the door. "Yes?"

Calder glowered at me. "Why didn't you answer?"

"Maybe because I didn't feel like company."

He brushed past me and into the house.

"Sure, come right in," I grumbled, shutting the door and locking it.

Calder moved in a flash, pulling me into his arms. "I'm sorry, Little Daredevil."

My throat burned, but I swallowed it down. "It's fine. I'm used to it."

"It's not fine." He pulled me tighter against him. "She can't help herself."

"I know that. But what am I supposed to do? Just let her constantly beat me down? I can't keep doing this." I'd said the words time and again, each time hoping that a solution would appear. It never had.

Calder loosened his hold on me, brushing the hair away from my face. "Your dad's having a pretty strong word with her right now. Hayes is backing him up."

That was something. "She has to be open to hearing it, though."

The wince on Calder's face told me that he wasn't sure she was. "They'll keep trying."

"Maybe one day it'll work." I glanced out the small window to the side of the door. "Where are Birdie and Sage?"

"Having a sleepover at the animal sanctuary with Everly and Hayes. They're over the moon."

My mouth curved a fraction. "Highlight of their week for sure."

Calder's hand came up to slide along my jaw, framing my face. "Hadley."

My gaze found his. "Yes?"

"I know you're hurting. It's killing me."

I let myself be weak. Just for one moment. My head fell to Calder's chest, and I fisted my hands in his shirt. "I'll never be good enough for her."

Calder wrapped his arms around me again. "That's only because she can't see."

A few more tears slipped free, my hands twisting the shirt tighter.

"It's her loss. She's missing out on truly knowing the most incredible person I've ever met."

I tipped my head back so I could see Calder's face and maybe I could understand the words that were coming out of his mouth.

His eyes bored into mine. "Trust me. I know the devastation of not truly having you in my life. Of looking away from the truth of who you are. It's bleak. And every second I blinded myself to that truth, there was a hole inside me."

"Calder…What is this?"

"I've missed you, Hads. So damned much. It was destroying me from the inside out."

"Why now?"

One of his hands slipped under my fall of hair, fingers tangling in the strands. "Something woke me up the day you went into that car at the ravine. Scared me straight. If I'd have lost you…I don't think I would've survived it."

His fingers tightened on my hair, tipping my head back even farther. "I'm sorry. You'll never know how much. I was scared out of my mind and trying to keep my head above water. It was all lies. I've wanted you for longer than I should've. But it's more than that. You've always been more. You own my fucking soul, and I don't ever want it back."

Tears slid down my cheeks. "You can't do this. It's not fair. What if you walk away again? What if you decide I'm too much and shut me out?"

He pulled me tighter against him. "Never. Not going to happen."

"You don't know that."

"Let me prove it to you."

I pulled in a breath, but it was painful. As if the air itself were made of tiny shards of glass. The thing I'd always wanted most was right in front of me, within reach. But if I lost my balance? The fall would kill me.

I pushed up onto my tiptoes and whispered two words against his lips. "Prove it."

Calder lifted me in one fluid move, and my legs wrapped around his waist. He took the stairs two at a time, and I couldn't help the giggle that sprang from my lips.

"Are you in a hurry?"

"Damn straight," he said, pushing open the door to my bedroom. "You give me even a hint of a shot, I'm taking it. Every time."

The ferocity of his words had everything inside me tightening. Slowly, so painfully slow, Calder lowered me to the floor. Sparks of heat danced across my skin as my center passed over the hard ridge in his jeans.

His hands came to my face again as my bare feet touched the floor. He found that spot on my jaw and neck that felt like his. "I want this with you. But I also want to know that you're ready."

My hands fisted in his shirt. "I've been ready for years."

It was all Calder needed. In a flash, he was kissing me, and there was nothing hesitant about it. The feral edge was a comfort. A reassurance that Calder was sure about this with me, that he wanted me as badly as I wanted him.

His lips left mine, trailing down my jaw to my neck and then my shoulder. "Your skin is so damn soft. You have no idea how long I've wanted to feel it against my tongue."

A pleasant shiver cascaded across my skin. "I'm pretty sure I have an idea."

Calder tugged the strap of my tank top down as my fingers went for the button on his jeans. Calder sucked in a sharp breath as my breasts sprang free. "No bra?"

I shot him a grin. "I'm in pajamas. I don't sleep in a bra."

One hand dipped between my legs, ghosting over my core through my sleep shorts. "What about here?"

I fought the urge to moan as sparks danced through my nerve-endings. "Guess you're just going to have to find out."

Calder's eyes heated, that golden amber starting to glow. "Are you trying to kill me?"

"Not before I have my way with you."

He chuckled and then launched me back onto the mattress. I landed with a whoosh of air leaving my lungs. Calder toed off his boots as he strode towards the bed. Then he pulled off his t-shirt, tossing it to the floor. His jeans were next. Then those black boxer briefs.

The man could've been a statue carved from marble at a major museum. All of those dips and curves on display for me alone had me swallowing. "You're beautiful, you know that?"

His stride stuttered and then he grinned. "I'll take that as a compliment coming from you."

"You are." But it wasn't just his muscled form. It was everything that lay beneath. His protectiveness. Care. Dedication. Kindness. It was all mixed together to make something that was uniquely Calder.

He bent over me, brushing his mouth against mine. "I've got nothing on you."

He trailed his lips down my neck to my chest. "You're this explosion of light in a world that's mostly gray. I've never seen anything like it."

Calder's lips found my nipple, pulling it into his mouth and sucking deep. I nearly bowed off the bed.

"Calder." It was a whisper and a plea.

"Yes?"

"Need you." I hadn't said those words to anyone in years. I'd made it my mission to become as self-sufficient as possible in the hopes of never being let down. But now, I needed Calder more than I needed my next breath.

"I've got you," he whispered against my skin.

In a flash, he pulled my tank top off and shorts down, letting them fall to the floor. When I was completely bare to him, it was more than simply my skin on display. It was my soul. I showed him everything and hoped he would stay.

His fingers trailed up the inside of my thigh. "This is beauty. Never really knew true beauty until I saw you, just like this." He stroked my center, delving in, teasing and toying.

Warmth spread through my limbs and pooled low in my core. "Calder."

"Love my name on your lips."

My legs hooked around his hips, pulling him closer to exactly where I wanted him.

"Shit," he muttered. "Condom."

"I'm on the pill. There hasn't been anyone since my last checkup."

His gaze bored into mine, all sorts of silent questions. "I'd never risk you if I didn't know for sure I was clean. You're sure?"

I had no idea how long this would last. I might only have Calder for one night. If that was the case, I wanted to feel *all* of him. "I'm sure."

His tip bumped against my entrance, and my back arched in silent request. Calder pushed inside, achingly slow. The stretch was just shy of pain. He groaned as I fully enveloped him, then stilled as he gave me time to adjust.

Calder's lips found mine. The kiss was so tender, it nearly hurt. Slow and deep. As he pulled away, he whispered, "Never felt anything better than this."

My eyes burned. "Me, either." *Completeness* wasn't the correct word, but there was a simple *rightness* to it. The way truth felt when you discovered it for the first time.

My hips began moving of their own volition, rocking back and forth and creating delicious friction. Calder started to move. He glided in and out of me, slowly picking up speed. His thumbs brushed across my nipples, teasing and toying.

The cascade of sensations had my body crying out for more. I arched into Calder, bringing him deeper. The movement had him hitting a spot inside me that made light dance across my vision. My fingers dug into his broad shoulders. "I'm not going to last."

Calder thrust impossibly deeper, my walls tightening around him. "Hell."

His thumb found my clit. He circled and pressed down. It was the spark that lit a chain reaction of feeling. The world around me blurred as I lost myself in whatever this was that Calder and I had created. Our own little universe of sensation.

I cried out against his shoulder as I came apart. And I never wanted to be put back together. Not as I was before.

Chapter Twenty-Three

Calder

I HUMMED AS I FLIPPED THE BACON IN THE PAN. THE EGGS were on warm in Hadley's toaster oven, and biscuits were almost done baking. I should've been dragging. The amount of sleep we'd gotten had been minimal. But once I'd finally given in to exhaustion, I'd slept better than I had…ever.

"You sound way too chipper," Hadley grumbled from the entryway.

I turned as I took the bacon off the heat, fighting a chuckle. Hadley was *not* a morning person, and she needed her full eight hours. An eight hours she hadn't come close to last night.

I crossed to her, pulling her into my arms and kissing her soundly. When I released her, Hadley blinked a few times before her gaze refocused. The corner of my mouth kicked up. "Feel better?"

She smacked my chest. "You're too cocky for your own good."

"That might be true, but I'm also the cocky bastard who made you breakfast."

Hadley sniffed the air. "Bacon?"

The timer went off, and I moved to the oven, grabbing the hot potholders off the counter. "Bacon, eggs, and biscuits."

"I didn't have stuff to make biscuits."

"You had pancake mix. That can be used for biscuits."

She eyed me skeptically. "You sure about that?"

"You taste them and tell me."

Hadley moved in behind me, peering over my shoulder. "They look legit."

"Grab us some juice, would you?"

We moved around the kitchen with practiced ease. That was the thing about being with someone you'd known for most of your life. You had each other's rhythms down without even trying.

We settled at a small breakfast nook in the corner of Hadley's kitchen. She broke off a piece of the biscuit and popped it into her mouth. Her eyes widened. "This is good."

I sent her a droll look. "You don't have to sound so shocked."

Hadley's lips pressed together as she tried to keep from laughing. "Sorry. I should never doubt your cooking prowess."

"Damn straight."

"You're still not as good as Mac."

"No one is as good as Mac." I swore the guy could open a restaurant and put all the others in town out of business.

We were quiet for a bit as we ate and let the caffeine from the coffee I'd brewed settle in our systems. Hadley traced a design in the condensation on her glass. "So, what are you up to today?"

The early teasing was gone from her voice and expression. Uncertainty had taken its place. I hated it. "I was thinking about seeing if you wanted to take the girls for a bike ride. If your back isn't bugging you too much."

I hadn't thought of that at all last night, and Hadley hadn't seemed as if she were hurting, but now, I wondered.

"My back's fine."

"So, bike ride?"

"Yeah, that'd be good." She was quiet for another moment. "I just need to know, so I'm prepared. Was this a one-time deal or…?"

I dropped my fork, letting it clatter on my plate. "Seriously?"

She shrugged. "I'm not going to be someone who assumes—"

I moved in closer to Hadley, taking her mouth in a hard kiss. "How's that for assuming?"

"Uh…"

"Hadley. I wouldn't have gone there with you if I didn't want this. In a very real way. I hope you feel the same."

If she didn't, I wasn't sure what I'd do. I didn't think I could walk away, but I didn't want casual, not with Hadley.

Hadley looked down at her plate. "I want this with you. But I'm scared something will happen, and you'll change your mind. That you'll freeze me out again."

I slid my hand across her jaw and neck, bringing her gaze to mine. "I can't promise you that this will work out, but I can promise to give it everything I have. We fit, Hads. It won't always be easy, but it always feels right. I feel an ease with you that I'd never felt before."

"Me, too," she whispered.

I brushed my mouth against hers. "Good."

"What about the girls?"

"We ease them into it. I'm not going to maul you in front of them—"

Her mouth quirked. "I would hope you'd never do that."

I pulled Hadley in closer against me. "I'm not hiding this."

"I don't want to hide it, but I also want a minute to be in this with you before we tell my whole family."

It made sense, but I couldn't help but feel annoyed. I was ready to scream from the rooftops that Hadley was mine. I hadn't been the one hurt before, though. Sure, I'd been in pain, but it was something that I'd caused myself by walking away from Hadley. She'd felt left out in the cold.

I squeezed the back of her neck. "I can give you time to trust me, to get used to the idea that I'm not going anywhere."

"Thank you." She gave me a quick kiss. "Now, let's go get the girls."

"Sounds good to me."

We brought my SUV to a stop outside the house Hayes and Everly had built on their mountain property. As we climbed out, the sounds of all sorts of animals filled the air. I could hear a pig, goats, horses, and who knew what else.

The screen door opened, and Birdie and Sage came running out. "We got to collect the eggs this morning," Sage called.

"How cool is that?"

"And I got to feed scraps to Petunia," Birdie said.

I looked questioningly at Hadley. She grinned. "That's the pig."

I wrapped an arm around Birdie as she flung herself against my side. "Better you than me."

"Pigs are cool, Dad. They're really smart, and they're actually really clean."

"She's right," Sage agreed, burrowing into Hadley's side. "Pigs get a bad rap. You shouldn't judge them like that."

I held up a hand. "Sorry."

Everly appeared on the steps, Hayes behind her. She smiled sheepishly. "I might've had a few teaching moments with them."

"Anything you can teach them to take Calder down a peg is good in my book," Hadley told her.

"Hey, now," I warned.

"We should so put you in your place," Birdie cheered.

Hayes barked out a laugh. "You're done for now. It's four against one."

"Laugh it up."

Hayes lifted his chin to the bikes on the rack at the back of my SUV. "You going somewhere?"

"Hadley and I were thinking of taking the girls on a ride down by the creek."

He looked from me to his sister. "I'm surprised you were willing to get up this early on a day off."

Pink hit Hadley's cheeks. "He bribed me with food."

"The way to get you to do anything," Hayes muttered.

"What can I say? I'm a smart woman."

Sage brightened at Hadley's side. "I bet we'll see some wild-flowers for my book by the creek."

"I bet so, too. Do you have your book with you?" Hadley asked.

"It's in my bag."

"You guys are welcome to come with," I offered to Everly and Hayes.

Everly shook her head. "I think I could use a lazy day at home. We've been too busy lately."

Hayes wrapped an arm around her. "I could use a day with you alone. I don't know about being lazy, though…"

"Hayes," she chastised, but he kissed her long and hard.

Birdie made a gagging sound. "Ew, gross."

"That's what I like to hear," I muttered.

"I think it's sweet," Sage argued. "I'm gonna find a husband like that one day."

My gaze zeroed in on my daughter. "One day, a *very* long time from now."

Hadley choked on her laughter. "You're in for it, Dad."

The wind whipped against my face as we rode down the trail. The path along Cleary Creek was well-worn and easy to navigate. There weren't any stray roots or rocks that would send someone flying. It was perfect for a relaxed bike ride, with just enough peaks and valleys to keep things interesting.

"Dad, watch this," Birdie cried in front of me. My youngest daughter by five minutes pedaled harder and then raced down a dip in the trail. The hill was steeper than I remembered, and I held my breath as Birdie flew down it.

She whooped and hollered as she reached the bottom, but I couldn't hear what words she yelled over the roaring of the blood in my ears. Hadley came to a stop next to me on the trail, Sage behind us. She rested a hand on my forearm. "You okay?"

I tore my focus away from Birdie and took in Hadley's expression. Wariness filled it as if she were bracing for me to lose it. She had reason to. I let out a shaky breath. "I'm fine."

"I want to do the hill," Sage piped up from behind us.

"You sure, Buttercup?" I asked.

She nodded. "I'm gonna fly."

The corner of Hadley's mouth kicked up as a wistfulness took over her expression. "Flying was always my favorite."

I guided my bike to the side of the path. "Go for it, kiddo."

Sage grinned and pushed off. She didn't go as fast as her sister, but her dark hair flew behind her in waves. I didn't let out my breath until she reached the bottom. I turned to Hadley. "You next?"

"I never pass up a chance to fly." She sailed over the edge of the hill, putting Birdie's speed to shame. Her head tipped back as she went, and she let loose one of those uninhibited laughs.

I couldn't help the smile that spread across my face as I watched her, completely free and alive. Without giving myself a chance to think about it, I took off after her, pumping my pedals to get even more speed. Instead of staying on the trail, I went to the side of it, aiming for a gulley. I hit it with just the right speed and at just the right angle. The air I caught was nothing short of sheer beauty.

It had been so long since I'd felt this. The hitch in my breathing. The dump of adrenaline. The moment of feeling nothing but the wind around you. I couldn't believe I'd ever given it up.

Chapter Twenty-Four

Hadley

Jones sent me a curious look for the dozenth time in the past hour.

I bugged my eyes at him over my playing cards. "What?"

His lips pressed together as if he were trying to hold in a laugh. "Nothing."

"Not nothing. You keep giving me weird looks."

He glanced around the room to see who might be within listening range and then leaned forward. "When are you going to tell me what's going on with you and Calder?"

I froze. "What do you mean?" It had been a week since things had changed. I'd carried that night with me since. We hadn't had much alone time in recent days, but we'd found stolen moments wherever we could. I'd also thought we were being discrete. Apparently, not.

Jones made a humming noise in the back of his throat. "Sure, doll."

"Don't *sure, doll* me."

"Look, you might think you're keeping this thing under wraps, but everyone sees the way you two look at each other."

"They do not." My gaze darted around the room, and sure

enough, Calder's eyes were pointed directly at me. I immediately turned around. "Shit."

Jones let out a snort of laughter. "Why are you hiding it? That man is gorgeous. I'd be parading him all over town and staking my claim."

Part of me wanted to do exactly that. Especially when I knew Jackie was lurking around, just waiting to pop up. "We're taking things slow. Giving ourselves time to get used to the new normal."

"That because of you, or because he's your big brother's best friend?"

I winced. I had no idea how Hayes would react to Calder and me seeing each other, but I knew the longer we put off telling him, the worse his reaction would be. "I hate small towns," I grumbled. "This wouldn't be an issue if I lived in New York City."

"You'd go crazy if you were locked inside a concrete jungle."

"I know." It was wide-open spaces for me and nothing else.

"Glad you got your happy, doll."

I looked up and met Jones' gaze. We'd been partnered since I'd started. He'd never once complained about being stuck with the new girl, one who'd been so young on top of it. He'd shown me the ropes and had been kind when I made mistakes. "I'm so lucky to have you."

"Damn straight. Now, enough with this mushy stuff. Draw a damn card."

I chuckled and pulled one from the top of the deck. I placed the Jack between a Queen and ten of the same suit and discarded an eight facedown. I grinned at Jones. "Gin."

"You cheat. I swear to God, I will find out how you do it one day."

I stood and bent over the table, kissing his cheek. "Don't be a sore loser."

Jones grumbled something under his breath and tossed his cards down onto the table.

"Why don't you play with McNally? He's horrible at cards. It'll make you feel better."

"I heard that," McNally called from one of the couches by the TV.

"I meant for you to," I hollered back.

Jones picked up the deck and shuffled. "What do you say to a little poker, McNally? We could make this afternoon interesting."

McNally groaned. "Cindy's gonna kill me."

His wife would likely make him sleep on the couch if he lost two hundred bucks the way he had last time. I shook my head and started for the bunk rooms. "I'm going to grab a nap."

I hadn't slept nearly as well since that night with Calder. It was as if my body had gotten used to Calder's presence and resented that he was no longer there. A flicker of annoyance surged in me at that knowledge. I'd slept alone for a long time. I mostly loved it. I could sprawl across the bed and take all the pillows. But nothing compared to the warmth and comfort of Calder's body wrapped around mine.

I pulled open the door to the small room and stepped inside. There were two twin beds and a little nightstand in between. There were only two women on the crew, so this was our own little room. I set my phone down on the nightstand and toed off my boots.

As I lay back on the bed, I stared up at the ceiling. Jones' words about everyone knowing what was going on with Calder and me played in my head. If that was the case, we needed to tell my brother. Everyone else could wait, but I didn't want to hurt Hayes by hiding this from him.

My phone buzzed on the table next to me. I reached out without looking and grabbed it. There was a notification for a new email. It wasn't from an address I recognized. I silently prayed for normal fan mail. A little girl telling me she'd gotten her first mountain bike. A backpacker wanting to know the best, hidden spots around Wolf Gap.

I scanned the email. There were only four words and a link. *Look what I found...*

I knew the last thing I should do was click on a link from someone I didn't know, but I couldn't seem to stop myself. An internet browser window popped up, and I froze. The shock melted into nausea, the urge to empty my stomach so strong that I reached for the small trashcan.

My lungs seized as my stomach roiled. It was a porn site. Photo after photo of naked women in all sorts of provocative poses, but on each and every one, my face replaced the woman's.

A text popped up on my screen.

Toby: *What the hell is going on with the feed on the channel? You're being tagged in all these insane pictures.*

I exited out of my texts and the internet browser, moving to the *Voyeur* app. There was a tab for my uploaded content, and then there was a tab where people could tag me. It was usually of people showing me them mastering tricks I'd done. Sometimes, drawings kids did. But there was none of that now.

The entire feed was those naked photos. My eyes burned with the urge to cry. Some of the photoshop jobs were horrible. Anyone would be able to tell they were fake. But others were so realistic, they had me doing a double take.

My breaths came quicker and quicker, my ribs tightening around my lungs. A soft knock sounded on the door, but I couldn't get the words out to answer. It opened slowly, just a fraction, and then the whole way.

Calder moved into the room, shutting the door behind him. "Hey—" His greeting cut off when he saw my face. "What's wrong?"

I still didn't have words. I simply held out my phone.

Calder took it, and his eyes flared as he scanned the screen. "What the hell?"

"It's on my channel and some porn site. They're everywhere. Too many to count."

He sat next to me, pulling me against him. "We'll figure it out. Can you revoke the ability to tag you in things? Or will we not be able to find the photos again?"

My hand shook as I took the phone. "No, I can hide the tag tab from the public, but I'll still be able to see it." My thumb moved across the screen, changing my settings. At least, there was that. But how many people had seen? How many were already thinking that they now knew every inch of my body? "I feel sick."

Calder held me tighter against him, pressing his lips to my temple. "I want to kill whoever's doing this. I need to send this information to my friend Mase. He's having people look into your case."

I pulled back. "You told someone what was happening?"

"I had to." He gripped the back of my neck, squeezing gently. "I needed to do *something*."

I swallowed back the frustration and annoyance. I understood. I truly did. Calder wanted to keep everyone he cared about safe. This was flipping every single one of his triggers. He'd given me space to do what I needed and tried to meet me there in the ways he could. "I get it. You should've told me, but I get it."

The tension running through Calder's shoulders relaxed a fraction. "Thank you." His lips met mine in a kiss. Everything about it was reassuring. That he was here. I wasn't alone.

I let my head fall to his chest. "How do I fix this? There are photos on some porn site. I have to get them down—"

Calder stiffened again. "Let me call Mase and see if he has any ideas or resources. But, Hadley, we have to tell Hayes. And it needs to be now."

All the things I'd built for myself, this secret life that was mine alone, would all come crashing down. I'd been playing with fire, hoping for just a little longer, but that time had run out.

Chapter Twenty-Five

Calder

I DID EVERYTHING I COULD TO KEEP MY FURY UNDER CONTROL as I spoke to Cap and told him Hadley and I needed to leave for about an hour. The sheriff's station was just a couple of blocks down, so he let me take my radio and told us to hurry back.

I continued to battle as Hadley and I walked down Aspen Street, my eyes darting to every person we passed. I didn't want my anger to scare Hadley, but beneath that rage was fear. The fact that someone would take the time to do this to her didn't spell good things.

"Will you say something?" she asked softly.

My steps faltered as I looked down at her. "What?"

"I need you to say something. Anything. Yell at me for doing some insane trick on my bike. Tell me I shouldn't hike alone. Anything but this pissed-off silent thing you've got going on right now."

I wrapped an arm around Hadley and pulled her into me. I inhaled the familiar flowery scent of her shampoo. I had no idea what it was, but it lingered in rooms long after she was gone, marking the space. "I'm sorry. I'm just going through every angle

"Well, it's freaking me out, so stop."

I kissed the top of her head and started walking again, but this time I linked my fingers with hers.

"Calder," she whispered, looking down at our fingers.

"I'm not hiding this."

Hadley's teeth pressed into her bottom lip. "Okay. I hope my brother doesn't punch you in the face."

Her matter-of-fact tone startled a laugh out of me. "I'm sure you'll patch me up if he does." I'd take a punch or whatever other punishment Hayes wanted to throw my way. Hadley was worth it all.

"Men," she grumbled under her breath.

We climbed the steps to the sheriff's station, and I pulled open the door for Hadley to go ahead. Once we were inside, I took her hand again.

Officer Williams looked up from behind the reception desk and smiled. That smile widened a fraction when he saw our linked hands. "Hey, guys. What can I do for you?"

"Is my brother around?" Hadley asked.

"Should be. Let me call back." He picked up the desk phone. "Hey, boss. Your sister and Calder are here." Silence for a moment. "No problem." He hung up. "He says to go on back."

I led Hadley through a maze of desks and then to Hayes' office. I didn't bother knocking, I just opened the door.

Hayes looked up from a stack of paperwork. "Hey, what's—?" His words cut off as he took in our hands. Then his gaze jumped from my face to Hadley's and back again. "I'll be damned."

Hadley began to giggle until it turned to hysterical laughter.

Hayes pushed to his feet, eyeing his sister. "Is she all right?"

"It's been a long day," I explained.

He continued to study both of us as Hadley tried to get herself under control. "It's certainly been an eventful one. When did this happen?"

"About a week ago," Hadley said, finally defeating her bout of laughter.

I pulled her closer to me, looking down at those arctic blue eyes. "But years, too."

Hayes looked as if he were watching a game of tennis, his gaze jumping back and forth between the two of us. "I can't say this is something I expected, but if you guys are happy, then I'm happy for you."

It was a weight off my shoulders that he wasn't pissed, but it still felt as if I were carrying the heaviest of loads. "That's not actually why we're here."

Something in my tone put Hayes on alert. "Sit down and tell me what's going on."

Hadley and I settled in the chairs opposite Hayes' desk, and suddenly everything felt official. Hadley's fingernails dug into the back of my hand. I knew she needed to be the one to make the jump. As much as I'd pushed to tell Hayes, Hadley had to be the one to share her story in her own words.

It took a couple of minutes, but Hayes had honed some patience over the years working this job. He knew he had to give people the time to find their words, their strength.

Finally, Hadley looked up and met her brother's gaze. "Someone's been messing with me. A stalker, I guess?" She glanced over at me. "Maybe that's too strong a word."

"It's not. Whoever this is, they're the definition of a stalker."

Hayes' jaw flexed. "Start at the beginning."

To Hadley's credit, she did. From her alter ego to the troll comments to the emails and texts, and finally today's events. She didn't leave a single detail out.

Hayes listened quietly, making notes on a pad of paper. When Hadley finished, he got quiet for a moment. "Why the hell didn't you tell me when this first started? I'm your brother. And I'm a fucking sheriff."

She flinched as he spat the words.

"Hayes," I warned. "Watch your tone."

His focus flicked to me. "You should've told me, too. You know she likes to keep things from us. You should've brought me into the loop."

"That's what we're doing right now," I pointed out.

"Too fucking late!" Hayes pushed to his feet and began pacing. "This kind of thing can be deadly. We have to assume that since this person has Hadley's phone number, they know her identity. They could hurt her or worse."

"I'm not so sure about that," Hadley argued. "If they knew where I was, don't you think they would've done something in person by now?"

"No. There are sick people out there who get a thrill out of scaring women. Right now, they're fulfilled by these kinds of pranks, but what happens when they're not? What happens when they escalate?"

"Hayes," I gritted out.

Hadley squeezed my hand. "No, I want to know what he thinks. It's why we're here."

Hayes let out a shaky breath and seemed to get himself a bit more under control. "First thing's first, I don't want you staying alone. You can stay with Everly and me."

"She can stay with me," I cut in. Hadley staying over wasn't anything new for the girls. The only difference would be that she'd sleep in my bed.

Hayes' mouth pressed into a thin line. "You're not a trained officer."

"I know how to keep the people I care about safe."

Hadley released my hand and squeezed the bridge of her nose. "Can we dial down the testosterone? I have an alarm system at my house. It's safe."

I turned towards her. "You're also ten minutes outside of town. Ten minutes from help. That's not a good idea."

She slumped against the chair. "Fine, I'll stay with you."

"You could sound a little happier about it," I grumbled.

The corner of Hadley's mouth kicked up, and she leaned over to give me a quick kiss. "I can hardly contain my excitement."

"That's a little better."

Hayes made a gagging noise. "This is too weird."

Hadley picked up a rubber band from his desk and shot it at him. "Don't be a jerk, or I'll tell Everly."

His lips twitched, but all humor fled as he focused back on the task at hand. "I need all the passwords to your accounts. We'll have to get the admins involved on that app you're on. But for now, I think you need to stop posting altogether."

Hadley winced. "I have people who count on those videos to make money."

"Toby and Jinx?" I asked.

She nodded. "They have a couple of side-gigs, but most of their respective income comes from their cut of my videos."

Hayes leaned against the wall. "Just how much money are you making on this site?"

Hadley nibbled on her bottom lip. "It's decent."

"Hads," he pressed.

"More than I could ever make as an EMT."

I blinked a few times. I honestly hadn't given much thought to the idea that Hadley could be making a living off her hobby. "You didn't pay for that house with the inheritance from your grandparents, did you?"

When Hadley had bought the property and had her house built two years ago, her family had warned her to be wiser with her money, not to use all of the cash her grandparents had left to her. Hadley had taken their grief without once fighting back.

"No. The inheritance is still in my investment account."

Hayes stared at his sister. "Why didn't you say something? We would've been proud to know you'd found this kind of success."

Hadley met his gaze dead-on. "Do you really think that's how you would've reacted? Seeing me diving off cliffs, flipping my bike, doing skate tricks? Or do you think you would all be telling me how reckless and irresponsible I am? Do you think I wanted to hear Mom blaming me for making her sick with worry?"

Hadley pushed to her feet. "I wanted one thing just for me. No judgments from any of you. Something where I could be *me*. But it looks like I can't have that, either." She flicked her gaze to me. "I need some air. I'm going to walk back to the station."

"Okay," I said quietly.

The door didn't slam behind her, but it wasn't quiet, either.

Hayes sank into the chair that Hadley had vacated. "Hell. There's so much hurt there, and every time I try to fix it, I make it worse."

"I know how you feel." As Hadley had spilled her challenge to Hayes, there had been so much pain in her words. I had been a part of causing that pain. I'd tried to push her to be someone she wasn't. To be less than she was.

Never again.

Chapter Twenty-Six

Hadley

WE WERE MOSTLY QUIET AS CALDER AND I MADE THE drive out of town and towards my house. The sun hung lower in the sky, casting a golden glow over the landscape.

"Did Addie pick up the girls today?" I asked. My mom got them once a week, and I didn't have it in me to face her today.

"Yup. They're making dinner right now so it'll be ready when we get home."

Home. A war of emotions started up in me at that one word. Warmth at being included in Calder's world. Frustration that I had to give up my safe space for the foreseeable future. And there was fear there, too. That someone might somehow be watching, even now.

I'd sent Hayes all of my passwords, and he was coordinating with Mason's team to do some digging into who could be behind all of this. So far, all Mason's contacts had found were dead ends of burner cell phone numbers and email addresses.

Calder reached over and linked his fingers with mine. The movement brought more comfort than was safe. I should've resisted, but I couldn't help sinking into the feeling. When he returned to the station after our meeting with my brother, he'd kissed me in front of everyone.

The crew had hooted and hollered so loudly, Cap had come running. There had been lots of uttered, "*About damn time*" and "*Keep him in line, would you?*" But, overall, I'd felt joy from them all that we'd found our little piece of happy. I just hoped it lasted.

"You're thinking awfully hard over there."

"There's lots to think about."

Calder traced circles on the back of my hand. "We'll find out who's doing this."

I knew they would. Eventually. But in the meantime, my entire life would be upended. "I'm annoyed that I have to leave my home."

Calder pulled to a stop in front of my house. It wasn't massive, but it wasn't small, either. A four-bedroom modern farmhouse with high ceilings and lots of windows. A sprawling porch in the front and a large deck in the back. I'd put myself into each little choice from the double ovens for my baking projects to the soaking tub with a view of the mountains.

"Why didn't you tell me you were making a living from your videos?"

I looked over at Calder, trying to read his tone. "It never came up." He was silent for a moment as he studied my house. "Does it bother you?"

"That you're making a killing doing what you love? Why would it?"

I tugged at a loose thread on the jeans I'd changed into at the station. "Some guys wouldn't be a big fan of that."

Calder's hand slid along my jaw, turning my face towards him. "Hads. I was surprised, and I'll admit a little annoyed that you didn't share you'd found that kind of success. But that has nothing to do with me being intimidated by how much money you make. Any man who has a problem with that isn't much of a man at all."

I leaned forward and brushed my lips against his. "You say all the right things."

His fingers tangled in my hair, keeping me just a breath away from him. "Glad you think so. Now, let's go pack some of your stuff so I can get fed."

"You do get grumpy when you're hungry."

Calder grunted. "Like you don't?"

"Fair point." I could be downright evil if someone kept me from my food.

We climbed out of the SUV and walked to the house. I pulled my keys out of my pocket and unlocked the door. We both paused for a moment, looking for some sort of destruction or waiting for the bogeyman to jump out, maybe. But everything was just as I'd left it.

Calder followed me up the stairs to my bedroom. Energy hummed over my skin as I took in the bed. Memories of Calder's hands and lips on my body cascaded through my brain.

"Don't get that kind of look, or we'll never make dinner," he mumbled.

My cheeks flushed. "I'll just get a duffle." I hurried to my walk-in closet and pulled two bags down from a top shelf. I tossed clothes into one with no real rhyme or reason, hoping it would be enough to last me as we got all of this figured out.

I slung the bag over my shoulder and tossed the empty sports duffle at Calder. "I need to put some of my gear in that one." I might pause the videos for a while, but I wasn't giving up the outlet I needed to stay sane.

"Just call me your pack mule."

I gave his butt a little pat as I passed. "But what a cute pack mule you are."

Calder growled. "Did you just call me cute?"

"Calling 'em like I see 'em."

"I'll show you cute." He grabbed me around the waist, tossing me over his shoulder and heading down the stairs.

"Put me down! You'll drop me, and I'll get some crazy concussion."

"If you had a pool or a lake, I'd throw you in it right now."

As Calder reached the bottom of the steps, I went for a spot under his ribs that I knew was particularly ticklish. He let out a grunted yell, pretty much tossing me from his shoulder. "You're evil, woman."

I waved my fingers like I might go for him again. "Play with fire, and you might get burned."

Calder shook his head but did it while grinning. "Do you want to clean out your fridge while we're here? You can take anything that might go bad over to my place."

"That's not a bad idea." The last thing I wanted to come home to was a fridge full of rotting food and a kitchen that stank to high heaven.

We moved towards the bright space, but Calder's steps faltered in front of the French doors out to the back deck. "What the hell?"

I peeked over his shoulder. "What—?" My words cut off as bile choked me. A dead deer lay gutted on my back picnic table.

Calder muttered a slew of curses and moved me away from the doors. "You locked up after we came in, right?" I nodded. He ushered me farther into the center of the house, away from all the access points. "There are too many damn windows in this house."

"I like light." It was an automatic response, but all I could see in my mind was the torn-up deer.

He pulled me into his arms as we reached the side of the fireplace in the living room. "I know." He pressed his lips to my forehead as he pulled out his phone. "Hey, we might have a problem."

I could barely hear the familiar tone of my brother's voice on the other line.

"Someone left a dead deer on Hadley's back deck." Calder paused for a few moments. "Yup, we're not going anywhere, and the doors are locked." He hung up. "Hayes will be here in a few."

I nodded woodenly.

"I'm guessing that wasn't out there when you left for work?"

"No," I whispered.

"Have you seen anyone hanging around?"

"No one." My breath gave a slight shudder as I inhaled. "But, Calder?"

He pulled back so he could fully see my face. "What?"

"I go out to my deck every day after work. I pour an iced tea and sit and watch the sky. It's how I decompress." I could slowly let the worst days go, sitting out there. Sometimes, I brought my dinner out, too, watching one color melt into another.

But while I'd been doing that, someone had been watching *me*.

Chapter Twenty-Seven

Calder

I PULLED HADLEY INTO MY SIDE ON THE COUCH, WRAPPING an arm around her. She stiffened for a moment, her gaze flicking to Birdie and Sage, but they were focused on the brownies they were eating at the coffee table. She relaxed into me. "I feel like I could sleep for a week."

"Maybe you should call out sick tomorrow. Everyone would understand."

Hadley groaned and pressed her face into my chest. "Then someone else would have to cover for me, and that's not fair. I'll just try to go to bed early tonight."

Birdie made a smacking sound as she licked icing off her thumb. "These are my new favorite, Hads."

Hadley raised her brows. "Really? Even more than double-fudge cake?"

Birdie tapped her lips with her finger. "Yup. Because with this, you get the chocolate of the brownie and the vanilla of the frosting. But I should probably have the cake tomorrow to make sure."

Hadley barked out a laugh. "You're a girl after my own heart."

"Me, too," I muttered. "She's got no shame."

"She goes after what she wants. I like it."

I pressed a kiss to Hadley's temple. "I do, too. Especially if it means I get cake tomorrow."

Sage studied us carefully, a small smile on her lips. "I can help you make the cake."

"Me, too, if I can lick the bowl," Birdie chimed in.

"Group baking project tomorrow afternoon," Hadley announced.

Sage nibbled on her bottom lip, and I knew my girl was choosing her words carefully. "Are you gonna move in for good?"

Hadley gave a small jolt. "I'm just staying for a little while, Goose."

Sage's shoulders slumped a little. "It would be fun if you were here all the time."

I squeezed Hadley's shoulder but kept my focus on Sage and Birdie, trying to read their expressions. "She'll be here a lot, though."

"More than usual?" Birdie asked.

"More than she used to."

"Because you're boyfriend and girlfriend?" she probed further.

I fought the urge to laugh. I was thirty years old. The idea of calling someone my *girlfriend* seemed ridiculous. But I was committed to Hadley and wanted her to know that. "We are. Do you guys have any questions about that?"

Sage leaned forward, elbows on the coffee table. "Are you gonna get married?"

Hadley made a sort of strangled noise in the back of her throat.

I pressed my lips into a firm line to keep from laughing. "This is pretty new. It takes time to figure out if you should marry someone. So, we don't know yet." But the question had visions flaring to life in my mind of Hadley walking towards me in a white gown. Of a little boy with her white-blond hair, and my dark eyes.

"So, you don't make a mistake like you did with our mom, right?" Sage asked softly.

All visions promptly flew out of my head as I zeroed in on my daughter. "Your mom and I were young when we got married—"

"'Cause she got knocked up," Birdie cut in.

I sat up straighter, my hand falling off Hadley's shoulders. "What? Where did you hear that?"

Birdie shrugged. "Susie's mom at school."

I muttered a curse. These small-town gossips needed to get a life. "Your mom and I didn't know each other well enough to get married, but I wanted you to have the best life possible, so we tried." I ran a hand through my hair. "Your mom was sick. She has a disease that makes it hard for her to make good choices."

Sage tore at the corner of a paper towel she'd been using as a napkin. "That's why she got in the accident?"

"It is," I told them.

Tears welled in Sage's eyes. "Why didn't she love us enough to make good choices?"

Hadley was moving before the question had a chance to truly land in my brain. She pulled Sage onto her lap, and my daughter burrowed into her. "Goose, it has nothing to do with you. This is such a hard lesson to learn, especially when you're still so young. But how people act often has nothing to do with us. It doesn't mean we're unlovable. It means they have something broken in *them*. So many people love you. Your dad, me, every single Easton, but what's most important is that you love yourself. Think about all of the things that make you amazing. Your kind heart. That beautiful brain. How you see the world. All of that makes you the most worth loving."

Part of me knew that I'd loved Hadley all her life. That love had shifted and changed over the years. From protective big-brother figure to friend and then to something more. But in this moment, seeing her pour that kind of truth into my daughter's heart, every doubt was swept away. I loved this woman with everything I had, and I was never letting go.

"Love you, Hads," Sage sniffed.

"More than all the stars in the sky."

Birdie pressed into Hadley's other side. "What about more than brownies with cream cheese frosting?"

She wrapped an arm around Birdie's shoulders, laughing. "Even more than brownies with cream cheese frosting. And that is saying *a lot*."

"No kidding."

A knock sounded on the front door, and I pushed to my feet. "I'll get it." I glanced quickly through the peephole, unlatching the lock when I saw Hayes on my front porch. "Hey, man. Come on in."

Birdie hopped to her feet. "We've got brownies! You want one, Hayes?"

"I'd never turn one down."

Sage looked up from Hadley's lap and gave a little wave.

"How are you, Little Goose?"

"Good," she whispered.

Sage might not be completely okay right now, but with Hadley in her life, I knew she would be in the long run. "It's almost bedtime. You guys want to head upstairs and get ready?"

Sage nodded, climbing off Hadley's lap.

"Aw, man," Birdie whined.

Hadley climbed to her feet. "Come on, Birds, we need our sleep if we're baking chocolate cake tomorrow."

Birdie's eyes flashed. "I gotta rest my mixing muscles."

She chuckled. "Right you are." Hadley glanced at her brother. "Do you need me, or can Calder fill me in tomorrow? I need a shower and bed."

Hayes pulled his sister in for a quick hug and dropped a kiss to the top of her head. "He can fill you in tomorrow."

"Thanks, Bubby."

"Love you."

I watched as the people I loved most climbed the stairs and disappeared.

Hayes cleared his throat. "You got a beer I can have with this brownie?"

"You know it."

I grabbed two beers from the kitchen and ushered Hayes out to my front porch. We had a few rockers there that made for a good way to end the day. I only hoped the easy back-and-forth rhythm could keep me calm with whatever Hayes had to say.

I handed him his beer. "So?"

"I don't have a whole hell of a lot."

I gripped the arm of the rocker a little bit tighter. "What about fingerprints or trace evidence?"

"We're running everything we can, but I'm not overly optimistic. Whoever this is, hasn't shown up in person. They've used burner phones and email addresses, so I doubt they'd all of a sudden not use gloves."

"What about a hair or something?"

Hayes took a pull of his beer. "I had techs go over every inch of that deck, and deputies searched the entire property. If there was something there, we got it." He scrubbed a hand over the scruff on his jaw. "That deer was cut up bad."

"That's rage. And whoever this is, knows where Hadley lives."

A muscle in Hayes' cheek ticked. "I know."

"I'm gonna stick close, but you know Hadley, she won't let someone be with her twenty-four-seven."

He grunted in agreement. "You'd have better luck locking her in the basement."

"She'd kick my ass first."

Hayes let loose a low chuckle. "That she would. And she's got a hell of an uppercut." He paused, looking out at the street. "You're sure about this?"

"About what?"

"A relationship with Hadley. I'm not trying to be a dick, but she's been hurt a lot by the people who love her most. I was surprised you two were together, but I'm not blind to the way she looks at you. To how she's *always* looked at you. If you change your mind midway through this thing, it'll kill her."

I stopped my slow back and forth rocking. "I'm not going to change my mind. Hadley was my refuge, too. I needed her just as much. I just let myself run scared. I pushed her away, and I'll never forgive myself for that."

Hayes studied me. "Just wanted to hear that you were sure."

I was. I'd never been more certain of anything in my life.

Chapter Twenty-Eight

Hadley

"**I**'M NOT GOING INTO WORK AN HOUR EARLY WITH YOU so that I can twiddle my thumbs."

Calder's jaw hardened as he glared at me from across the kitchen. "I don't like the idea of you being alone right now."

I set my empty bowl in the sink. "I get that you're worried, but Hayes left me a terrifying goody bag of all sorts of things to keep me safe." There was pepper spray, a taser, some spiked thing to put on my key chain, and a personal alarm. "No one is going to kidnap me when I go get coffee downtown. I'll park right in front of the coffee shop."

Calder said nothing, simply leaned against the counter with his arms crossed.

I crossed the space and laid my hands on his arms, stretching up on my tiptoes and brushing my lips against his. "I need a little bit of normal. I want to get coffee for Jones and me. If you're nice, I might even get one for you."

"Fine," he grumbled. "But text me when you get there and when you leave for the station."

"Deal." I would take it and run. "Now, go so you aren't late for your meeting."

"Bossy," he muttered.

I slapped his butt as he walked out of the kitchen. "Or am I just a boss?"

"I'll take it either way."

I chuckled as I heard the front door close and Calder's SUV start. Thankful we'd picked up mine on the way home last night, I grabbed my bag and headed out, locking the door behind me.

I found a spot almost directly in front of The Bean, which was lucky since tourist traffic was picking up. It would be June before we knew it, and the season would be in full swing. I hopped out of my vehicle and headed towards the coffee house.

I inhaled deeply as I entered. Had to be one of my favorite scents in the universe. I waved at Meghan, working the espresso machine, and then smiled at Calla behind the counter.

"Hey," she greeted. "You okay? Toby showed me what happened to the channel."

That little happy buzz I felt at the scent of coffee fled in a flash at the memory of all those photos. "I'm hanging in there. Just need to be a little more careful for now. We need to keep with no new videos or posts for a while longer."

Calla winced. "Does Toby know?"

"I texted him, but I'm pretty sure he thinks I'll change my mind."

"I'm so sorry this is happening, Hadley."

So was I. The thing that had given me community and purpose was now showing me its dark side. I'd always known it had been there to some degree, but this was a whole other level of messed up. "Hopefully, they'll figure out who's doing this, and we can all get back to normal."

Calla gave me a reassuring smile, but I could see the doubt around the edges. She knew as well as I did that finding someone who was harassing you online was like searching for a needle in a haystack. "I hope so. And in the meantime, I can make sure you're caffeinated."

"That would be greatly appreciated. I'll take Jones' and my regular orders."

"Coming right up."

The bell over the door tinkled, and I glanced over my shoulder. My appetite for coffee soured as Jackie strode towards me. As she approached, I took in everything about her. The angles of her face were sharper, everything about her harder somehow, but I guessed that was what happened when you went to prison.

Jackie bypassed the register and came straight to me. Her gaze was assessing, sweeping over my face and body. I suddenly wished I wasn't wearing my uniform. Jackie wore figure-hugging black pants and a shirt that dipped in the front, showing off a hint of cleavage. My uniform consisted of cargo pants and a button-down that weren't exactly the height of fashion.

She came to a stop in front of me. "Hadley, it's good to see you."

"Jackie," I greeted. I couldn't return the rest of her sentiments. If she'd never returned to Wolf Gap, I would've been a happy camper.

"How are you?"

I studied her, trying to read beneath the question. The woman had a vibrating energy, something humming just below the surface. "I'm doing well."

Jackie's lips pursed when I didn't reciprocate the question. "Listen, can I talk to you for a minute?"

I glanced up at the clock on the wall. "I've got two minutes. Then I need to head to the station."

"That's plenty of time." She moved away from the counter and towards an empty corner of the shop. I didn't know what she thought she'd accomplish with that. The eyes of the five people currently in The Bean were glued to us.

Jackie picked an invisible piece of lint from her pants. "Hadley, this isn't easy for me to talk to you about, but I'm beyond having any sort of ego at this point."

I braced myself for what might come out of her mouth next.

"I made a lot of mistakes years ago."

"You did," I agreed.

A flicker of annoyance passed over her features. "I'm trying to make that right. I want to put my family back together again, but you're standing in my way."

My mouth slackened, falling open a fraction. If a fly had been in the area, it could've flown right in. "Excuse me?"

"Birdie and Sage are my daughters. I know you like to play at being their mother, but you're not. You never will be. What's best for them is for Calder and me to give them a family again. To heal some of those hurts. I know you're not a bad person. You want something that simply isn't yours to have. It's time you realized that."

I blinked a few times. "Did you take a hit to the head recently? You might want to get that checked out by a professional."

Heat hit Jackie's cheeks. "You can't brush this off with your sarcasm, Hadley. It won't change the truth. Calder married *me*. He gave *me* two daughters. Not you. He had plenty of time to choose you, but he never did. Not until I was out of the picture. He's still mad, but he'll come back to me."

I wanted to laugh, to scoff and tell her she was being ridiculous. But some of her words hit their mark.

"Hadley, your order's ready."

I sent a million silent thanks up for Calla in that moment but kept my focus on Jackie. "You can live in whatever delusional world you want, but I'll be over here in the real one. The one where I'm in Calder's bed every night."

I turned on my heel and grabbed my coffees. Everything was a haze as I left. The drive to the station was a blur. I barely remembered handing Jones his coffee.

As I walked to my room to drop off my stuff, an arm caught my elbow. "Hey, you okay?"

I blinked, bringing Calder's face into focus. "Fine."

"Let me rephrase. I know something's wrong, so why don't you tell me what it is."

I needed to work on my poker face, but something told me even if I could fool the rest of the world, I'd never be able to fool

Calder. "I had a lovely little encounter with your ex. Is there a reason you didn't tell me she was in town to get you back?"

I wasn't one hundred percent sure she'd revealed that little tidbit to Calder, but he wasn't an idiot. He would've read between the lines of her approach, even if she hadn't outright said as much. The wince he gave at my words told me that Jackie had already made her pitch to the man in front of me.

"It doesn't matter what Jackie wants because she's not getting it."

I stared into those dark eyes that had been my refuge for so long. God, it would kill me if he walked away. "You might want to make that clear to Jackie because she's pretty sure she has an opening."

I turned and strode towards my room. I needed space to breathe. What I really needed was a good ride, taking my bike over jump after jump and down a hellish mountain pass. I needed to remember that I was alive and breathing, that I'd made it through worse before, and I'd make it through this, too. Even if Calder walked away.

Chapter Twenty-Nine

Calder

I MANEUVERED THE SUV AWAY FROM HOME AND TOWARDS the small resort a few minutes outside of town. I hadn't wanted to leave. Hadley and the twins were wreaking all sorts of havoc on our kitchen in an effort to make the best chocolate cake of all time. But the wariness still clinging to Hadley had told me I needed to go.

I turned onto the private road that led to The Wolf Gap Lodge. The buildings themselves were gorgeous, the resort catering to high-end tourists looking to escape city life for a while. I pulled into a parking spot in the guest lot. Sliding out of my SUV, I strode towards the main structure.

The Lodge had several restaurants, and I had no idea which one Jackie worked in, but I started with the main one. The hostess looked up from her stand. "Good evening, sir. How many in your party?"

"I'm actually looking for someone. Jackie Evans."

"Oh, yes. Just a second." The young woman scanned the space before she landed on Jackie. "Let me go get her for you."

I waited, watching as she approached my ex-wife. She spoke a few quiet words, and Jackie's head snapped in my direction.

The smile that stretched across her face only fueled my rage. She thought this was some sort of victory.

Jackie moved swiftly in my direction, her hips swaying. "Calder, it's so good to see you."

"Cut the shit."

A bit of the smile faltered. "Please don't curse at my place of employment."

When had Jackie ever cared about things like that? I guessed she was trying to create a new persona for herself. "Then maybe we should have a word somewhere more private."

That damn smile was back, but it had more of a sly quality this time. "Of course." She guided me down an empty back hallway. "No one uses this route. I only have ten minutes, but I could come by after I get off work and—"

"I only need one minute." I looked Jackie directly in the eyes, letting my expression go hard. "Listen and really hear me. You and I will never happen. Not if you were the last woman on Earth. I'm not trying to be mean, but it's the truth. You will not approach the woman I love and try to mess with her head. This is my only warning. You keep this shit up, and I will file a restraining order. Do you understand me?"

Jackie widened her eyes in shock, but I could tell it was fake, just like the rest of her. "I don't know what Hadley told you, but I did no such thing. I simply told her how important it was for me to get my family back, to fight for you."

"We aren't yours to fight for," I growled.

"You'll always be mine, Calder. I'm sorry I didn't see just what I had years ago, but I see that now."

"I'll give it to you, you're still good at that manipulative bull-shit, but I see through you. I know what you pulled with Hadley today, and it makes me that much more confident in my decision not to let you around the girls."

Jackie's mouth thinned. "You may not have a choice about that for much longer."

"What are you talking about?"

"I met a lawyer while I was working here. Told him about my situation, and he thinks a judge might overturn that old ruling since I've changed my life for the better. He said he'd take my case pro bono."

My rib cage tightened around my lungs, making it feel as if I couldn't take a full breath. I had no idea if that was even a possibility or if this was some middle-aged lawyer, who hoped he'd get lucky by stringing Jackie along. "You want to play it that way, fine. Just remember everything that'll get dredged up when you do. Every police report and witness statement. The drugs found in your car and your little hidey-hole in our damn house—somewhere Birdie and Sage could've stumbled across accidentally. I will find out every last thing you have ever done, and I will make sure the judge knows about it."

"Calder," Jackie said softly. "That isn't what I want. Just give me a chance. I'll prove to you that we can be good again."

She moved in closer, reaching out as if she might lay a hand on my chest. I stepped out of the way. "You don't get to touch me. Stay away from me. Stay away from the girls. And stay away from Hadley."

I turned on my heel and strode down the hall. My spine jarred with the force of my footsteps as I made my way to my SUV. Hell, none of this was good. Jackie was like a starving dog with her last bone when it came to something she wanted.

I pulled out of the parking space and made my way back to the private road. Instead of heading home like I wanted to, I made the turn for the sheriff's station. I pulled into an empty spot right out front and jogged up the front stairs.

An officer whose name I didn't remember greeted me.

"Hey, is Hayes still in?"

"He is. Let me call back."

Within a few seconds, the young guy told me to go on back.

It was past quitting time, so the space was full of mostly empty desks. But as I passed, I gave chin lifts to the few remaining folks.

I knocked twice on Hayes' door when I got to his office but didn't bother to wait for an answer.

"Is Hadley okay? Did something happen?" Hayes asked before I even crossed the threshold.

"She's fine. Baking a cake with Birdie and Sage."

"Then why do you look like you're about ready to murder someone?"

I scrubbed a hand over my face as I sat down in one of the chairs opposite Hayes. "Jackie's creating problems."

Hayes leaned back in his desk chair. "She's good at that."

"Understatement of the century."

I grunted in response.

"What's going on?"

I cracked my knuckles on one hand, trying to alleviate a small portion of the tension running through me. "She approached Hadley this morning. Told her that she was here to get her family back and that Hadley was standing in her way."

Hayes let out a low whistle. "Did Hadley deck her?"

"No. But when I went to have a stronger word with Jackie just now, she told me that she's been talking to a lawyer. She's going to try to get some of her rights back."

Hayes straightened in his chair. "You call your lawyer?"

"I will first thing tomorrow. I want to say it's just posturing, threats to get me to let her in a little, in the hopes that she won't take this to court."

"You gonna do that?"

"Hell, no. All this proves is that I'm right not to want her in Birdie's and Sage's lives. She doesn't care about them. She's using them as pawns."

Hayes' jaw worked back and forth. "Want me to do some digging?"

"Nothing that would get you into trouble, but I think I might need to file a restraining order."

"I'll look into things as much as I can. Making some phone calls isn't illegal. I'll be clear that it's in an unofficial capacity."

I pushed to my feet and held out a hand. "Appreciate it, brother."

Hayes gave me a half-slap, half-shake. "I'd do anything for you. You know that."

I grinned at him. "Bury a body in the desert?"

He chuckled. "It would depend on who it was."

"Cold. I wouldn't even ask who if you called me for my shovel."

"I guess you're the better friend."

"And don't you forget it."

The truth was, Hayes was the best friend I could ask for. I had a bountiful life in so many ways. Amazing friends who were more like family. Two girls who gave me more purpose and joy than I could measure. A job I loved. And now, I had Hadley in a way I never thought I would. But that seemed to be the final piece clicking into place. I wouldn't lose that, not for anything or anyone.

Chapter Thirty

Hadley

I TWISTED THE EARRING IN MY LOBE. THEY WERE LITTLE SILVER stars I had bought myself years ago. They reminded me of Calder, and those late-night rides we took. The ones where we chased the starry horizon. Those memories were my touchpoint, even after the horizon seemed tattered and broken, I could still hold on to those few beautifully perfect memories.

"Are you sure this is a good idea?" I whispered across the front seat to Calder.

He glanced in the rearview mirror, but Birdie and Sage were engrossed in a heated thumb war game. "It'll be good. I've been thinking about it a lot the past few days. She might go easier on you."

You never knew how my mother would react to anything, and it was possible she'd already heard the town gossip of Calder and me being out and about together. I didn't have it in me for another knock-down, drag-out fight with her. I was too tired.

Hayes had promised not to say a word to my parents about the stalker upon penalty of dismemberment. But taking that pressure off me didn't clear the slate. I still looked over my shoulder constantly. For Jackie, for some anonymous asshole who used a keyboard for a weapon, for someone who would gut an animal and leave it for me to find. I couldn't take my mother harping on me on top of it.

Calder wove his fingers through mine. "Just take it one step at a time. I've got your back."

I stared over at Calder, the angles of his face so familiar and yet different now, too. Different because he was mine for the first time. Three little words teased the tip of my tongue, but I swallowed them back. It was way too soon. Yet, it wasn't. Because I'd known Calder all my life. Loved him nearly all that time. Instead, I settled for two words. They weren't enough, but they were something. "Thank you."

He squeezed my hand. "Always."

Calder pulled into an empty space in front of the house. The girls immediately jumped out of the SUV and ran towards Shiloh, who was over by the barn.

Their speed had a smile teasing my lips. "Think they're excited about the new colt?"

Shy's new baby had arrived two days ago, and Birdie and Sage had been talking about little else. It would be special for them to see how Shiloh trained and cared for the little guy.

Calder turned in his seat, sliding a hand along my jaw. "You're amazing. Don't let anything she says make you think otherwise."

He knew me too well. That even though I was talking about something else, my mind was still bracing for what was to come. "I hate that family dinners feel like prepping for battle."

Calder pulled me against his chest. "I hate that, too."

"What if we just stay out here all night?"

He chuckled. "Somehow, I don't think that will solve the problem."

I didn't either. Someone would eventually come looking. I pushed off his chest. "Might as well get it over with."

We climbed out of the SUV, and Calder came around, taking my hand.

"Are you sure? Maybe it's better if she hears from one of her friends that we're dating."

Calder's lips twitched. "That would make her furious. That there was something about her daughter she didn't hear firsthand."

"Dammit, why do you always have a point?"

"Because I'm incredibly smart, not to mention ruggedly handsome."

I scoffed. "No ego problems here."

He pulled me in closer. "Not when I've won you over."

"I wouldn't say you won me over. I might still be making up my mind."

Calder skimmed his lips over the column of my neck. "Totally won you over."

A pleasant shiver ran over my skin, proving his point. "Show-off."

We climbed the steps to the porch, and Calder opened the front door without knocking, keeping hold of my hand. Everly and Hayes were on stools at the kitchen island, seated next to my mom, while Dad worked on something at the counter.

"Hey, guys," Hayes greeted.

Everly immediately slipped off her stool and hurried over to me, letting out a little squeal and pulling me into a hug. "So happy for you two."

"Thanks," I said softly, releasing her. As I stepped back, Calder took my hand again.

I looked past Everly to my mom. She'd turned on her stool, and her gaze zeroed in on Calder's and my joined hands. Her mouth opened and closed and then reopened. "No, you're not..."

Calder hurried to fill the awkward silence. "Hadley and I are seeing each other."

Mom's gaze jumped to me. "Hadley, you didn't."

I stiffened, my back going ramrod straight.

"What about Birdie and Sage? You can't live your life the way you do with children involved. How will they react when you get bored with your fling and decide to take off for a month?"

Everyone was stunned silent. The only thing I could hear was the blood roaring in my ears. "It's not a fling." I spoke the words softly, hoping they crossed the space.

My mom's lips pressed into a firm line. "Everything is dispensable to you, Hadley. You pick things up and put them down on any little whim. Cancel plans, disappear whenever you want. The same goes with the people in your life. Something gets hard or complicated? Someone asks something of you that you don't want to give? You simply walk away. I won't let you do that to Birdie and Sage. Calder, either. You'll stop this right now before someone truly gets hurt."

Fire burned my throat. "The only person I've ever walked away from was you, Mom. Because you don't seem to have a care in the world that you destroy me on a weekly basis. Why would I choose to put myself in that kind of position?"

Her shoulders straightened, her chin jutting out. "If you are hurt by me stating the truth, then maybe you need to look at your life a little more closely."

"It's not the truth! It's your twisted interpretation, and I'm done with it."

"Calder deserves better than someone who will leave him high and dry. He's been through enough already."

"And you get to decide who he deserves? And that's Addie, right? She's the daughter you wished you would've gotten. She does whatever you ask."

Color hit my mother's cheeks. "Do I think Addie would be a better match for Calder? Yes. She's steady, responsible—"

"Enough!" Calder barked. "What about what I want? This beautiful, kind, strong woman next to me? The one who has put up with your nonsense for all these years because she doesn't want to put her family in a tough spot? That's who I choose. The one who has cared for me even when I didn't deserve it. That's who I choose. The one who makes me feel alive. That's who I choose."

Tears burned the backs of my eyes as my hand gripped Calder's tighter.

Mom clasped her hands in front of her, knuckles bleaching white. "I love my daughter, but I also know her. You can't strap a child to a bike and leave for weeks on end. Or take them repelling down a cliff. You must see that."

But it wasn't that. It was that she truly didn't think I was good enough for Calder. Something in me would always be a disappointment to her. Less than. Unacceptable. Never, not once, good enough.

I pulled my fingers from Calder's grasp. I didn't have any words to say to my mother or anyone else in the room. It hurt too much. I simply turned on my heel and walked out the door.

Chapter Thirty-One

Calder

THE DOOR DIDN'T SLAM IN TYPICAL HADLEY FASHION. I could only hear the soft snick of the latch because the space was deadly quiet. No one moved for a few beats.

Hayes was the first to do so, standing from his stool and moving to face his mother. "What is wrong with you?"

Julia blinked a few times as if bringing her son into focus. "Hayes, you know she isn't ready to be a mother. I don't want Birdie and Sage to get hurt—"

"Hadley's been a constant in their lives since they were born. They love her, feel supported by her," Hayes argued.

It was more than that. My daughters felt *seen* by her. I was starting to realize that precious gift came from her pain. Hadley knew what it was like to feel constantly overlooked and misinterpreted. She knew how much it hurt to have the person who was supposed to love her the most think the worst of her.

Hayes shook his head. "This isn't okay. You need to get some help."

Julia's mouth slackened as she looked around the room, her gaze jumping from one person to the next.

There was only one word to describe Gabe's expression.

Ravaged. As if for the first time, he truly realized the damage his wife had done over the years. "Julia," he whispered.

Her spine snapped straight. "You know, Gabe. What she's put me through over the years. All the unnecessary worry to go chase whatever flight of fancy she has. Now, *I'm* the bad guy for pointing out that she's irresponsible?"

"You're the one who's irresponsible," I cut in.

Julia whirled in my direction. "Excuse me?"

"You're irresponsible with the words you throw around. You know how much they hurt her. I think something in you enjoys it. It might not even be anything conscious. But you like paying her back for the worry she caused you. That isn't love."

The red on her cheeks deepened. "I never thought you of all people would say that to me."

My jaw worked back and forth as I tried my best to keep the rage at bay. "You've been more a mother to me than my own, but I will *never* let you treat Hadley like that again. I've stood by for too long. I'll never forgive myself for it. But this stops now."

"He's right," Hayes added. "I'm not coming to another family dinner until you start seeing a therapist. You need to work through why you can't love your daughter for who she is instead of trying to beat her down and turn her into someone she's not."

"Hayes," Julia whispered. "You can't let her turn you against me."

"Look around, Mom. Hadley's gone. You're the one turning us against you. These are your actions. No one else's."

I started for the door. I didn't need to stick around for this. I needed to find Hadley. A hand caught my elbow, and I turned to see Gabe.

"Let me know how she is?"

My back teeth ground together. "You should be asking her that question. You should've asked it a long time ago."

"I know." The words were low and anguished, barely audible.

"Then start doing it now. Make a stand and get your wife the help she clearly needs."

Gabe nodded but didn't say another word.

I started for the door again. Julia called out my name, but I didn't even falter. I let the door slam behind me as I scanned the area in front of the house. I didn't see Hadley anywhere.

She wouldn't have gone to the barn because Shiloh and the twins were there. I started down the path towards a field where several horses grazed. The land dipped to where a small creek ran alongside the pasture. There, hunched down in the small gulley, was Hadley.

Her shoulders shook as she sobbed. I'd never seen tears like this from her, not once in the twenty-four years I'd known her. Not even when she'd fallen out of a tree. She'd broken her arm and needed eight stitches along her hairline, but she'd only shed a few tears.

I moved down the embankment, but Hadley didn't hear me approach. She jolted as I lifted her off the grass and into my lap. She only fought me for the briefest of moments before burrowing her face into my chest.

I held her as she let everything go. All the pain she'd been holding inside for so long. The hurt I hadn't been there to help her find an outlet for. I felt it all hit me in waves. Blow after blow. I took every single one.

I rocked back and forth with Hadley in my arms, pressing my lips to the top of her head. "I'm so sorry. I should've been there."

She only cried harder.

"I'm here now. I'm not going anywhere."

Her hands fisted in my shirt. "I can't do this anymore. It's killing me."

"You're not going to do this anymore. No more family dinners or any of that shit. Not unless Julia gets some serious help."

"It won't happen," Hadley said through hiccupped cries. "She doesn't have the ability to see that she might be wrong."

I brushed my hand over her hair and down her back. "Hayes

said he isn't coming to dinner again unless she starts seeing a therapist."

Hadley reared back. "Hayes?"

I nodded. "It's taken us all too long to see how much this was hurting you." Because Hadley hid it way too well.

Hadley loosened her hold on my shirt, smoothing it down. "I don't want to ruin anyone else's relationships. I just...I don't want to keep hurting like this."

I pulled her against my chest again. "Sometimes, things need to break to be put back together right. I'm hoping tonight was that. Things might be messy for a while, but maybe we'll all get to a better place. No matter what, it's not your responsibility to deal with. Let everyone else shoulder that responsibility for a bit."

She slumped against me. "I'm so tired."

"I know." I pressed my lips to her hair again, inhaling that scent that was forever Hadley to me. She'd been carrying way too heavy a load for too long. And she'd been doing it alone. "I should've been there."

"You're right. You should've," she said quietly. "But I also understand why you weren't. We were both dealing with our own demons."

"We do a hell of a lot better when we deal with them together." I should've seen that a long time ago. There was so much more balance and peace when Hadley was in my life. When I was truly open with her. From the tiny details to the life-altering decisions, she made me see everything more clearly.

Hadley tipped her head back so she was looking into my eyes. "I like dealing with things together." Her fingers traced over my lips to the scruff of my beard. "But I'm scared I'll get used to having it again, then something will happen, and you'll get scared and bolt."

My hold on her tightened. "I'm not going anywhere." I wanted to give her every promise right now, to tell her that this was forever, but I knew it was too much, too soon. That I needed to build up her trust slowly. "I have so much hope for our future, but if for any reason we decide we don't work as a couple, I'll promise you one thing. You will never lose me as a friend."

"I don't want to lose you as either."

That was the thing. We had always been more. Something that transcended friends or even lovers. Hadley knew every corner of my soul, even the darkest, hidden ones.

I slid my hand along her jaw, tipping her face up to mine. "I love you, Hadley. That's something you'll never lose."

Chapter Thirty-Two

Hadley

I woke to Calder pulling me tighter against him. His heat surrounded me, seeping deep into my bones. There was nothing better. His arms around me, those three words dancing in my mind. Despite all of the awfulness of last night, I'd been given the greatest gift.

I glanced at the clock on the nightstand opposite me. It was almost eight. I was surprised Birdie and Sage hadn't woken us up yet, but it had been a late night.

I hadn't gone back inside my parents' house at all. Calder had given me his keys and went to get the girls. They'd sent me concerned looks at the sight of my swollen and tear-streaked face. When Calder had stopped to pick up burgers in town, Sage had climbed over the seats of his SUV and right into my lap. She'd hugged me tightly and whispered that she loved me.

My throat burned just thinking about it now. I might never get what I wanted or needed from my mother, but I had it in spades from the other people around me. My cup overflowed.

Lips skimmed my neck. "You're thinking pretty hard over there

My mouth curved as pleasant shivers danced across my skin. "Thinking about how much I love you."

Calder smiled against my throat. "Say it again."

"I love you. Always have, always will."

He pulled me closer. "Love you, Hadley. We'll make it through everything that's going on right now. The fact that we've found each other in the midst of all the insanity of the past month just shows how strong our relationship is."

I loved the sentiment. As if our love were the strongest steel because it had been formed in the hottest fire. Amidst stalkers, exes returning, and the height of family drama. That knowledge fueled my hope.

Calder's hand curved around my waist and slipped beneath the waistband of my pajama pants. I sucked in a breath as his fingers began exploring, and I arched back.

Footsteps pounded against the floor. "Dad!" Birdie yelled. "Hayes is here. I see his SUV. Can I open the door?"

I scrambled to a sitting position, pulling the covers over my chest, even though I was fully clothed.

Calder barked out a laugh. "She knows she's not allowed to come in without knocking and waiting for an answer."

"She's *nine*. She could forget," I hissed.

"Daaaaaaaad."

"I'm coming, Birds. You can open the door if you check the window and see that it's Hayes."

"Okay." Footsteps sounded again, ones that resembled an elephant instead of a nine-year-old.

Calder leaned in to kiss me, but I put a finger on his lips to stop him. "Your girls are awake, and my brother is downstairs. No. Just no."

Calder chuckled and dodged my finger to kiss my neck. "I bet I'll be able to change your mind later."

I swore my skin started to hum with energy at his promise. We needed a lock for this door, maybe some solid soundproofing for the walls. I couldn't help but think about my house. The main bedroom was on the opposite side of the house from the secondary ones.

"You're thinking about it, aren't you?"

I shoved at his chest and hopped out of bed. "Your ego really needs some work." I grabbed Calder's robe from the hook in the closet and wrapped it around myself.

"I like you wearing my clothes, Little Daredevil."

I could feel the heat rising to my cheeks. "Would you stop it?"

"Never." He dove for me, hiking me over his shoulder and heading out of the room.

"What is it with you and carrying me like this? Put me down."

I could hear the girls' giggles coming from the bottom of the stairs.

"What are you doing, Dad?" Sage asked.

"Just making sure Hads gets down the stairs safely."

"I'm sure," Hayes mumbled.

I squirmed once we reached the bottom and Calder put me down. It took a second for the world to right itself again. The living room was a lot fuller than I expected.

Everly stepped forward, holding out bakery boxes. "We brought breakfast."

Addie stood next to her with a tray of coffee cups, and Shiloh moved around them into my space, pulling me into a hug so quick, I wondered if I'd imagined it. She kept hold of my shoulders. "I'm sorry."

I blinked a few times at my sister. "What?"

"If I hadn't been taken, Mom wouldn't be like this. You guys wouldn't. I should've fought harder."

I didn't move, couldn't even breathe. Shiloh *never* spoke of her kidnapping. Not once in all the years since. I itched to pull her into my arms, but I knew it wouldn't go over well. Instead, I ducked my head to meet her downcast gaze. "None of this, not one single thing, is your fault. If you take it on, I'm going to be royally pissed."

Hayes moved in closer. "She's right, Shy. Mom's actions are hers alone. So many people in this world carry trauma, but it's each person's responsibility to process and deal with it so they don't hurt others because of it. It's time for her to do that."

Shy's gaze traveled from me to Calder and back again. "Don't let her ruin this. You deserve to be happy."

"So do you, Shy."

She gave me a smile that looked more like a grimace. "I am happy."

I wasn't so sure about that, but I wouldn't push. "So, what's for breakfast?"

Everly wiped under her eyes. "We've got egg sandwiches and donuts. How does that sound?"

"Sounds perfect to me." I drilled a finger into Sage's belly. "What do you think? Could you force a donut down?"

She linked her fingers with mine. "I think I could handle that."

We crowded around Calder's dining table, moving in extra chairs from the garage. We stuffed ourselves silly and didn't talk about anything serious.

Calder slipped his hand under my hair and absentmindedly traced a design on the back of my neck. "What do you want to do today?"

I leaned back in my chair and looked around the table. "I think we should all do something. Take a picnic to the park or go on a hike." I wanted to spend the day with these people who'd gotten up early on a Saturday to make sure I knew they cared.

"Park!" Birdie shouted. "We can bring our skateboards."

Calder's fingers stilled for the briefest of moments, and then he picked up his ministrations again. "That sounds good to me. What do you guys say?"

"We're in," Everly agreed.

Shy nodded, and I sent her a grin. My sister rarely volunteered for more group time, but she loved me and knew I needed her today.

"What about you, Addie?"

Her head popped up. "I don't want to intrude."

"You're not intruding," I argued. "I'd love for you to come."

She sent me a soft smile. It was just like the rest of her, gentle and warm. "I'd love to see some of your skate tricks. Birdie told me all about them."

"We'll have to get you up on a board."

Her smile wavered slightly. "Maybe."

"Okay, let's get everything cleaned up, and we can head out."

"Ev and I will get sandwiches from the deli for lunch. Calder, can we borrow your cooler?" Hayes asked.

"I'll get it."

The cleanup began. Addie and I did the dishes while Shiloh and the girls cleared the table. She was quiet as we worked, but as she loaded the last dish into the dishwasher, Addie spoke softly. "I know what it's like to have someone make you constantly feel less than. To beat you down with words. It's the words that hurt so much more than the fists. I'm so sorry you've been hurting, Hadley."

Tears burned my eyes. I couldn't imagine what Addie had gone through. But there were hints of her story in the way she flinched if someone moved too quickly around her, and the way she always avoided being alone with any man, even those in our group I knew she trusted. I moved on instinct, pulling her into a hug.

"You have the kindest heart. I'm so sorry he hurt you. I'm always here if you need to talk."

Addie's arms trembled but she wrapped her arms around me. "Thank you."

As I straightened and released her, I caught sight of Calder in the entryway to the kitchen. He cleared his throat. "You guys need anything?"

Addie shook her head, darting past him and into the living room. He strode towards me, pulling me into his hold. "You okay?"

I nodded into his chest. "We've all been through so much, but we're still damn lucky."

"I don't disagree, but why are you saying that now?"

"We have each other. Family. It's not all by blood, but that doesn't matter. We have the kind of people in our lives who will always show up, especially when the chips are down. So many people don't get that."

Calder bent his head, brushing his lips across mine. "Love you."

"Love you, too." And I felt each word in my bones.

Chapter Thirty-Three

Calder

OUR PARADE OF FRIENDS MADE THEIR WAY DOWN THE sidewalk towards the park. I had a bag of skate gear for Birdie and Hadley slung over one shoulder and my other hand wrapped around Hadley's. Everything about the moment was normal. A kind of everyday pleasure that I'd been missing, one where Hadley was mine, and I was hers.

She looked up at me as she almost skipped. "Do you care if I invite Jinx, Toby, and Calla?"

"Of course, not." I'd always held a hint of bitterness when it came to Hadley's other friends. They had somewhat replaced me after things had fallen apart between us, but knowing all that she'd been going through, and that I hadn't been there to help, I should be buying them all beer.

Hadley pulled her phone out of her back pocket and typed out a text. Within a few seconds, I heard multiple dings. "They'll head over in a bit."

Birdie and Sage started running as the park came into sight. It was still early enough that it wasn't especially crowded. Addie motioned to a spot with shade from a large tree that also gave us

"Perfect," Hadley called. She released my hand to help Addie spread out two large blankets.

Birdie darted over to me, tugging on the bag on my arm. "I gotta gear up, Dad."

My gaze met Hadley's, humor lighting both of our eyes. "We've got all day, Birds."

"I know, but I want to get started. Think I can do a trick today?" she asked Hadley.

"We'll see how it goes."

The word *trick* had something heavy dropping in my gut.

As if she could see it happening, Hadley reached out and squeezed my arm. "Don't worry. We'll go easy."

I pulled her into my arms and pressed a kiss to the top of her head. "Thanks."

Birdie slid her helmet into place, fastening the clasp. "Enough with the gross mushy stuff, let's go!"

Hadley turned her face into my chest, laughing. "Sorry, Birdie. I'm ready."

I released my hold on Hadley even though it was the last thing I wanted to do and watched as she led my daughter over to a cement surface where they could practice.

"Addie, want to go see if there are any new wildflowers?" Sage asked.

Addie looked to me for silent permission. I waved them off. "Have fun."

They headed for the small creek that ran alongside the park that was blanketed by trees. It was only Shiloh and me now. She opted to lean against a tree set a little bit apart from the blankets, giving her the space she always seemed to prefer. Her gaze remained on Hadley as she helped Birdie balance on her skateboard.

"Is she okay?" Shiloh asked quietly. Her voice wasn't soft the way Addie's was, but it was unassuming.

"I think she will be. But Hadley was right, none of this is your fault."

Shiloh didn't say another word, simply pushed to her feet and started for the creek.

"What's wrong?"

I looked over at the sound of Hayes' voice. "She was asking about Hadley, and I told her that what happened wasn't her fault."

Hayes' jaw tightened as he set down the cooler on the edge of the blanket. "Doesn't like talking about it."

"That much is clear."

"I'll make sure she's okay," Everly said and started after her.

"You got a good one there."

Hayes grinned. "I certainly do." The grin wavered a beat. "I don't want to wreck this day for you, but I heard from one of my contacts in Salem."

"About Jackie?"

"The one and only." He lowered himself to one of the blankets. "Take a load off. We'll talk it through."

He wasn't running off to arrest Jackie, so it couldn't be that bad. I sat down, leaning against the trunk of the tree. "Spill."

"On the surface, she was honest about staying out of trouble. No convictions or arrests."

"But…"

Hayes plucked up a piece of grass and began ripping it to tiny shreds. "She's been involved with people who are definitely not on the straight and narrow. They just sentenced her last boyfriend to ten years for distribution."

I muttered a curse under my breath. I should be relieved, my instincts to keep her away from Birdie and Sage were right on the money. "Jackie didn't go down with him?"

"Nope. Apparently, she played the innocent victim. Had no idea what her boyfriend was up to. Even volunteered for a drug test."

"And?"

"It came back negative."

I scrubbed a hand over my face. "So, she might be sober."

"Might be. But that's not the only kind of high Jackie goes

after. She likes being caught up in that whole world. Makes her life feel exciting—"

"When it's anything but," I finished for him.

"Nail on the head."

"I left a message for my lawyer. We'll see what she says on Monday."

Hayes clapped me on the shoulder. "I'm sorry, man. I'm still digging. There might be more to find. The cop I talked to in Salem was a straight shooter. She said this whole crew Jackie was mixed up with is bad news. Jackie likely took off after her man went to prison because there was no one left to protect her. She didn't want to be exposed."

My fingers dug into the blanket at my sides. "So, she comes back to Wolf Gap, thinking I'll shield her from this bullshit."

"That's what I was wondering."

"She bringing trouble back here?"

Hayes opened the cooler and pulled out a Coke. "That, I don't know. But I asked the detective I talked to if she would keep her ear to the ground, and she said she would."

At least, there was that. We should have an early warning if shit was about to hit the fan. "I need her gone, Hayes."

"I know you do, and I think she'll go once she realizes she doesn't have a prayer of a shot with you."

"I don't know how I could make that any clearer." But Jackie was used to getting what she wanted. She had a natural bent towards manipulation and twisting the truth. Maybe she'd end up shacked up with that lawyer she talked about and would leave me the hell alone.

My gaze lifted at movement in the distance. Hadley hugged a young woman who I knew was Calla, and then Toby enveloped her in an embrace. The hold went on for a beat longer than was friendly, and my eyes narrowed on the man.

Hayes barked out a laugh. "Are you going to go piss a circle around her now?"

"Shut up," I said, climbing to my feet. "I think it's time I officially meet these friends of hers."

"If that's what you want to call it," Hayes said through his chuckling.

He could laugh all he wanted. I had a woman who meant the world to me, and I wouldn't let anyone screw that up.

Chapter Thirty-Four

Hadley

TOBY RELEASED ME. "FEEL LIKE I HAVEN'T SEEN YOU IN forever."

"It's been less than a week," I said with a laugh.

"Usually, we're filming a couple of times a week, at least," he grumbled.

"Toby," Calla said quietly as she slipped her arm through his. "You know it's not safe for Hadley to do the videos right now."

"Yeah, yeah. I just think it's a bunch of BS that we're letting this creeper win," he argued.

"What creeper?" Birdie asked as she skated up.

I glared at Toby. "No one, Birds. Hey, you're looking pretty great. How do you feel?"

"Awesome! Is it time for me to learn a trick?"

Toby grinned at Birdie. "Looks like we've got another Little Daredevil in the making."

Birdie beamed up at him. "Hadley said she's going to teach me all the tricks she knows."

"There's no one better to learn from than Hads. She's a total

I coughed, cutting off the swear that was about to come out of Toby's mouth.

He winced. "I mean, she's a total beast."

An arm slid around my waist, pulling me against a muscled form. I sank into Calder's heat. He reached out a hand to Calla. "I'm Calder. I know you've helped me at the coffee shop before, but we've never officially met."

Her eyes flared the tiniest bit, and I didn't blame her. Calder was a whole lot of handsome man to take in. "Calla. Nice to meet you, too."

Calder gave Toby a chin lift. "Good to see you."

Toby was quiet for a moment, staring Calder down in some weird battle for dominance. "Yeah, sure."

I cleared my throat. "So glad you guys could come hang. I've got all my favorite people in one place."

Birdie pushed off on her skateboard, clearly done with adult conversation.

Toby rested his foot on his skateboard, glancing back at Calder. "Yeah, it's a shame you avoided Hadley like the plague for so long. We could've hung out sooner."

I sucked in an audible breath.

Calder simply pulled me tighter against his body. "I get that you might be a little protective of Hadley, so I'll let that one slide. But hear me when I say that we have a closeness you'll never understand."

Toby scoffed. "One that involved you blowing her off for years? You were nowhere, man. We were her friends. Her *family*. Never saw you once."

"Toby, stop it," I begged. He'd seen how much Calder had hurt me. That pain had still been so incredibly raw when we began hanging out more. But just because he'd seen it didn't give him the right to lay into Calder.

Calder didn't even flinch, keeping his gaze firmly on Toby. "I've seen the way you look at Hadley. Friendship has very little to do with it. You might be pissed we're together, but don't make her life harder because of it."

Color hit Toby's cheeks. "Bullshit, I've got a girl. But Hadley will always be important to me. I'll always look out for her. Just because you decided you wanted to pay attention to her again doesn't mean she'll throw us over for you. And you won't last. You've proven your lack of loyalty already."

"Both of you, stop!" I slid out of Calder's hold. "That's enough. Toby, my relationship with Calder is none of your damn business. Calder, you have no idea what you're talking about."

There was a niggling kernel of worry in the back of my brain that my statement to Calder wasn't entirely true. There were times I could feel Toby's gaze on me for longer than a friend should look. The tears glistening in Calla's eyes right now told me she'd seen it, too.

She quickly wiped under her eyes. "I'm gonna go."

"Calla, no—" My sentence was cut off as she turned on her heel and fled. I spun to face Toby and Calder. "That is on both of you."

I took off to find Birdie. I wanted nothing to do with either of the men in my wake.

I lay curled on my side, facing the wall. I kept my eyes closed as I heard Calder move from the bathroom to the dresser. I heard the sound of a drawer opening and closing, then clothing being tossed into a hamper. A moment later, the other side of the bed dipped. Then, I was being pulled against a bare chest.

I struggled out of Calder's hold.

"Going to finally admit you were faking being asleep?"

I scooted over to my side of the bed. "I was not. You woke me up when you got into bed and manhandled me."

Calder raised a brow. "Manhandled, huh?"

"Yes. Freaking *men*," I muttered.

"Little Daredevil." He spoke the words softly, reaching a hand to gently brush the hair away from my face.

"Don't you be all sweet now."

He moved into my space, pressing his lips to my temple. "I'm sorry. I shouldn't have said that in front of Calla, but Toby pissed me off."

"I don't care if he punched you in the face. You shouldn't have said those things in front of his *girlfriend*."

Calder twisted a strand of my hair around his finger. "You're right." He was quiet for a moment. "Do you guys have a history?"

"Me and Toby?"

He nodded.

"No. He made a move on me once, years ago. Not too long after everything blew up with you and me. I told Toby that I wasn't interested in him like that, and it hasn't been an issue since."

Calder's twisting of my hair stopped as I spoke. "I'm so fucking sorry. I feel like I'm always going to pay for the mess I made of things."

There was so much pain and grief in those words, and it ripped away the worst of my anger. I pressed a palm to Calder's chest. "I love you. I've forgiven you. Hell, there's no one I've loved in this world more than you. There's nothing for you to be jealous or worried about."

Calder's hand slid along my jaw to my neck. "You're the only person I've ever been in love with, too."

My eyes flared. "Calder—"

"It's true. I'll never regret that Jackie gave me those two beautiful girls, but I never loved her."

"There were times I saw you two together that I would've thought otherwise."

"Jackie was good at putting on an act, and she was always intimidated by you, by the connection we had."

"Seriously?"

"It's true." Calder brushed his lips against mine. "Everyone but you could see how much you owned me, way before you should've.

Never feel more alive than when I'm with you. You're like a fire that lives inside me. Even when I thought it was all burned out, there were still embers that lived in my bones. They'll always be there, and I wouldn't want it any other way."

I'd felt those embers in me. I'd done everything I could to snuff them out. But they kept right on burning. I thought I was broken because of it. Now, I wondered if it was because Calder and I were always meant to be.

I pressed my lips to the spot above his heart. "Trust those embers. I don't want anyone else."

Calder's hand slipped beneath the hem of my tank top. "I do. Today wasn't about not trusting you. It was about not liking how Toby looked at you. It was about hating myself for giving him an opening."

My fingers sifted through Calder's hair, tilting his head so I could look him in the eyes. "The time we were apart only showed me how much better life is with you."

Something about the words broke the last of Calder's resolve. His hands were desperate as he tugged my tank top free and then my sleep shorts. His mouth devoured mine, tongue stroking in and out.

His fingers found my core, teasing and then entering. My hand slipped into his pajama pants. His skin was so soft, and the juxtaposition of that softness against the hardness underneath sent a pleasant shiver through me.

Calder's thumb circled my clit, and I arched my back. Each pass was another step up a mountain we were climbing together. Each twist of his fingers inside me brought me closer to the edge of that cliff. We'd chased the horizon together so many times. This time, we were building one of our own.

"Calder." His name came out on a hoarse whisper. He didn't need anything else. He knew exactly what I was asking for.

He shucked his flannel pants and settled between my legs. The weight of him wasn't too much. That pressure of him on top of me as his tip bumped my entrance only made me feel more connected to him.

I let out a moan as he pushed inside. My legs came up, hooking around his waist. Then he was driving into me.

There was that familiar, feral edge to the movement, as if we were both trying to imprint this moment onto each other's bones forever. I met him thrust for thrust as we climbed even higher, to a place I'd never been before.

Our gazes locked, neither of us looking away as we pushed each other even more. My muscles trembled as I began to tighten. "Calder." His name was a breath, a plea. A coming together and a falling apart.

As we spiraled off that cliff together, I felt it all—everything that was between us. The joy and pain. The depths of understanding and the unknown future. The hope of what we were becoming.

But most of all, I felt free. In that moment, I realized I'd found a different kind of freedom in life with Calder. It wasn't something I had to chase, like flipping off mountains or any of my other daredevil tricks. This was something that would always be there. A constant. It was steady and warm and light. It didn't fence me in or force me to be someone I wasn't. It let me fly.

Chapter Thirty-Five

Calder

I CAME UP BEHIND HADLEY AT THE SINK, WRAPPING MY ARMS around her and kissing her neck. "How are you feeling?"

A hint of a blush filled her cheeks. "A little sore but good."

I grinned against her neck. "What does it say about me that I'm glad you'll remember me all day long?"

"That you're a barbaric caveman."

I chuckled and kissed her again. "I've been called worse." I released her and took the bowl she'd been rinsing, placing it in the dishwasher. "Plans for this morning?"

So far, since Hadley had been avoiding posting videos on her channel, there had been no other emails, text messages, or phone calls. That didn't mean I loved the idea of her being alone right now.

"After I walk the girls to school, I thought I'd go get a coffee. I'm hoping Calla is working so we can talk."

I closed the dishwasher and leaned a hip against the counter. "I really am sorry I said something that hurt her."

Hadley pressed a lip to the corner of my mouth. "I know. I think I can soothe over the worst of the hurt, but Toby has some serious apologizing to do, too. He needs to get his head out of his ass because she's a great girl. If she dumped him, I wouldn't blame her."

From what I'd seen, that was exactly what Calla should do, but I held my tongue on that. "Let me know if you think I should stop by and apologize. I'd be happy to." But there wouldn't be a word of apology to Toby.

"I don't think that's the best idea."

"Probably not."

Hadley dried her hands on a towel. "What time is your meeting with Cap?"

"Fifteen minutes. I'd better hit the road." I let out a whistle. "I'm heading out, girls."

Footsteps thundered before two small forms hit me with a force that had me rocking back on my heels. "Can we have pizza tonight, Dad?" Birdie asked.

Sage burrowed deeper into my side. "Pizza would be good."

I chuckled and looked up at Hadley. "What do you say to pizza?"

"Do I look dumb to you? I say yes."

Birdie let out a little whoop and then proceeded to do a sort of shimmy-shaking dance all over the kitchen. Hadley grabbed her hands and danced in circles with her.

Sage curved a finger through my belt loop. "They're kinda nutty."

"But we love them that way."

She grinned. "Life would be pretty boring if they were normal."

Truer words had never been spoken. I pressed a kiss to the top of Sage's head. "Don't let them be late walking to school."

"I won't."

"Bye, guys," I called as I headed for the front door.

I made the drive to the station in my typical three minutes. Soon, that three would stretch to ten if I made the drive later in the day. Tourist traffic would clog the streets and have locals cursing.

I pulled into an empty parking spot and climbed out of my SUV. The birds sang overhead as I moved to the front door. Pulling it open, I called out greetings to the guys scattered around the living room and kitchen. Shift change wasn't for another hour, but they were ready to head home and get some decent sleep.

I made my way down the hallway. As I turned a corner, I almost ran smack-dab into someone. "Sorry about that." I took a half-step back as I recognized the man we'd saved from the accident at the ravine. "Evan, right?"

The man nodded, extending a hand. "Good to see you again, Calder."

"You, too. What brings you back to our neck of the woods?"

"Just had a meeting with your captain about how I can help support you guys."

"That's kind of you." Just as long as helping wasn't buying anyone ridiculously expensive gifts.

Evan twirled his cell phone between two fingers. "Hey, you're friends with Hadley Easton, aren't you?"

The false casualness in his tone set me on edge. "She's my girlfriend, actually."

It was the first time I'd said the word. It felt both right and like not nearly enough. She was so much more than that.

Evan straightened, his shoulders tensing. "She told me that she wasn't interested in dating anyone."

Hadley had conveniently forgotten to mention that this idiot had made a move on her. I sent him an easy grin. "We've known each other our whole lives. Timing just wasn't right until now."

His jaw tightened, the muscle there flexing. "Sure. Tell her I said hi."

"Will do. You have a good day."

Evan grumbled something under his breath and took off towards the building's entrance.

I flexed and clenched my hands, trying to get blood flow back into my fingers. Hadley was a beautiful woman. She was charming and caring and lit up a room. I'd have to get used to the fact that I wasn't the only person who saw that. It didn't mean I had to like it.

I moved down the hall and quickly knocked on Captain Murray's open door. "Morning, Cap."

"Morning, Cruz." He inclined his head to an open box on his desk. "I got donuts if you want one."

"Wouldn't say no." I plucked up a glazed pastry and a napkin from the stack. "So, Evan Gibbs."

Cap let out a sigh, shaking his head. "Someone's feeling the need to make his reach known."

"How so?"

"I think he's determined to let everyone in town know just how big his bank account is. He wants to put on a ball to raise money for the widows and orphans fund."

I choked on the bite of donut I'd just taken, and Cap handed me a bottle of water from his mini fridge. I took a gulp, clearing my throat. "Wolf Gap isn't really a *ball* kind of place."

"I tried explaining that to him." Cap rubbed at his temples. "Apparently, our lovely mayor thinks it's a great idea. Hell, it's barely eight in the morning, and I already have a headache."

"Does this mean I'm going to have to wear a tux at some point in the future?"

"Welcome to politics, Cruz."

I shifted in my seat, setting my donut down on his desk. "Actually, that was what I wanted to talk to you about."

Cap leaned back in his chair, taking me in. "You having second thoughts about wanting my job?"

"I am." I didn't have any other words to give him at the moment. All I knew was that being with Hadley, letting myself love her, had shown me all the ways I was trying to be someone I wasn't. I loved fighting fires with my team. I hated sitting behind a desk and making nice with people like Evan Gibbs. It was a recipe for a miserable life for me.

"Thank God."

"Excuse me?"

Cap shook his head. "You're an amazing leader, Calder. But your gift is being on the ground with your crew. You lead by example. Sure, you can soothe egos and hobnob if you have to, but that's not where your true gift is. This firehouse would lose a lot if you decided to leave your post as lieutenant." He paused for a moment, eyes widening a fraction. "Please tell me you aren't quitting to do something else altogether."

I chuckled. "I don't want to leave. Some things lately just made me realize that I love what I do. I don't want to lose it, even if my job is riskier than most."

"Life is risky. I could have a heart attack right here at this desk. I could cross the street and get hit by a truck. We aren't guaranteed a certain number of days on this planet. You know that better than most. It's about the life we can fit into the days we have."

A burn lit down my throat. I'd spent so much time since the accident trying to mitigate every risk. To keep my girls safe. To keep myself safe. To keep us all from experiencing more pain. But in doing that, I'd made our lives smaller.

"I want to do what will make me happy, and that's staying in the lieutenant position."

"I have a feeling Hadley's a part of that, too."

The corner of my mouth kicked up. "She is."

"Don't know how you two stayed away from each other for so long. A blind man could see how much you meant to each other."

I leaned back in my chair. "Because I was an idiot."

Cap chuckled. "Us guys tend to be that way." The humor slipped from his face. "Don't go back there. Whatever it takes, don't lose her. A love like that…it only comes along once in a blue moon."

"I won't." The words were rough, panic edging in. Because now that I knew what it was like to live with Hadley by my side, I wasn't sure I'd survive without her. If I did, it would be as a shell of a man.

Chapter Thirty-Six

Hadley

I GRABBED A PARKING SPOT A FEW STORES DOWN FROM THE coffee shop and hopped out of my SUV. The morning sun gave downtown an almost pink glow. It was one of the things I loved about Wolf Gap in the spring and summer. It was even more beautiful when you saw the mountains lit up in the same way.

I pushed my door closed and beeped my locks. Stepping onto the sidewalk, I paused. Toby strode down the street in my direction, his head down.

"Toby."

His head snapped up, and he grimaced when he saw me. "Hey, Hads." He glanced around the street as if looking for someone.

"I was just heading to the coffee shop to check on Calla."

That grimace deepened. "She's not there."

"Okay…"

Toby ran a hand over his buzzed head. "She's pissed. Went to stay with a friend for a couple of days. Said she needed to think."

My stomach cramped, the hope for everything blowing over evaporating in the wind. "I'm sorry, Toby."

He let out a chuckle, but nothing about it was pleasant. "Shouldn't your boyfriend be the one to apologize?"

"Calder is sorry. He was out of line, but you didn't exactly help."

Toby's gaze hardened. "I didn't help? Your boyfriend basically accused me of panting after you in front of Calla. Of course, she's upset."

He was right, but there was more. If Calla didn't already see those signs in Toby, wouldn't she have blown the whole thing off? Or put Calder in his place?

"Toby," I said quietly, "you know I love you, right? But that kind of love will only ever be a friendship. You were there for me when my life was falling apart—"

"You mean when Calder ripped it apart. And now you're spreading your legs for him."

My palm itched to strike out and slap, but I fisted my hand, keeping it firmly at my side. "Don't you *ever* say that kind of thing to me again. You might be my friend, but you have no right to speak to me that way."

"Fuck!" Toby spun around and punched the side of the building.

I winced at the cracking sound the wood made.

"Hell!" He shook his hand, blood dripping from his knuckles.

"Come on, you big idiot." I ushered him towards the building where his and Calla's apartment was. Toby was silent as I led him through the bike shop and up the stairs. I opened the door, knowing Toby never bothered to lock it.

The place was a mess, pizza boxes and beer cans strewn across the coffee table. A blanket rumpled in the corner of the couch told me Toby had likely crashed right there.

"Sorry," he mumbled. "Jinx came over last night."

I was sure Jinx had helped Toby drown his sorrows. Normally, I would've been there, too, an extra shoulder and listening ear, but things were changing.

I moved into the small kitchen, grabbing the first-aid kit I kept stocked for them from below the sink. "Come here." I started the water, and Toby stuck his hand under the flow. I tore off a couple of paper towels and patted his hand dry. Toby winced. "Do you think you need an x-ray?"

He flexed his fingers, grimacing. "No. It'll be swollen, but it's not broken."

When you took as many falls as we did, you could tell what was a break and what was a bruise. I inclined my head to one of the stools at the kitchen island. "Sit."

He did as I told him and rested his hand on the counter. I opened an alcohol wipe. "This is going to sting."

"I deserve it."

"You kind of do." I lightly swiped the pad across Toby's knuckles, and he hissed. "What's going on with you anyway?"

"I don't know, man. Things are changing, and I just want them to stay the same. Life is good the way it is."

A pang lit along my sternum at the almost boyish tone to Toby's voice. "There's only one constant about life: it'll always change. Nothing stays the same forever."

"I guess," he grumbled. "I'm sorry I was an asshole. I just hate the idea of Calder getting the chance to hurt you again."

Toby had always been protective. He'd once knocked a guy out for slapping my butt at a skate park.

I spread some antibiotic ointment across his knuckles and covered it with gauze. Then popped one of the instant ice packs and handed it to Toby. "I appreciate that you don't want me to get hurt, but you can't protect me from everything. The whole reason we started doing what we do was to feel that rush of being alive. It comes with risks, and I'm okay with that."

He looked up and met my gaze. "Even if he breaks your heart again?"

I shuddered at the thought, at how crushed I'd been the last time around. If it happened again, it'd flatten me. But I couldn't stop moving forward. It was too late, anyway, I was already gone. Head over heels for a man who'd grown to mean everything to me. "I'll find a way to deal with it if it happens."

"I hope you're right."

I glanced at the clock on the wall. "I need to get going, or I'm going to be late for work."

"Sure. Thanks for—" Toby held up his hand.

"Of course." I didn't move towards the door for a moment. "Are we going to be okay?"

He nodded, but the movement was jerky. "Of course, we are."

Something in Toby's tone didn't quite ring true. It had a stinging sensation hitting my nose. He and Jinx had been my partners in crime for years. I didn't want to lose them. "When your hand's feeling better, we'll go for a ride."

"Sure. Now, get out of here before you get fired."

I sent him a smile that I knew was forced, but it was the best I had. I made my way out of the apartment and down the stairs to the bike shop. The stinging in my nose intensified as I swallowed back tears. I didn't even notice the figure ahead of me on the street.

"Hadley."

My head snapped up. "Mom."

She studied me, her eyes narrowing as she focused on my face. "What's wrong?"

"Nothing, just running late for work."

"You should make sure—" She cut herself off. "I'll let you go, then. Maybe we could talk later this week?"

I looked at the woman in front of me, and my chest physically ached as if it were holding all the hurts and disappointments that had built up over twenty-four years. It didn't change that I knew part of her loved me, in the same way I would always love her. But I couldn't be around her, not when it built up more of that pain that I would have to carry around with me every day.

"I'm not ready for that."

My mom's lips thinned. "Hadley, my entire family is royally pissed at me. You need to give me an opportunity to make things right."

My fingers tightened around my keys, the grooves in the metal digging into my flesh. The tiny bite of pain helped, kept me from screaming right there on the street. "If your family is royally pissed at you, then maybe you should talk to them. It's not my job to smooth things over. Not anymore."

"I didn't mean that you should. I simply meant that I would like for you to hear me out. You might not believe me, but I don't want my family to be at odds."

I did believe her. She wanted us to be one big, happy family. But to be that, we had to be as she wanted us to be, fall in line and play the role she gave us. I was never much good at acting. "I really don't have time for this right now. I'm sorry." I started towards my SUV.

"Hadley," she called after me.

I kept right on walking, another weight added to that cavity in my chest. I climbed behind the wheel. My eyes burned as I pulled out of my parking spot, my mother staring at me from the sidewalk. It felt as if someone had poured acid in them by the time I pulled into the fire station.

I grabbed a spot at the edge of the lot and took several deep breaths. Calla. Toby. My mom. It was all too much. I stared at the front doors of the station, focusing on the letters above them as I continued to breathe. I tried to picture the stress of the morning melting away into a pool on the floor of my SUV.

I had no room for my personal baggage when I walked through those doors. None of us did. The only thing that mattered once you were inside that station was the people who needed your help.

That helped. Putting the focus on something outside of me. People in need.

My phone dinged, but I didn't pick it up, I simply kept breathing. Another ding sounded, and then another. My phone let alerts fly, one after the other.

I pulled the device out of my cupholder, silencing it as I went. Text after text popped up from numbers I didn't recognize.

Unknown Number: *Is this really Little Daredevil? Please text me back! I'm your biggest fan! I started BMX racing because of you.*

What the hell was happening? Another number popped up on my screen.

Unknown Number: *Dude, if this really is the Little Daredevil send me some of those sweet ass nudes that were on your account.*

My stomach pitched as incoming calls started popping up on my screen, email after email. I could barely get rid of one before another notification appeared. I struggled to navigate to my settings but finally made it there and put my phone in airplane mode. The notifications stopped, but one had frozen at the top from a new sender.

Unknown Number: *I'd like to fuck you, tear you up, and show you your place.*

No amount of breathing would help me now. My thumb trembled as I tapped the message icon. There were over a hundred new texts in less than two minutes. I scrolled through them. It was a mixed bag, everything from fans to things that made me want to vomit, but my thumb hovered over one in particular.

Unknown Number: *This is me helping karma along. Liars and sluts deserve to be punished.*

My gaze flew up from the screen, darting around the parking lot. I searched the trees that lined one side of the space, half expecting a masked serial killer to jump out. I scanned the street our station sat on. A couple jogged with their dog, and a woman walked with a baby in a stroller.

Nothing was out of place. But as I stared down at the screen, I couldn't help but feel like someone was watching me.

Chapter Thirty-Seven

Calder

"**H**AND ME THE CAYENNE PEPPER, WOULD YOU?" MAC asked as he stood in front of the stove in the station's kitchen.

I opened one of the cabinets and grabbed the spice but held it just out of his reach. "You're not going to burn our mouths off, are you?"

"Y'all are a bunch of sissies."

"No, we just weren't born in hell," McNally shot back from his spot at the counter where he was reading the local paper.

Mac grinned. "Not hell, Louisiana. Now, give me the damned pepper."

I tossed him the spice. "You make me cry, and I'll dump this in your coffee when you're not looking."

Mac shook his head and sprinkled a light dusting of the pepper onto whatever egg creation he was making. "I'm making it mild for the crybabies."

McNally sent him a salute. "We thank you."

I looked up at the sound of the front door opening. The same way I'd looked up every time, just waiting for Hadley.

"You've got it bad," Mac muttered.

"Shut up."

As Hadley moved through the entryway and into the living space, the light from the large windows hit her face. There was no typical blush staining her cheeks. In fact, there was no color in her face at all.

I was moving towards her before I consciously gave my legs the order. My hands went to her face, brushing strands of hair away that had fallen out of her bun. "What's wrong?"

"I think someone posted my phone number online somewhere. I started getting a bunch of texts and phone calls. So many, I'll have to shut off the service."

As she gave me the device, her hand trembled. That miniscule movement sent rage pumping through me. Hadley was one of the strongest people I knew. The fact that this asshole had her shaking made me want to rip them limb from limb.

I scanned through the missed calls and text messages. My grip on the phone tightened as I read disgusting messages about what some guys would like to do with Hadley. I slowed as I read one that made bile creep up my throat. "What in the actual fuck?"

"It's bad, right?"

"I don't want you looking at these." I didn't want her to see one ugly word that graced this phone. "Come on and sit down."

I guided her towards one of the couches, easing her down onto it. I pulled out my phone and hit Hayes' number.

"Hey, man. What's up?"

"You need to get over to the station. Hadley's phone number was posted on a website somewhere. She's getting some pretty ugly messages."

"I'll be there in five."

We both hung up without another word.

I sat down next to Hadley, pulling her into my arms. I didn't give a damn that we were at work or that half a dozen people were staring. I hauled her right into my lap. "Baby, I'm so sorry."

Her hand fisted in my shirt. "Some of those messages, Calder…"

"Don't think about them. They don't exist for you." Rage

pumped through my veins, thick and heavy. My hands itched to break something. I focused on not holding Hadley too tight. I ran a hand down her hair. "It's going to be okay."

"Is it, though? Who hates me that much? I stopped making videos. I don't even go on the damn site anymore."

"I don't know. God, I wish I did." But I couldn't be trusted if I found out who.

The door to the station banged open, and Hayes charged into the space, a female deputy on his heels. He'd made it way under five minutes. "Hadley," he barked.

"Tone it down," I warned.

Hayes took a steadying breath. "Sorry. Are you okay?"

Hadley straightened, sliding off my lap. "I'm fine."

"You're not fine," he shot back.

She pinched the bridge of her nose. "If you already know how I am, then why did you bother asking?"

Hayes took the seat on Hadley's other side and pulled her into a hug. "Sorry, baby sister. I'm worried about you."

She patted his chest. "I know, but I really am okay. Not physically hurt in any way."

Emotionally was something else altogether. I stared down at her phone, the list of messages taunting me. I handed it to Hayes. "You should see these."

"It's on airplane mode now," Hadley said. "Don't turn that off unless you have to."

Deputy Adams appeared with a tall glass of water. "Here you go, Hads."

She sent the woman a grateful smile. "Thanks."

Hayes scrolled through the messages, and his face got redder and redder. His jaw was granite when he met his deputy's gaze. "Get a tech over here. See if we can get that James woman from Fox River, she's the best with this kind of thing."

"I'll put the call in now." Adams stepped away from our group, scrolling through her cell phone.

Hayes turned himself so he faced Hadley and me. "Start from the beginning of your day. Don't leave anything out."

Hadley didn't give him any grief. She told him about making breakfast with me and the girls, going into town, her run-in with Toby, and then with her mother.

I wove my fingers through hers as she spoke. I needed that point of contact, something to assure me that she was safe. "It might be worth having a conversation with Toby."

Hadley's head snapped in my direction. "Seriously, Calder?"

"We need to consider every possibility. He has access to your phone number and email. He's not happy that you and I are together."

Hayes typed out notes on his phone before looking up at his sister. "Do you guys have a romantic history?"

"No, we don't."

"He made a move on her, and we had a run-in at the park yesterday that wasn't exactly pleasant."

Hadley pushed to her feet. "Stop it. Both of you. Toby doesn't want me to get hurt again, that's why he's upset that Calder and I are together. He saw how much it hurt me when we had our falling-out, that's all. He'd never do something like this."

Hayes held out a hand in a placating gesture. "Okay. Just calm down. He may not be the one doing this but talking to all of your friends involved in those videos will be a necessity. They may have noticed something you haven't."

"Okay," she whispered.

I grabbed Hadley's hand and tugged her back down to the couch. "We need to look under every rock."

"Fine, but this isn't Toby. You don't know him like I do."

"I'll be the first to apologize when Hayes crosses him off the suspect list."

She burrowed into my side. "You'd better."

Hayes typed out a few more things. "Is there anyone else you've noticed hanging around? Someone paying you more attention than feels comfortable? Anything."

Hadley pinched the bridge of her nose as if a headache were forming. "Besides Jackie?"

"Jackie's a bitch, but unless she got a tech degree I don't know about, I don't think this is her," I said. Jackie was more of a make-a-public-scene-in-the-middle-of-town kind of person.

Hadley stiffened in my arms. "Evan Gibbs."

Hayes' eyes narrowed. "The real estate guy you pulled out of the wreck?"

"Yeah. He tried to give me some really extravagant gifts, and I keep running into him."

"It is a small town," Hayes pointed out.

"He was out at Painted Rocks when I was cliff diving with my friends. That's not exactly a popular trail."

"When did that happen?" I asked.

"Not long after the accident, before you and I, uh, got together."

I squeezed Hadley's hand but looked at Hayes. "He was here this morning, too. Wants to host a ball to raise money for the fire department."

"Inserting himself into her life potentially," Hayes muttered.

"I hate this," Hadley whispered. "It's going to make me look at everyone around me differently."

I pulled her in closer to me. "For now. We'll catch whoever's doing this, and then things will go back to normal."

"Will they? I don't see how. Everything's different. Those videos used to be a way for me to connect with people looking to break free. Now, I know how much hate is hiding behind those screens."

I pressed my lips to the top of Hadley's head. "It's not just hate. There's inspiration and love there, too. I've seen some of the videos little girls have made, showing you their first tricks on a bike or skateboard. I've seen the hiking trips people have taken because you showed them how amazing it can be. I've seen comments thanking you for what you do. Don't forget all of that."

Hadley's eyes shone as she looked up at me. "Love you."

I brushed my lips against hers. "Always have, always will."

Chapter Thirty-Eight

Hadley

I SAT HUDDLED ON THE COUCH, WRAPPED IN A BLANKET. EVEN though night had fallen, it was still relatively warm outside, but I was freezing. I hadn't been able to get warm since I'd read those text messages.

I couldn't stop thinking about what made a person say such vile things to a complete stranger. The hate had to be a living and breathing thing inside them. It had to be burning them alive.

My mind drifted again to the anonymous puppet master behind it all. Hayes had found listings on several social media sites with not only my phone number and email but also my physical address. That was what killed the most: that my respite from the world had now been exposed to it. Those vile people full of hatred could walk right up to my front door if they wanted to.

Calder had gone out and bought me a new phone with a brand-new number, but he couldn't wipe away the words burned into my brain. He couldn't make my home safe again, though he was trying. He'd already called a security company to put in a gate and cameras.

I just sat here as the world kept spinning around me. Any sort of movement felt like too much. My arms and legs seemed as if they weighed one hundred pounds each, and my head throbbed. I was exhausted down to my bones, but when I'd tried to nap, the words from the messages had danced in my head, taunting me.

The couch dipped, and Sage crawled into the spot next to me. She linked her little fingers through mine. "Love you, Hads."

"Love you, too, Goose."

"Want to talk about it? Sometimes, that makes me feel better."

I leaned my head so that it rested on top of hers. "Have I ever told you that you have the best heart?"

Her mouth curved. "Once or twice."

"I'm telling you again. Seriously, the best."

"I'm sorry you're sad. Dad said some people said mean things to you."

I winced at the thought of Calder having to explain this to his kids. "Some people are being pretty awful."

Sage was quiet for a moment, but she tapped out a beat with her thumb on my hand. "There was a girl who was real mean to me last year. She said my mom tried to kill me."

I sat up straight. "Who?" I didn't care if she was nine years old. I'd give that little girl a piece of my mind.

Sage shook her head. "It doesn't matter who, but it hurt. I was sad for a long time, but then I realized she doesn't really know me. She didn't take the time to get to know me. If she had, she wouldn't have said that. I bet these people don't know you, either."

I pulled Sage into a tight hug. "You're the wisest nine-year-old I know. Thanks for reminding me of what I already knew."

She burrowed deeper into my hold. "We know you and we love you the most."

My eyes burned for the hundredth time today, but this time, it was happy tears trying to escape. "Love you so much, there's not a word for it."

Calder strode into the room from the kitchen, but his steps faltered as he took in Sage and me. "What's going on here?"

Sage smiled at her dad. "Just having a heart-to-heart."

"Am I interrupting?"

I shook my head. "Come get in on this cuddle puddle."

Calder chuckled. "A cuddle puddle, huh?" He eased down on my other side, pulling both me and Sage against him.

"That's the technical name, trust me."

Sage giggled. "It's a good name."

I drilled a finger into her side. "Just like Goose is a good name."

Her giggles turned to laughter. "Did you know there's a wild-flower named Goosefoot?"

"Really?"

"Yup. Pinyon Goosefoot. It's not that pretty, though."

"We still need to try to find it. Make a pressing in your book," I said.

Calder pressed his lips together to keep from laughing. "Pinyon Goosefoot?"

Sage rolled her eyes. "Yes, Dad."

"What other good names are in that book of yours?" I asked.

"There are some weird ones, like Bastard Toadflax."

Calder sat up straighter, taking us with him. "Sage, we don't use that kind of language in this house."

"It's the name, Dad. Swear."

"What kind of book did Addie give you?"

I couldn't hold in my laughter. God, it felt good to let it free. As if the action unburdened all of the tension of the day. "Bastard Toadflax?" I laughed harder.

Calder held onto me but looked at his daughter. "I think she's losing it."

"I think you're right."

The back door slammed, and Birdie came in through the kitchen. "What the heck is going on?"

Sage grinned at her sister. "Hadley's losing it."

"I think we have to go looking for Pinyon Goosefoot and Bastard Toadflax," I said through my laughter.

Birdie's brows drew together. "What is she talking about? Is that another language?"

"Wildflowers," Sage explained.

Birdie rolled her eyes. "Oh, geez. Not that again."

Sage pushed up to a sitting position. "Hey, I like them, don't make fun. I'm not mean about your skateboarding, even when you fall on your butt."

"I don't fall on my butt."

"You did earlier today, right on the sidewalk."

Calder waved a hand in the air. "Girls, that's enough. Take a breath." Both of them glared at him. "Okay"—he pushed to his feet, taking me with him—"I think we all need to get out of this house."

"I don't know—" I began. The idea that whoever was behind this might be watching set my teeth on edge.

Calder gave my shoulder a squeeze. "Family bike ride. To get ice cream."

"Yes!" Birdie did a little shimmy shake around the living room. "I'm getting cookies and cream."

"I want strawberry," Sage chimed in.

Calder turned to me, brushing the hair out of my face. "What about you? What are you going to get?"

"Salted caramel all the way."

He brushed his lips against mine. "Think you'll let me have a bite?"

I linked my fingers with his. "Depends on what you'll give me in return."

"I can think of a few things…"

Birdie made a gagging noise. "Enough with the mushy stuff. I need ice cream!"

Calder leaned in close, whispering in my ear. "I love them more than anything, but they're kind of a cock-block right now."

I barked out a laugh. "Come on, Casanova, let's get some sugar."

We geared up and got our bikes from the garage. The ride wasn't horribly long, but the drive-in ice cream shop was on the other side of town. The evening air was still warm from the heat earlier in the day, and our bike lights cut through the twilight.

The girls' laughter and good-natured ribbing floated on the air. The breeze lifted my hair off my back as I rode. It was heaven. More than that, it was freedom. That different kind, the steady warmth of love making me feel lighter than I would've thought possible given the events of the day.

Yet that was exactly what I felt. Free. With Sage and Birdie and Calder, winding our way through neighborhood streets in search of ice cream. It was so simple, yet it was everything.

Chapter Thirty-Nine

Calder

"**W**E'VE GOT A LITTLE TIME. YOU WANT A COFFEE and a breakfast burrito?" I asked as I parked in front of the sheriff's station.

Hadley's stomach rumbled in answer. "I think that's a yes." She started to climb out of the car when her phone rang. She pulled it out of her pocket, scanning the screen. "It's Beckett."

"Answer it. I'll go get food and coffee and be back."

She leaned over, giving me a quick kiss. "Thanks." Then she tapped her screen. "I'll be damned. You are alive."

I grinned as I climbed out of my SUV. Hadley loved her eldest brother fiercely. I was sure she admired how he'd taken off for parts unknown to follow whatever dream popped into his head. I should be counting my lucky stars that she hadn't done the same.

I made it halfway to the coffee shop before I heard someone call my name. Turning around, the good mood I'd been holding onto after waking up and losing myself in Hadley fled. "Jackie."

"Did you move her in?"

"Excuse me?"

"Stop playing games. I want to know if you moved Hadley

I studied the woman in front of me, searching for signs that she was on something. I didn't see glassy eyes or pinprick pupils, but there was an almost frantic energy to Jackie. Her fingers tapped out a beat against her thigh in a staccato rhythm.

"Jackie, that's *my* house. Who lives there or doesn't is none of your concern."

Her eyes narrowed. "It will always be my concern. You're my family."

"Jackie—"

"You're all I have."

The faintest crack appeared in my armor as her voice broke. "Shit," I muttered. "You may need some support, but I can't be that person."

Jackie gripped my arm, her nails digging into my skin. "You're the only one who can help. There's no one else. You're it. You and Birdie and Sage. We can be a family again."

I pulled my arm from her grasp. "We can't." My tone was firm but not cruel. "Look, there are support services—"

"Did you cheat on me?"

My eyes flared. "What?"

"You heard me. Were you fucking Hadley the entire time we were together? She was barely legal back then. It's sick."

"I *never* cheated on you. Not once." I knew the same couldn't be said for Jackie. I'd never forget having to go to my doctor for an STD test, wondering if something would come back positive. I'd never forget the relief when I found out that I was in the clear.

"She's manipulating you. She always has. So, her sister was kidnapped. Boohoo. She's fine now. I'm the one who needs you, not her."

"Enough, Jackie," I barked. "This has to stop. I can't help you. We'll never get back together. And I won't have you bringing dangerous people into my daughters' lives."

Jackie paled. "W-what are you talking about?"

"I know you got mixed up with some seriously bad people,

Jackie. If you really loved Birdie and Sage, you'd be moving to the other side of the country to keep them safe."

"They don't know where I am. I swear, they don't—"

"How hard do you think they would have to look before they found you? This is where you used to live, where you have ties to a community."

"No, they won't find me here."

I bit back the urge to scream. "Come back to reality. Of course, they can."

Tears filled Jackie's eyes. "Hadley stole you from me. All of you. If she would've just stayed away—"

"The outcome would've been exactly the same." Only I'd be living a half-life, that same half-full existence I'd lived for years after the accident. I wouldn't ever go back there.

I pulled out my wallet, searching for a card. I handed it to Jackie. "This is a therapist in town. She's good. She can help you." I'd sent a number of folks to her after traumatizing accidents or fires. "But you have to stay away from me now. From Birdie and Sage. From Hadley."

Jackie stared down at the card. "Why are you throwing me away?"

"You threw yourself away the moment you drove high with Birdie and Sage in the car. That was your choice. You can make amends for that one day, but not by pulling what you are now. Get your head straight. Deal with the mess you've made. Then maybe one day you can have a relationship with those girls, but a relationship with me is off the table."

Jackie's gaze rose to meet mine, her eyes glittering. "You'll see. One day you'll realize we're meant to be. And I'll be here, waiting."

There wasn't anything else to say, I had to simply walk away. I turned around and headed for the coffee shop. I ordered Hadley's latte and breakfast burrito in a blur. I barely remembered what I ordered for myself and Hayes.

As I headed back out into the morning light, I scanned the

street, looking for any sign of Jackie. There was none. It was as if she had simply vanished into thin air. I wished it were that simple. That I could beam my ex to the other side of the country.

I strode down the sidewalk, the sheriff's station coming into view. Hadley had the back hatch of my SUV open and sat perched on the back bumper, her face tipped up to the sun. My steps faltered for a moment as I took her in. God, she was beautiful. Everything about her pulled me in.

Those ice-blue eyes opened and looked straight at me. "Hey." The peaceful happiness slipped from her expression. "What's wrong?"

I must've carried more of the residual tension from my encounter with Jackie than I realized. "Let's go inside. I'll fill you and Hayes in at the same time." I didn't want to have to recount it more than once. I didn't want that garbage in Hadley's head.

"Hell," she muttered, closing the back of my SUV and then taking the tray of coffees from me.

With my free hand I tugged Hadley closer to me. "No matter what, we'll be okay."

"That isn't making me feel better."

I leaned in and took her mouth in a slow kiss. "What about now?"

"That helps."

The corner of my mouth kicked up. "Glad to hear it."

We made our way up the stairs and inside. Officer Williams greeted us with a smile and a wave. "Head on back. The boss is in his office."

"Don't call him the boss," Hadley quipped. "It'll go to his head."

Williams chuckled. "I'll keep that in mind."

We wove through the desks where deputies were beginning to take their seats. Hayes' door was open, and he waved us in, his gaze zeroing in on the bag in my hands. "Please tell me you brought me breakfast."

I riffled through the bag, handing him an egg sandwich. I set Hadley's burrito in front of her and took my breakfast out. "I'd never leave you hanging."

"You're a godsend. I haven't had time to grab anything this morning."

Hadley sat in one of the chairs opposite Hayes' desk, toying with the rim of her coffee cup. "Spill."

Hayes' gaze went from his sister to me. "What's up?"

I lowered myself into the second chair. "Unrelated to Hadley's case. I had a run-in with Jackie just now."

"She threaten you?" he asked.

"No talk of lawyers, but I'm worried this might escalate. I don't want her approaching Birdie and Sage. Something isn't right there. She's fixated on me, and she needs help. I gave her Dr. Kensington's card, and I'm hoping she'll use it."

Hadley shifted in her seat. "What do you mean, threaten? Did she do something before?"

I realized I hadn't filled Hadley in on that little conversation with Jackie. "She said she was talking to a lawyer about filing a request to reinstate her custody or visitation rights."

Hadley's jaw slackened. "Can she do that?"

"She can file anything she wants, but I don't think it's what she's actually hoping for."

Hadley didn't look away from me. "She wants you."

I winced. "Not really, but she thinks I'll make her feel safe again. Protect her."

She leaned back in her chair. "You are good at that."

I reached over and slid a hand under Hadley's hair, squeezing her neck. "It doesn't matter what she wants. You know that, right?"

"I do. I just—ugh, she makes me so mad. And I almost feel bad for her, which just pisses me off more."

Hayes chuckled, and Hadley cut him a glare. He held up both hands. "Sorry. I'd say go for a restraining order, but she hasn't made any overt threats, has she?"

I shook my head. "I just need her to back off."

Hayes drummed his fingers on his desk. "I'm going to send Adams to have a word with Jackie. She might be able to convince her to get some help, and at least then Jackie knows we're watching."

"Appreciate that, man."

"Of course." Hayes looked back at his sister. "How are you hanging in?"

"I'm doing a lot better. Tell me you found something."

A muscle in Hayes' jaw ticked. "Not yet. We've got our best tech on it, but every time she finds something, it's just another false trail."

I linked my fingers with Hadley's. "Did you at least have any luck getting her address taken down?"

"Every post we saw is now down, but that doesn't stop whoever this is from posting again. I'm sorry, Hads, but you're going to have to stay with Calder until we find whoever's doing this. It's not worth the risk."

I had no problem with her staying forever. I wanted her to. But I wanted it to come from a place of choice, not force.

Hadley glanced at me. "Is that okay?"

I leaned over and brushed my lips against hers. "I love waking up with you every day."

Hayes let out what sounded like a strangled cough. "I really don't need to be reminded about what's going on with you and my sister."

Hadley blushed but scowled at her brother. "Then mind your own beeswax."

"You're sitting right in front of me. It's a little hard to ignore."

I swallowed the chuckle that wanted to break free. "Do I need to give you both a time out?"

They both glared at me.

"I'm just saying, a time out might do you both some good."

Hadley looked at her brother. "He's too smug for his own good."

"Amen to that. You need to put him in his place a little more."

"Trust me, I'm working on it."

This time, the laugh burst free, and there was no stopping it. We needed this little slice of normal, even if it came in the form of bickering and giving each other a hard time. Because what was between the lines of Hayes' report was that he had no idea who was harassing Hadley. And that meant the culprit could be anywhere.

Chapter Forty

Hadley

I BOUNCED THE QUARTER AGAINST THE TABLE AND CURSED when it missed the cup by a millimeter.

The couch dipped next to me. "Are you playing quarters without any alcohol?" Amusement lit Calder's tone.

"That, I am."

"Can I ask why?"

"I'm freaking bored." We hadn't had a single callout all day. I'd tried reading, watching a movie, but I couldn't focus. Quarters was the best I had to entertain myself.

"We've only got a few minutes left on the clock for the day."

"Hallelujah." I rolled my shoulders back, trying to relieve a little of the tension that had been living there lately.

"Sore?"

"Just tense."

"Here." Calder turned me so that I faced away from him and began kneading my shoulders.

I let out a little moan. "Please never stop doing that."

"I'll keep going if you promise not to moan like that again. If I get a hard-on at the station, I'll never hear the end of it."

I bit my lip. "You know, the house will be empty when we get home. We won't have to pick up Birdie and Sage from their friend's house for almost an hour."

"Stop, seriously. Talk about anything but that."

I burst out laughing.

"You're a witch. You know that, right?"

I twisted in my seat. "But you love me for it."

He gave me a quick kiss. "I do."

There were a few hoots and hollers. Calder glared at anyone making the sounds. I stood, tugging his hand. "Come on, let's go home."

"Thank, God."

We made our way out of the station as the next shift settled in. Calder's pace was a little quicker than normal.

"You in a hurry?" I asked.

"Damn straight," he shot back, beeping his locks. "I want you home and naked."

Heat began to simmer low in my belly. "Sounds like a good plan to me."

Calder made the short drive in half the time it usually took. We were climbing out of his SUV when a familiar truck came to a screeching halt in front of Calder's house, Hayes' SUV hot on its heels.

My mother slammed her door and stalked towards Calder and me.

Hayes jumped out of his SUV. "Mom, you need to dial it back a notch."

She held out her phone to me, her arm trembling. "This is what you've been blowing off your family to do? Some reckless stunts that could get you killed?"

A still of the jump I'd made off the cliff showed on the screen. I remembered the high I'd gotten as I sailed through the air. How free I'd felt. Then I focused on my mother's face, splotches of red on her cheeks and neck.

"Hi, Mom."

"Don't you 'hi, Mom' me. I want an explanation."

I glanced at Hayes, who looked poised to pull our mother back as if he were worried she might strike. Is that what we'd come to? Why? Because I couldn't play by her rules?

I looked back at the woman who had raised me. I did my best to keep my voice calm and even. "I don't owe you an explanation."

"The hell, you don't. I want to know why you would put me through this. How you could be so selfish."

It was the familiar refrain. I was selfish and cruel for simply wanting to live my life the way I wanted. As her voice rose, so did the pressure in my chest. "It has nothing to do with you! It's me. What I want. I'm not going to apologize for doing something that makes me happy."

"But it's fine that it could destroy your family if something happened to you? How can you see it that way? We'd be ruined. You know what it was like when we almost lost Shiloh. You know that it almost killed me. Why would you do this?"

"People die every day. Heart attack. Stroke. Car accident. Freak happenstance. I'm not going to stop living in hopes it will make *you* feel safer. I can't live my life for you, Mom, and you shouldn't want me to."

Calder's hand came down on my shoulder. "Okay, let's all take a breath. No one wants to say something they'll regret."

My mom's gaze shot to him. "You couldn't have possibly known about this. You wouldn't have put Birdie and Sage at risk that way. You wouldn't have put yourself at risk."

Calder's jaw hardened as his hand dropped from my shoulder.

The anger inside me turned up a notch. She didn't get to do this. Try to turn the people in my corner against me. "At risk of what? Being loved and cared for?"

"At risk of losing you! You're putting yourself in danger for no good reason."

"Why is it only me you're so fixated on? Hayes puts himself at risk every day he puts on that badge and gun. Beckett is in the trenches in war-torn countries. But you never say a thing about either of them."

Mom's spine stiffened. "Those are their jobs. They are doing them in service of others. You're just—just—"

"Doing something for myself? How dare I?"

She looked pleadingly at Calder. "You need to explain to her why she can't do this."

"I can't," Calder said. His tone was flat; no emotion in it at all. "Hadley is a grown woman. She knows the risks, and she knows the rewards. I won't force her to be someone she's not."

The briefest flicker of doubt swept through me, wondering if a part of him wished I could be that someone else. If he hoped that maybe I would lose interest in all the things that made him worry. The back of my throat burned.

My mom turned to Hayes. "Surely, you have something to say."

"Mom, we all take risks every day. Somehow, in your mind, you think some are acceptable, and others aren't. There's no truth in that. None of us are guaranteed tomorrow. You have to let Hadley be free to live her life the way she sees fit."

My hands fisted at my sides, nails digging into my palms. I was desperate for that bite of pain, anything to take me away from the scene in front of me.

Mom shoved her phone into her pocket and brushed the hair out of her face. I could see her putting the pieces of her armor back in place, becoming the picture of composure. "Hayes is right. You're free to live your life however you choose. But I don't have to sit around and watch it. It's too much. I won't look on as you rip another family apart."

Her gaze met Calder's. "Don't put your girls through this. Don't put yourself through it. It'll end in disaster. You three have been through enough already. Protect yourself and them the way I couldn't protect my family."

Every word cut as if she carved each letter into my skin.

Bringing pain that would leave a permanent scar. "Mom," I whispered. "Don't do this."

Her head snapped in my direction. "You're free to make your choices, Hadley, but so are the rest of us. And you'll have to live with the consequences."

With that, she turned and strode to her truck. She didn't storm off or slam the door. She calmly got behind the wheel and drove away. But she left wreckage in her wake.

Chapter Forty-One

Calder

BLOOD ROARED IN MY EARS. A THUNDERING PULSE THAT created a sort of tunnel. The only thing I could hear was Julia's words. *Don't put your girls through this. Don't put yourself through this.*

Hadley stood there, watching her mother drive away. She wasn't crying, but the pain was carved into her face. It was so deep, I didn't know what could ever erase it.

I pulled her into my arms. She came willingly, her face pressed to my chest. I stroked a hand over her hair as I held her to me. I met Hayes' gaze as I did. He was ravaged, too. He ran a hand through his hair, tugging harshly on the ends as he stepped away to give Hadley and me some privacy.

Their family was being destroyed from the inside out, and I didn't know if anything could fix it. The shattered pieces were so small, I wasn't sure they could be glued back together. And it wasn't for lack of love. It was because fear drowned out that love—for both Julia and Hadley.

Julia was petrified to once again experience the pain she'd felt when Shiloh had been taken. Hadley was terrified that she would be trapped, never able to breathe freely again. Neither of them was wrong at the root of it, but I couldn't see how they would ever find middle ground.

Hadley let out a shuddering breath, straightening in my hold. "Did she get to you?"

"What?"

"What she said, did it get to you?"

The question pissed me off, sending sparks of heat cascading through muscle and sinew. "I love you."

Hadley's throat worked as she swallowed. "I know you do. Is that enough?"

I slid a hand along her jaw. "It's always enough." God, I prayed it would be, that I wasn't making the biggest mistake of my life. Because I couldn't imagine being without Hadley. She had been a part of me long before I realized that was even the case.

"Then why do you look as if you're in pain?"

Sometimes, it sucked that Hadley could read me so damn well. "I see where she's coming from—" I kept hold of Hadley as she tried to pull back. "Though not in the way she's expressing it. But I do understand that fear. I've lived it. Nothing is more terrifying than the fear you'll lose your child. Nothing. They were yours to care for and protect, and when the worst happens, and you aren't there to do that…it can break something inside you."

Tears welled in Hadley's eyes. "So, I'm supposed to live in a bubble for the rest of my life, so you two don't have to worry?"

"No, baby. No." I pressed a kiss to her forehead. "You have to live your life. But I think it helps to understand where she's coming from. It's not malicious."

"I know that. I know she loves me." Hadley's eyes turned to mine. "I know you love me, but I don't want your loving me to cause you pain." Her voice broke on the words.

"Love is pain. One can't exist without the other. The more you expand your heart, the more you have the possibility of being hurt. The deeper you let someone into that space, the more it will kill if anything ever happens to them. That's life. I shut it off for years after the accident, but I don't want to anymore. You will always be worth the risk to me."

A tear slipped out of the corner of Hadley's eye, cascading down her cheek. "I love you, Calder."

"I know. I love you, too."

She buried her face in my chest again, hands fisting in my shirt. I pulled her tighter against me. "Everything's going to be okay. Maybe not right now, but one day."

She nodded against my chest. We stood there for...I don't know how long, Hayes almost standing guard in case Julia decided to return. Finally, Hadley straightened. She brushed any remaining tears from her face. "I need to go for a ride."

"Okay, let me change, and I'll go with you—"

She cut me off with a shake of her head. "I need some time to think. It's been weeks since I've truly been alone. I need that. I promise I'll let you know what trail I end up at, and I'll take my phone. I just need a little time with my thoughts."

I studied her carefully. "You're not running on me, are you?"

She stretched up onto her tiptoes and pressed her mouth to mine. "Never."

A little of the pressure in my chest released. But not enough. Hadley was worried that her mother's thoughts had gotten into my head, but I was worried about the opposite—that Hadley might bolt, thinking she was saving me potential pain and heartache.

I slid my hand under her hair, giving it a little tug so her head tipped back. "You know I always beat you at hide-and-seek. I'll find you."

Her mouth curved. "Did you ever think I hid in easy spots because I *wanted* you to find me?"

My eyes flared. "You little minx."

Hadley gave me another quick kiss and pulled away from me. "I'll be back in an hour or so."

"Call if you need me."

"I will."

I watched her jog to her SUV parked next to mine in the drive and climb in. As she disappeared down the road, I ran a hand through my hair, tugging on the ends. "Hell," I muttered.

"That would be one word for it," Hayes agreed.

"You want a drink?" I asked.

"I'm on call, but I wouldn't say no to a Coke."

"You got it." I wished we could go for something stronger. I needed something to take the edge off, but I wouldn't drink a beer while Hayes had to abstain.

We walked up the path to the house and went inside. I grabbed two sodas from the fridge, handing one to him. "Front porch?"

"Always a fan of a rocker."

We were quiet for a while as the rockers' rails made an almost hypnotizing sound against the porch. I took a sip of my cola. "I don't know how I fix this for her."

"You can't." Hayes stared out at the street. "I used to think I could fix it all, make sure no one I loved ever got hurt, but it's impossible."

"Everly a part of you realizing that?"

Even with the heaviness of the last thirty minutes, his fiancée's name made him smile. "She's a big part of it. She helped me make peace with the fact that I can't control everything. That doesn't mean I won't try, but I'm able to release a little more when something doesn't go the way I've planned."

"I need to learn a little of that release."

Hayes glanced over at me. "Give yourself a little grace, you've been through a lot."

I picked at the tab on my can. "I don't want my issues to ruin what Hadley and I have."

"And you're worried they will?"

"I'll never like that she throws herself off cliffs and rides hell-bent for leather down a mountain. It scares the hell out of me."

Hayes halted his rocking. "Because you love her. It scares the snot out of me when Everly gets in the ring with a skittish horse. I see a million ways she could get hurt or worse. It's ridiculous to think you won't fear, but you have to let her do what makes her happy anyway. Celebrate it. Hell, do it with her and make sure she's as safe as possible. Just don't clip her wings."

"I've tried not to, but maybe I haven't done as good of a job as I should've."

He started rocking again and raised his can to me. "Like I said, grace. You guys are new, still finding your way. You'll get there."

I hoped he was right because I couldn't imagine life without Hadley's fire.

Chapter Forty-Two

Hadley

As I headed out of town, I didn't opt for the music typically pumping through my speakers. I didn't want to lose myself in lyrics and melody. I wanted to sink into everything I was feeling. For the first time, I wanted to face it. All of the hurt and doubt. The pain and second-guessing.

I rolled down my windows, the air flowing in and lifting my hair around me. It felt like a warm blanket, the perfect temperature and weight. The scent as comforting as an old friend, the kind who knew all your secrets.

Yet even with the smell of pine and the warm caress of the breeze, my chest ached. There was no solution. None that I could see, anyway. And I'd been looking for seventeen years. Ever since Shiloh had been returned to us, and my mother had started seeing monsters everywhere. I'd been looking for a way to break free without hurting anyone.

It was impossible. I either broke my mother's heart or slowly starved myself to death. I'd tried for short periods. Times when I stayed carefully between the lines my mom had drawn. I hadn't asked for trips to town with my friends or sleepovers away from home. I'd answered every call and text within thirty seconds. I'd stayed home instead of exploring the land around our ranch. And, within days, I'd wanted to crawl out of my skin.

It always began as an itch just below the surface. Soon, I'd be pacing my room and dying to get out. I'd tried everything I could think of. Running sprints, jumping rope, helping the ranch hands throw hay to the horses. Nothing helped.

Not until I found that adrenaline high. Not until Calder had shown me how to release all that pent-up energy into the ether. I remembered one of the first times Calder had taken me down a mountain on our bikes.

It had been drizzling when we started. By the time we were halfway down the mountain, it was pouring. It was unlike anything I'd ever experienced. All of the anxiety I'd been consumed with flew away on the breeze. It had felt as if we were chasing the rain itself. There was no space for worry, fear, or frustration. There was only us, the mountain, and the rain.

I'd wanted more, and Calder had given it to me. Sometimes, Hayes came with us. Other times, it was only Calder and me. I had fallen in love with him one mountain at a time. From snow-capped summits to the cliffside plunges. One ride after another had carved him into my heart.

But I'd found myself on those mountains, too. I'd learned to trust my instincts, to test the boundaries of my control. I'd learned to work hard and see just how far I could push my body. I'd gained a confidence I'd so severely lacked from being kept so close to home.

I couldn't give that up. Not for my mother. Not even for Calder.

The thought had a sharp pain lighting along my sternum. I'd seen his face when my mother had told him what he was risking by being with me. I'd seen pain and worry.

I didn't want to be the one responsible for putting it there, but I couldn't become half a person to save him from it. It would slowly kill me, and I would take that pain out on him. Tears stung the backs of my eyes as I tried to see a path through. I could barely see the first steps, let alone into the distance.

I turned off onto one of the roads that curved around the mountains. I hoped a ride and the sights would give me some clarity. Restore some of my faith. I'd take anything right about now.

As my SUV climbed higher, another vehicle appeared behind me. The dark truck wasn't one I recognized, and it was going far too fast for these windy roads. I tapped on my brakes, signaling for them to slow down. Whoever was behind the wheel didn't get the message, only accelerated.

"Hell," I muttered. I'd responded to too many calls of idiots who thought they were speed-racers on these back roads. Many of them hadn't made it out alive.

As the road flattened out a bit, I moved to the side, giving the person behind me room to pass. Instead of veering around me, they slammed into my bumper.

My head snapped forward, chin hitting my chest as my teeth clacked together. The impact left my ears ringing. As my vision cleared, I saw the truck reversing. They aimed for me again. As the vehicle shot forward, I pressed on the accelerator.

I moved out of the way, just in time for the truck to miss me, but they were hot on my heels. My heart hammered against my ribs as nausea rolled through me. I tried to picture the rest of this road in my mind. It curved around the side of the mountains and eventually spilled back out onto the two-lane highway. But there were what seemed like an infinite number of hairpin turns and steep drop-offs before then.

I sent my SUV to a higher speed. The only thing I had going for me was that the truck was larger than my sport-utility. Maybe one of the turns would have them spinning out.

I hit the button on my wheel for my hands-free phone. "Call Calder."

It rang twice before he picked up. "Hey. Want me to come meet you?"

"Someone's trying to run me off the road."

"What? Where?"

I could hear him standing, footsteps echoing, and then Hayes asking something in the background.

"I'm on 132, the mountain pass." The truck rammed my bumper again. "Shit!"

"What's going on?"

"They hit me again. They have to be crazy. They're going to kill us both."

Calder barked something at Hayes, and I heard an engine start up.

Before I could increase my speed, the truck hit my bumper once more. As it did, a face came into view. A familiar one, full of rage.

"Calder, it's Jackie. I can see her in my rearview mirror." The truck slammed into my SUV, sending my tires spinning. I barely got control in time to make the next turn. I forced myself to suck in air because the burn in my lungs told me I hadn't been breathing.

"Hayes called in reinforcements. We're on our way. Where are you on the road?"

His voice was calm, even, but I could hear the fury bubbling just beneath the surface.

"I don't know. I'm just trying to stay on the road."

My gaze locked with the turn ahead. I had to slow down, or I'd go over the side. I knew the ravine there. Several jagged drop-offs layered the side of the mountain.

I eased off the accelerator the slightest bit. It was too much. Jackie went full-throttle, sailing into my SUV with a sickening crunch. I slammed on my brakes, but they did nothing. My wheels only spun in the gravel on the road.

I felt as if I were flying. But there was no freedom in it like when I cascaded down a mountain on my bike. No lightness. There was only fear, my blood roaring in my ears, Calder's voice yelling in the distant background.

Then, there was nothing at all.

Chapter Forty-Three

Calder

"**H**ADLEY!"

I heard a brief scream and then a sickening crunch.

"Hadley, talk to me." My hand shook as I held the phone to my ear. All I could hear was a sort of hissing sound and groaning metal. "Hads," I whispered, my voice hoarse.

"You need to go faster," I shot at Hayes.

His fingers tightened around the wheel. "I'm going as fast as I can. It won't help Hadley if I crash, too."

I kept the phone pressed to my ear, listening for any signs of life. As if by keeping that line of communication open, I could keep Hadley with me.

Hayes turned off the highway and onto the two-lane road that wove through the mountains. How many times had Hadley and I come up this pass? Too many to count. We'd hiked trails and biked the paths. We'd talked about things that weighed us down and, other times, we said nothing at all.

I squeezed my eyes shut for a moment. I held her face in my mind. Those blue eyes that could freeze me to the spot. The way her mouth quirked when she was up to something mischievous. Hadley had to be okay.

"There," Hayes said.

My eyes flew open, taking in the missing guardrail up ahead. I couldn't breathe. The drop-offs around here were deadly. I'd seen half a dozen accidents on this road over my career, and very few had a happy outcome.

Hayes screeched to a stop in the middle of the road. I was already out of the vehicle before he had it in park, running to the embankment. My breath stalled in my lungs as I looked over the side.

Two vehicles had gone over, but I only had eyes for the SUV. It was caught on a ledge. This stretch of mountain had what were almost steps carved into it. Hadley's SUV was balanced precariously on one.

My vision blurred as I fought the onslaught of memories. Birdie's screams from the ravine below. Sage's lifeless form as they brought her up on a backboard.

Hayes' hand landed on my shoulder. "Hell."

I could hear the faint strains of a siren, but it was too far away. "I have to get down there."

"Calder, you can't. We have to wait for backup."

I whirled on him. "That's your fucking sister down there. The woman I love more than life. Are you really going to tell me that you won't do everything you can to save her life?"

A muscle in Hayes' jaw ticked, and he looked as if he were a second away from decking me. "I've got a harness in my trunk."

I followed him to the back of his SUV. We moved in quick, tandem motions. I slid on the harness, checking each buckle and strap as Hayes tied a rope onto his trailer hitch and put his own harness on. When he finished, he looked up at me. "You sure you can handle this? I could go down—"

"I'm going."

Hayes tugged on a pair of gloves. "All right, then."

I strode to the edge of the ravine. The truck was at the bottom, smoking. I wasn't sure there was any way someone could have survived that, but I couldn't think of Jackie now. The woman who had sent Hadley hurtling off a cliff.

I focused on the path to the SUV. It had landed on its side, and the driver's side door was up. That was good. I couldn't make out Hadley's form, only a shadow. My back teeth ground together. "Ready. Slack."

Hayes gave me a few feet of rope, and I started my descent. I picked my way around rock formations, focusing only on the next steps, not what I might find when I got to the ledge.

The sirens got louder and then shouts filled the air. I shut them all out, focusing on the next place to put my feet. The SUV came into my line of vision.

"Hadley," I called.

Nothing.

"Slack," I yelled. I took the final two steps, holding my breath, my lungs and eyes burning as Hadley came into view. I stilled, watching her chest. It rose and fell. Air left me in a whoosh as I stuck a hand through the open window, brushing the hair away from her face.

"Hadley." It hurt to say her name, not knowing if I would get a response. As if each syllable were made of razor blades.

A low moan sounded as Hadley's eyes fluttered. As her head turned, everything in me locked. Blood trickled from her hairline and down the side of her face.

"Hadley, talk to me."

She blinked a few times. "Calder? What—?" Her eyes flared as she took in her surroundings.

"Don't move. Nice and steady now. I'm going to get you out."

The metal of the vehicle groaned as the wind picked up.

"Calder," she said, panic seeping into her tone.

"We're gonna move quickly but safely."

"Cruz," Mac called from up above. "You gotta move. SUV's shifting."

I fucking knew that, but him saying it would only scare Hadley. "Moving as quick as I can."

Hadley shut her eyes for the briefest of moments, and when she opened them again, she was calmer. That same steely strength I'd seen on so many callouts before. "I'm going to unbuckle my seat belt. I think I should climb out through the window. If we open the door, the SUV could fall."

"All right. Hold on to me with one hand, unbuckle with the other." Right now, the seat belt was holding the majority of Hadley's weight. If she fell, it would rock the vehicle off its axis.

She licked her lips and nodded. Reaching out the window, she locked a hand with mine. She kept her gaze on me as her other hand went to the buckle at her waist. I held my breath as she pressed down. The seat belt sprang free, and Hadley's weight shifted. She did her best to brace herself with her feet and hold on to me, but the SUV slid down another few inches.

"Grab my other hand!"

She reached for me, holding tight as she got her other hand free of the seat belt.

My muscles strained as I reached under her armpits, hauling her towards me. "I've got you."

"Calder!"

Metal groaned as pieces of rock fell away beneath the vehicle.

"Hold on to me," I called. I wouldn't lose her. Not like this. Not ever.

Just as Hadley slipped free of the SUV, the rock below it gave way. I watched as it sailed down the side of the mountain. Tumbling and landing with a sickening boom.

Hadley's arms locked around my neck, her body shaking.

"I've got you. Just hold on."

"Not letting go," she whispered.

"We do this nice and easy. Take our time."

"We've got your back," Mac called from a few feet above. He carried a second harness we could lock Hadley into.

We moved as quickly as possible, getting Hadley into the gear and tethered to another rope. As soon as she was secure, I pulled her to me, pressing my lips to the unmarred side of her head. "Can you climb?"

"I can climb," she said hoarsely.

"You go in front of me. I've got your back."

"Okay."

We picked our way over rock outcroppings and brush. Hadley's arms and legs shook as shock took hold, but she never gave up. As she reached the side, familiar hands reached out for her, pulling her to safety.

With one final push, I made it to the side of the road. But I didn't stop, not until I broke through the crowd. Not until Hadley was in my arms. I held her to me, trembling, running my hands over her body. "You're okay."

"I'm okay," she assured me, but her voice shook.

I framed her face with my hands as tears burned the backs of my eyes. "I love you. So damn much."

Tears slid down Hadley's cheeks. "I didn't think I would get to see you again."

I pulled her against my chest. "Never. You're stuck with me for good."

She sniffed. "I'm glad. I'm starting to get used to your ugly mug."

I couldn't find it in me to laugh. I simply pulled Hadley against me. I soaked in the beat of her heart against my chest, the knowledge that she was here and breathing and in my arms.

Chapter Forty-Four

Hadley

EVERYTHING IN ME ACHED AS IF I'D BEEN DUMPED INTO AN industrial dryer and set on super speed. I guessed in a way, I had. A slight shudder ran through me as images assaulted me. It had been close. Far too close for me to forget anytime soon.

Sage adjusted the blanket around me from her spot on the couch. "Do you need something else to drink?"

I looked at the coffee table. There was tea, water, and a ginger ale. I squeezed Sage's hand. "I'm fine, Goose. Promise."

"Your head," she whispered.

"I've had worse than this from a fall off my bike." It wasn't a lie, but the five stitches that traced my hairline would carry haunting memories.

Birdie hurried down the stairs and over to the couch. She nestled into my other side. "How do you feel now?"

"Better, Birds." The painkillers they had given me at the hospital had undoubtedly helped, but I didn't want to be zoned out right now, so I'd only taken the minimum dose.

She toyed with a corner of the blanket, tugging on a loose thread. "Do you hate us?"

"What? Why would you ask something like that?"

The pain in Birdie's face was a living, breathing thing. Her small fingers fisted around the edge of the blanket. "I heard Dad on the phone. It wasn't an accident. Mom pushed you off the cliff."

Sage gasped.

I let my eyes fall closed for a moment. Calder and I had decided that telling the girls it had been an accident was better. Our fire and rescue teams had gotten Jackie out of the bottom of the ravine. She hadn't lost her life yet, but she was currently in a coma, the doctors unsure if she would survive.

When we told Birdie and Sage, they'd been upset and confused. They'd been worried about me. They didn't need this, too.

"Birdie," I whispered.

"No! Don't lie to me. Dad always lies about Mom. We deserve to know the truth."

Footsteps sounded on the stairs. "Hey, what's with the yelling?"

Birdie's gaze shot to her father. "Tell us what's really going on."

I looked at Calder. "She heard you on the phone."

Calder muttered a curse under his breath and moved to the couch, sitting next to Sage. "This isn't something I want you guys worrying about. It's grownup stuff."

"No, Dad. It's our mom." She shook her head. "I don't even want to call her that. It's Jackie. But we deserve to know. We deserve to know if she did something that would make Hadley hate us."

I pulled Birdie into a hug, ignoring the flare of pain in my ribs. "I could never hate you. What Jackie did has absolutely nothing to do with you."

I wrapped my other arm around Sage. "Nothing. You hear me? I've loved you both from the day you were born." I swallowed back the burn creeping up my throat. In so many ways, Birdie and Sage had always felt like mine. I couldn't bear the thought of them worrying that I might cast them aside.

Sage's shoulders shook. "I'm so sorry."

"Goose." I pressed a kiss to her head. "It's not your fault. Nothing she has ever done is on you. Nothing."

Birdie burrowed deeper into my side but looked at Calder. "Will she go to jail?"

"If Jackie wakes up, yes. She'll go to jail."

"Good," Birdie mumbled.

My heart ached like nothing I'd ever felt before. For these beautiful girls who'd had their lives ripped apart again by a mother who should've put them first but never had.

Calder moved in closer, wrapping us all in his embrace. "We're going to make it through this."

"We're strong," Sage said with a sniffle.

"That's right. We've been through harder things and made it through with flying colors."

I looked into those beautiful dark eyes. "And we have each other."

He didn't look away for a moment. "Always."

Calder closed the door behind him with a soft snick. "They're finally asleep."

The bedtime routine had lasted three times as long tonight, a sign of how unsettled Birdie and Sage still were. We'd all put on pajamas earlier and zoned out with a movie and brownies, but the pain was still there, waiting just below the surface.

I patted the bed next to me. "They'll be okay. It's going to take time, but they will be. Birdie and Sage are two of the most resilient kids I know."

Calder eased down onto the bed, moving in close to me. "I know they are, but I hate that they've had to be."

I brushed the hair away from his face and then began massaging his scalp. "I know you do."

Calder's eyes fell closed for a moment as I continued stroking. When they opened again there was so much in those dark depths—pain, sorrow, fatigue.

"Calder," I whispered, leaning into his chest and wrapping my hands around his biceps.

He curled around me, holding me close. "I'm so sorry, Hads."

"It isn't yours to be sorry for."

"She did this because of me. I don't know if she thought having you out of the way would suddenly give her a clear shot at me or if she just completely lost it."

"Probably a little of both, but it's still not on you."

His body shuddered. "You could've been killed."

"But I wasn't. I'm right here." I tipped my head back so I could see Calder's face. "You have me."

"Do I?"

"Body and soul." I stretched up, bringing my lips to his. I meant the kiss to be one of comfort but that spark lit, those embers that lived in my bones coming to life again the way they always did when Calder touched me.

His hand dipped below the hem of my tank top as his tongue tangled with mine. I could live forever in the warmth that spread through me at the glide of his fingers across my skin.

"We shouldn't," he whispered. "You're hurting."

My hand tightened in his hair. "I need to feel, Calder. To remind myself we're still here."

He searched my face, looking for what, I wasn't sure. Then his head dipped, his mouth taking mine again. I could feel the restraint there. I wanted to break it, to feel that desperate need that always sprang to life when Calder and I were together.

I tried to light that fuse, to spur him on, but Calder wouldn't be rushed. Not as he peeled me out of my tank and sleep shorts. Not as his fingers danced along my skin.

His lips trailed down my neck to the peaks of my breasts. "Don't be in such a hurry." His mouth closed around my nipple, and I nearly bowed off the bed.

"Let me take my time." A single finger slipped inside me, then a second. He stroked. Teased and toyed.

My hand slipped into his pajama pants, finding him hard and

ready. I did my own exploring, watching Calder's face to see what got the best reaction.

"Hadley," he groaned.

"If you get to play, so do I."

His fingers inside me curled and twisted. I let out a whimper, and he grinned.

I nipped Calder's bottom lip. "No more. I want *you*."

His eyes bored into mine. "You have me."

"Then show me."

It was all he needed. Those flannel pants were gone in a flash, and he was settling between my legs. "You tell me the minute something hurts."

I nodded, my legs encircling his hips. I lifted a hand to rest on his stubbled cheek. "I love you."

"More than I thought possible." He slipped inside me with those words.

We never found that feral heat. This was something different. A heat lit by those embers that lived in both our bones. We moved as one, finding something that was more than lust or even love. Something that belonged to only Calder and me.

As we climbed that mountain, we clung to one another, assuring each other that we were here, alive and breathing. And when we came apart, it was with a bone-deep knowledge that this was always meant to be.

Chapter Forty-Five

Calder

"WELCOME TO CHAOS CENTRAL," I told Hayes as I ushered him out to the back porch. School had let out a couple of days before, and Birdie and Sage had the early summer burst of energy running through their veins. They let out shrieks as they chased each other around the backyard in a game I hadn't quite figured out.

Hayes grinned as he handed me a coffee. "Maybe this will help."

"God, I hope so."

"Where's Hads?"

I took a sip of the coffee and almost sighed. "She's going on a ride with Toby and Jinx."

Hayes lifted a brow in my direction. "And how do you feel about that?"

I lowered myself into one of the chairs, facing the yard. "I want her to be happy. Riding, climbing, boarding, it's all a part of her." I flicked the edge of the lid on my cup. "I don't want to change that. It doesn't mean I don't worry—"

"Because you're human."

I nodded, watching as Birdie threw herself into some sort of flipping roll. "I think Hadley gets that, too. We're both at peace with it. She knows I'll worry. I know she needs to live the life she wants. And we'll both try to make it as easy on the other as possible."

"I'm happy for both of you."

"Thanks, man." I looked over at Hayes, my friend from basically birth. "I love her. I'll do everything in my power to protect her. Everything I can to help her soar."

"That's good because if you hurt her, I'll have to kick your ass."

I barked out a laugh. "You could try."

"And I'd succeed."

I took another sip of coffee as Sage let out an especially high-pitched yell. "So, you gonna tell me why you're here first thing in the morning on a workday?"

Hayes leaned back in his chair. "First, I wanted to tell you that Evan Gibbs won't be giving Hadley any more trouble." His lips twitched. "And you and I won't have to don monkey suits to go to some stupid ball."

"What happened?"

Hayes shook his head, scrubbing a hand over his jaw. "Someone from the FBI field office in Bend showed up today. Wanted to give me a heads-up that they'd be taking Evan into custody. Turns out, he's been defrauding people all across the country."

"Shit," I muttered.

"No kidding. It's even worse. A lot of the organizations he stole from were charities."

I straightened in my chair. "You think he was going to try to steal from the widows and orphans fund?"

"I wouldn't put it past him, but he won't get that chance now."

"I knew that guy was an asshole."

"Understatement of the century."

Hayes was quiet for a minute. "Jackie woke up."

I watched as Birdie tackled Sage, and they both went down laughing. "Okay." I didn't know how to feel about that, exactly. A million warring emotions battled for dominance.

"Doctors believe she'll make a full recovery in time."

"She talking?"

Hayes shifted in his seat. "I spoke with her this morning. She said it was an accident. That she lost control of her car—"

"Bullshit," I hissed, sitting up.

Hayes lifted a hand to stop whatever was about to come out of my mouth. "It's not going to hold up. Hadley's testimony, the accident reconstruction, it all shows she's full of it."

I eased back in the chair, but nothing in me relaxed. "And now Hadley's going to have to go through the nightmare of a court case, having her life picked apart. What about the rest of it?"

"She's playing dumb. Said she didn't even know Hadley made videos."

I shook my head. "I don't know why I thought almost dying might change her. It didn't before."

Hayes squeezed my shoulder. "Hoping someone can change isn't wrong."

"Maybe not, but it's dumb when they've proven how heartless they are time and again."

"She's going to go away for a long time. Given her record, they'll push for the max sentence."

I gripped the edge of the chair, my fingers digging into the wood. "What's the minimum sentence?"

"Seven and a half years."

I let a slew of curses loose under my breath. "That means she'll be out before we know it."

"We're going to push for longer, and I've already got a restraining order in place. Word's out about what happened. No one in Wolf Gap will give Jackie a job if she comes back. No one will rent her a place to live, either."

That was something, but it wasn't nearly enough. I looked at Hayes. "How are you so calm about this?"

"I have to trust that the system will do its job." His jaw worked back and forth. "That doesn't mean I'm not pissed as hell and worried about my sister, but I have to choose trust. Hope."

Birdie and Sage climbed to their feet, still laughing. There was hope in my two girls. In the future I had with Hadley. I could hold on to that.

"I'm going to ask your sister to marry me."

Hayes had just taken a sip of coffee, and he began to choke. I pounded him on the back as he coughed. "Give a guy a little warning, would ya?"

I chuckled. "That mean you're all right with the idea?"

"Would it matter if I wasn't?"

"I'd still marry her, but I'd be sad not to have your support."

"Nothing would make me happier than to have you as family officially." Hayes grinned. "You gotta get her to say yes first."

"Details." I already knew exactly where I'd ask her. Our mountain. The one where we'd chased so many sunsets. Those sunsets had splintered once, but we'd put them back together. They were stronger now, and they meant more.

I now knew why I'd never given Jackie my grandmother's ring. I'd told myself that I was saving it for Birdie or Sage, but the truth was, it had always been meant for Hadley. Now, it burned a hole in my pocket, just waiting for that perfect moment when I could steal Hadley away to make her mine officially.

Hayes shook his head, a smile still on his face. "I can't believe this is happening."

"Me, either." I hadn't believed I'd ever get here, that I'd ever be this happy. I took in my friend. "How are things with your mom?"

Julia had stopped by once after Hadley's accident. She'd dropped off a casserole and stayed for all of ten minutes. I'd found Hadley crying in our bathroom that night, and it had nearly killed me.

Hayes' jaw tightened. "She started seeing a therapist, but so far, I haven't seen or heard a whole lot of difference."

I couldn't imagine having a wedding without Julia present, but I wouldn't let her do anything to ruin that moment for Hadley and me. "I hope she gets the wake-up call she needs."

"Me, too." Hayes' phone buzzed, and he checked the screen. "I gotta run." He stood and pulled me into a hug. "Always thought of you as a brother. Pleased as hell for you."

I slapped his shoulder as I released him, my voice going hoarse. "Thanks for having my back."

"Always will."

"Right back at you."

"Come over for dinner tomorrow night. Just the six of us," I said as he started around the house.

"Sounds good. Text me what we can bring."

"Will do."

Hayes disappeared, and I turned back to Birdie and Sage. "Hey, girls, come here."

They paused mid-run to the swing set and turned. "You're not gonna make us go do something boring, are you?" Birdie asked.

I chuckled. "No, I have something I want to ask you. But you have to keep it a secret. This is in the vault."

Both of them nodded, suddenly curious.

"How would you feel about Hadley living with us all the time, either here or at her house?"

Sage grinned. "She's got a ton of wildflowers at her place."

"I bet."

Birdie's face scrunched. "She's already living with us."

I fought back a laugh. "This would be something more official."

Sage let out a squeal. "Are you gonna ask Hads to marry you?"

I grinned. "I am."

Birdie looked down at her shoes.

"What is it, Birds?"

"Do you—do you think she'll want to be our mom?"

My throat burned as I struggled to get the words out. "We can ask her, but I bet she'd love it."

Birdie's head came up. "Really?"

"Really."

"Hurry up and ask her," Birdie urged.

I chuckled. "I'm waiting for my moment."

"It needs to be perfect," Sage added.

Birdie rolled her eyes. "Whatever."

"Hey," Sage started.

I stepped between them, trying to stop the fight before it started. "Let's go out to the ranch so you can visit Shy and the colt."

They both perked up at the idea, racing for my SUV. And while they were distracted with baby horses, I would ask Gabe for his blessing to marry his daughter.

Chapter Forty-Six

Hadley

"**T**HANK YOU FOR DRIVING US OUT HERE," ADDIE said as we headed up the trail.

"Of course. Any excuse to get out and enjoy these mountains."

Addie surveyed the forest around us as Birdie and Sage led the way. "I love the silence out here."

"Me, too." A bird called to another overhead, and the wind rustled through the leaves and pines. Even the girls were quieter than usual, seeming to enjoy nature's soundtrack. "I feel peace here that I was never able to find anywhere else."

Addie nodded as she stepped over a fallen tree. "Growing up, I spent as much time as possible outside. There are so many hidden gems all around here."

"You'll have to show me some of your favorites."

"I'd like that."

I side-stepped some brush that had grown onto the path. "How is Hayes' house treating you?"

"It's a beautiful home. I keep offering to find an apartment, but Hayes always says that he doesn't want to sell, and he likes someone living there." She paused for a moment, looking over at me. "Is that the truth?"

"I know he doesn't want to sell, so that much is true. I also know he's a born protector. He likes looking out for people, and you're important to him because you're important to Everly."

Addie flushed. "They've already done too much. I never thought I'd get out of the house I grew up in, but Hayes and Ev made it possible. That's enough."

I was quiet for a moment, searching for the right words. Ones that gently prodded but didn't push. "Have you seen your dad much since you left?"

Addie's fingers drummed a beat on her thigh. "A few times in town. If I see him, I go in the other direction."

"Probably smart." I wished there was a way for us to kick certain people out of the town's limits. Two people at the top of my list were Addie's father and Everly's brother. "I'm sorry you have to deal with them at all."

"It's so much better now. I'm free."

"Are you?" The question was out of my mouth before I could stop it. Because I'd seen how Addie lived her life. She worked for Calder a few days a week, she'd go to the library and the grocery store, but that was about it. Mostly, she stayed cooped up at Hayes' house.

Addie didn't say anything.

"I'm sorry. That was overstepping."

"No, it's okay."

"Addie, look!" Sage shouted.

We hurried over to where Sage was bent over a cluster of flowers.

"I think those are Pentstemons."

Addie crouched down to examine the blooms. "I think that's exactly what it is."

Sage beamed. "I've never seen them before." Her smile fell a little. "I can't pick one for my book, can I?"

"Not out here. If everyone picked one, there'd be nothing left," Addie told her.

"I know."

"Here." I pulled out my phone and bent to take a picture. "We can print this out and put a photo in your book."

Addie nodded. "That's a wonderful idea."

"Can we do that for everything we find?" Sage asked.

I ruffled her hair. "We sure can. We can stop on the way home and print them out at the copy shop."

"Thanks, Hads."

"Think we could stop for ice cream, too?" Birdie chimed in.

I chuckled as I stood, pulling her into a hug. "I think we can make that happen."

"Ice cream always tastes extra good after a hike," she said.

Addie pushed to her feet. "I agree."

Footsteps sounded on the trail behind us, and a figure rounded the bend.

"Calla. Hey. What are you doing out here?"

Her gaze jumped around our group, and her jaw tightened. "Thought it was a pretty day for a hike."

I cringed at the lack of warmth in her greeting. It might take us longer than I'd hoped to get back to even ground. "You're welcome to join us. We're moving a little slow because we're looking for wildflowers."

"When are you ever okay with moving slow? You usually mow over everyone in your path."

Addie shifted behind me, wrapping an arm around Birdie's shoulders. Sage climbed to her feet, eyeing Calla. Even the girls could feel the tension pouring off her.

"Calla, I don't think now is the time for this. Maybe you and I could get breakfast tomorrow and talk?"

Her eyes heated as if lit from the inside. "It always has to be on your schedule, doesn't it? Everything has to go Princess Hadley's way. Whatever she wants has to be hers."

I turned back to Addie. "Why don't you go on ahead with the girls? I need to talk to Calla for a bit."

Addie shifted her weight from foot to foot. "I think we should stay with you."

"No, really. I'll be fine. Go ahead." I didn't want Birdie and Sage to hear whatever ugliness was about to come out of Calla's mouth.

"I don't think so." Calla grabbed onto Sage's t-shirt, tugging Sage back towards her.

"What the hell, Calla?" I stepped forward but froze as metal glinted in the afternoon light. A gun. Pointed directly at Sage's tiny form.

"Tell me, Hadley. How does it feel? To know you might lose someone you love so much?"

I fought to keep my tone calm, even. "Calla, put the gun down. You don't want to hurt anyone."

"Don't I?" Calla jabbed the gun into Sage's back.

Sage whimpered, a few tears tracking down her cheeks.

"It's okay, Goose. Everything's going to be okay." My heart hammered against my ribs, those tears breaking something deep inside me. My gaze moved to Calla. There was so much hatred pouring off her, I wondered how I'd never seen it before. "What do you want?"

"What do I *want*?!" Calla's voice grew more and more shrill. "I want you to know what it's like to lose everything. Just like you took everything from me."

I needed to keep Calla talking, to buy time to get Sage away from her. But everything I said only seemed to deepen the woman's rage. I swallowed, taking a small step forward. "Take me instead."

Her gun swiveled to point directly at me. "Don't move."

I took another step. "I just want to trade places with Sage. That's all. You and I can talk as much as you want then."

"I don't want to talk! I want you to hurt!"

I saw Addie out of the corner of my eye, motioning for Sage to run to her. Calla's head snapped in her direction, the gun following. There was a crack of sound, and Addie screamed, her hand flying to her arm. She crumpled, her head hitting a log with a sickening thud.

I didn't think, I charged. Sage ducked out of the way just as I took Calla down. Calla screamed, clocking me on the side of the head with the gun. My vision blurred. "Run!" I shouted to Birdie and Sage. They didn't move for a moment.

I struck out at Calla's face, and she cursed, sending a vicious punch to my ribs. "You fucking bitch." She rolled so she was on top of me.

"Run!" I cried, my voice breaking as I grabbed a hank of Calla's hair, trying to distract her.

Birdie grabbed Sage's hand and pulled her into the woods. I wanted to feel relief, but all I felt was pain as the butt of the gun cracked across my skull again. My vision darkened before coming back into focus.

Calla was above me, gun pointed at my head. "They'll probably all die. And it's all your fault."

Chapter Forty-Seven

Calder

"**Y**OU ASK HER YET?"

I looked up from my laptop at Mac. "Ask who, what?"

He rolled his eyes as he sat down in the chair next to me. "Have you asked Hadley to marry you yet?"

"How do you know I'm going to ask her to marry me?"

Mac chuckled. "I see the way you look at her. You're both a hell of a lot happier now that you're together. I figured it was just a matter of time. Nice to see that my prediction was right. You got a ring?"

I pinched the bridge of my nose. I'd fallen right into Mac's trap, and he was a gossip. I'd have to make sure I asked Hadley in the next few days, or one of these nosy assholes would surely spill the beans.

"Come on. I'm not going to tell. I know when to keep a secret."

I arched a brow in his direction. "You have the biggest mouth of anyone I know."

He clutched his chest. "That hurts. You just *think* I have a big mouth. You have no idea how many secrets I really know."

"It's the truth. Now, tell me if you have a ring."

"I may have one…"

Mac motioned for me to hand it over. "Come on. I know you. You've got it on you."

I'd taken to carrying it around in my wallet. There was a perfect little hidden compartment that kept it secure but on hand in case the ideal moment presented itself. "The first person to see this ring will be the woman I give it to."

"Aw, man. You're no fun."

My cell phone rang, and I picked it up, swiping my finger across the screen. "Calder Cruz."

"Mr. Cruz, this is Ranger Moore. I have your daughters with me at the Larkspur Butte trailhead. There was an incident."

I was already moving, standing and shoving my chair back. "What happened? Are they okay? Where's Hadley? Addie? Are they hurt?"

My questions came out as rapid-fire bullets, but I couldn't help it.

"Both your girls are fine, just a little shaken up. We're not totally sure what happened yet. There was an attack. Your daughter, Birdie, told me there was a woman with a gun."

I froze. A woman with a gun? Jackie was supposed to be in the hospital, under arrest but cuffed to a hospital bed.

"I've got backup on the way, and they'll search the woods. Do you want to meet us here or at the ranger station?"

"I'll come directly there." I hung up without another word.

"What the hell is going on?" Mac asked, following me as I headed for the door.

"Tell Cap I had to go. Call in emergency backup. Someone attacked the girls. They don't know where Hadley is."

The words burned as they crawled out of my throat, leaving a trail I knew would scar. I'd almost lost her once. That had been more than enough. It couldn't be happening again.

I pulled open the door just as a sheriff's SUV came to a

screeching halt outside. Hayes rolled down the passenger side window. "Get in."

I didn't hesitate. I climbed in and slammed the door. "Tell me everything you know."

"Dispatch got a call from the ranger station. Birdie and Sage flagged down a hiker in the parking lot at the trailhead. They were dirty and distraught, kept talking about a woman with a gun."

"Did you check on Jackie?"

Hayes jerked his head in a nod as he pulled onto the two-lane highway. "She's locked down. It's not her."

"Then who? Some random person, who decided to take someone hostage?"

"I don't know," Hayes gritted out.

I let a slew of curses fly. "I'm sorry. I know you don't. I just—I can't…"—my voice broke—"she has to be okay."

Hayes pressed down on the accelerator. "She will be."

We didn't say another word on the twenty-minute drive out of town. It should've taken us almost twice as long, but Hayes kept his siren on and didn't let up on the accelerator. Gravel flew as he skidded to a stop outside a cluster of emergency vehicles.

There were a couple of ranger vehicles, three belonging to the sheriff's department, and an ambulance from a neighboring town. I jumped out of Hayes' SUV as soon as he hit the brakes, scanning the crowd.

"Dad!" Birdie launched herself off the gurney she'd been sitting on and ran towards me.

I caught her on the fly, still moving towards the gurney where an EMT held an ice pack to Sage's arm. "Are you guys okay? Are you hurt?"

Sage burst into tears and then jumped into my arms, as well.

I turned, sitting on the gurney to hold my girls. My heart shattered as my chest heaved. All I wanted to do was keep them safe, protected, and now they were terrified.

The EMT gave me a reassuring smile. "They are both uninjured. Sage just has a little bruise on her arm. That's it."

"Thank you," I choked out. "What about the two women who were with them? Any word?"

"The rangers found one woman. She's unconscious. They're bringing her out now."

Sage's small form shook, and she sobbed. "H-H-Hadley saved me. She tackled the woman. But the bad woman hurt her."

Birdie's head bobbed up and down. "She was gonna hurt Sage. Hadley tried to switch places with Sage, but the lady didn't want that. Then Hadley tackled her so she wouldn't hurt Sage."

I closed my eyes for a moment. My beautiful daredevil, through and through. "Do you know who it was?"

"Kind of. I saw her before," Birdie said. "But I can't remember her name."

"Where did you—?"

A commotion at the trailhead cut off my words. I didn't want to leave Birdie and Sage, but I had to see who it was. How badly they were injured.

I hugged the girls a little tighter. "Can you stay here? Just for a minute."

A truck pulled to a stop, and Shiloh jumped out, jogging towards us. "Hadley?"

I shook my head. "I don't know. Can you stay with Birdie and Sage?"

"Of course."

Shiloh, the woman who avoided all physical affection, didn't even flinch when the girls piled into her arms. She met my gaze. "I've got them."

"Thank you." The words were barely audible.

She carried them away from the melee and towards the edge of the woods, not once loosening her hold.

I moved to where a team carried a backboard out of the woods. I saw blond hair matted with blood first. Bile crept up my throat as I moved in closer. Addie's face came into view, her eyes fluttering.

"She's waking up," one of the rangers called.

Hayes and I were there in a flash as the team set her down. He leaned over her. "Addie, can you hear me?"

Her eyes opened fully, panic dancing through them.

"It's okay, Addie. Hayes and I are here. You're going to be okay. But we need you to tell us what happened."

"Calla. She has Hadley. She's going to kill her."

Chapter Forty-Eight

Hadley

"**W**ALK." I winced as Calla jabbed the gun into the spot just below my ribs. I had a feeling I had some bruised kidneys. Likely a concussion, as well. The trail in front of me blurred every few steps. "If you wanted me to move fast, you probably shouldn't have bashed me in the head with that gun."

"Keep talking like that, and I'll do it again."

I stumbled over a tree root, falling to my knees. I cried out as rocks bit into my palms.

Calla snorted. "A little less of a *daredevil* than usual, aren't you?"

I looked up and saw that her phone was pointed directly at me. "What are you doing?"

"Recording this for posterity. One final video to show everyone what a sniveling little bitch you really are. Smile pretty for the camera."

"Is that what this is about? My channel?"

Calla tapped something on the screen and dropped her hand to her side. "It's about you being a liar and a thief. Stringing Toby along, making him think there could be something between you. You used him."

"He's my friend, that's it."

Her foot struck out so fast, I barely saw it coming. It connected with my ribs, forcing all the air from my lungs. I curled in on myself, wheezing and coughing, trying to catch my breath.

"He's *nothing* to you. You treat him like dirt. But he never sees the truth. Always talking about how cool it is you do all those stupid tricks. I'm the one who's always there for him."

I let my eyes close for a moment, focused on my breathing. It hurt to inhale. A broken rib? More than one? "I'll never be what you are to Toby. He loves you."

Calla gripped my t-shirt, hauling me to my feet. "You're right. He does. But it's not enough." She shoved me farther down the path. "Toby saved me, took me away from my asshole parents. He's my everything. We were happy. Then he wanted to come back here after he finished school. Said he could make good money editing videos for his *friend*."

She kicked a rock into the trees. "I should've known by the way his eyes went soft when he talked about you. He would drop anything the second you called. I never came first."

I curved an arm around my middle, trying to hold my ribs steady as I walked. "That's just work. He and Jinx love what they do. It has nothing to do with me."

I eyed the tree line, searching for any foliage thick enough to give me a fighting chance. But I knew I couldn't outrun Calla, not with my current injuries. For now, my best option was to keep her talking. "So, you started sending the emails? The text messages?"

"I tried to warn you. Gave you so many chances. But you never listen, do you?"

"You could've talked to me. Told me what was bothering you. You could've talked to Toby."

"You don't think I tried talking to him?" she shrieked. "I told him you were coming between us, that Wolf Gap wasn't a good place for us. But he wouldn't listen. He told me I was jealous."

I stopped, leaning against a tree, trying to catch my breath. "Why didn't you tell me?"

Calla scoffed. "Oh, you would've loved that, wouldn't you? Me begging you not to steal my boyfriend." A muscle in her cheek ticked. "You have *everything*. This perfect family, parents who love you, a big brother who looks out for you, a sister who's your best friend, your dream job. I had none of that. All I had was Toby."

My mind stuck on the past tense. All she *had* was Toby. "My life isn't perfect. It's a disaster most of the time."

"Bullshit."

"It's true. My mom and I haven't had a real conversation in almost a month. She's pissed as hell at me."

A small smile flickered across Calla's face.

I straightened from the tree. "You're the one who told my mom about my videos."

She grinned. "Anonymous emails can be so helpful. Text messages, too. I found Jackie's number and fed her all sorts of things. I really thought that crazy bitch was going to take care of my problem for me. She came so close." Calla shrugged. "You know what they say, if you want something done right…"

Calla gave me a hard push. Pain sparked along my ribs as my head swam. "You're not going to get away with this. People saw you."

"I'll take my chances. Poor ol' Addie is probably bleeding out from that head wound. And those little girls, they'll never find their way back to the trailhead for help. I'd say the odds are in my favor."

My chest gave a vicious squeeze. *No.* Birdie and Sage were far smarter than Calla gave them credit for. They'd get help. Someone would find Addie and call the police. Hayes would come. So would Calder.

A sob ripped at my throat as an image of him filled my mind. Those dark eyes dancing with humor. Or how they'd heat to a golden amber when we made love. How they saw everything I hid away from the world and always understood. I wouldn't lose those moments. I refused.

"Where does Toby think you are right now, Calla?" He was my one hope, the only thing that might bring her back from the edge.

"He thinks I'm staying with a friend."

"Don't you think he might get suspicious? Put two and two together when I go missing?"

Calla jabbed the gun into my back to keep me moving. "Sure, he'll be sad at first, especially when they find your body. But then he'll forget all about you. He'll realize I was all he ever needed."

I stumbled a little as Calla so casually mentioned my death. As if I were nothing more than an annoying flea she wanted to be rid of. "If you kill me, you'll be competing with a ghost forever. That won't get you what you want."

Her footsteps slowed. "What are you talking about?"

"Haven't you realized that people always make those they've lost into gods? Their faults are wiped away, and their attributes are ten times greater. What you want is to take me down a peg. And you've already done that. The photos, the porn sites, the hate you've built in the comments of my site. You have what you want."

"It isn't enough!"

"Why not?"

Calla pointed the gun at my chest, her eyes blazing. "Because he broke up with me. He told me it wasn't fair for him to be with me while he was in love with you. That's why you have to die."

Chapter Forty-Nine

Calder

"Give us time to get a full team in place," Ranger Moore said, straightening from where he was bent over a map of the area.

"We don't have time," I gritted out.

Hayes gripped my shoulder. "He's right. We don't have enough daylight hours left to assemble a team. We'll start the search and stay in radio contact."

Moore's jaw worked back and forth. "Isn't she your sister? That's gotta be a conflict of interest."

"In a community this small, you have a relationship with just about everyone. That's just how things work."

Moore's gaze shifted to me. "He's not even law enforcement."

I was going to punch this guy. "No, but I'm trained in search and rescue, and I have my EMT license."

"It's a bad idea—"

Shiloh stepped up to the table. "Listen, you overgrown toad. My sister is out there with some psychopath. If you think you're going to stop Hayes and Calder from going after her, I'll shoot

"That's what I thought." Shiloh pressed a holstered gun into my chest. "Here. Hayes won't be able to give you one of his. I'm going to take Birdie and Sage to the ranch. They're upset, and this isn't helping."

I looked over her shoulder to where my girls were huddled together. I set the gun down on the table and walked over to them, pulling them into my arms. "Love you more than words."

"Where's Hadley?" Sage asked.

"I'm going to find her, but I need to know you're safe, so you're going to the ranch with Shy."

"No, Dad, we can help. We know where we were," Birdie argued.

"I can't be out there and worried about you. Please, just do this one thing for me."

Birdie bit her lip but nodded.

Sage burrowed deeper into my side. "You'll bring her back, right?"

"I'm going to bring her back." Everything burned, my eyes, my throat, my chest. The words were a vow, and I wouldn't settle for anything less. "Be good for Shy."

I straightened and met Shiloh's gaze. "Thank you. For everything."

Shy's hands flexed and clenched as she squeezed her eyes closed. "Just find Hads."

I wanted to pull her into a hug, but I knew that was the last thing Shiloh would find helpful at the moment. "I will."

I didn't look back as I returned to the table. I knew if I did, I would second-guess walking away from the girls. They were my world. But Hadley was a part of that world, too, and she was the one who needed me right now.

I picked up the holster and fastened it to the side of my uniform pants, checking the gun. Hayes handed me a Kevlar vest. "I keep an extra in the SUV, just in case."

"I'm glad you do." I pulled it over my head and adjusted the straps.

"Would you two idiots think about this? Another hour or two, and you'll have backup," Ranger Moore argued.

Neither Hayes nor I bothered to say another word to the man. Hayes slung a pack over his shoulder and handed me a radio. "I've got water, food, and first-aid."

"Let's go."

We took the trail at a jog, knowing we had to make up ground and hoping that Calla hadn't taken Hadley off the path. This trail was much less populated than other tourist traps, which might mean that Calla would risk it.

We slowed when we reached the spot where Addie had clearly been injured. There was a disturbance in the brush and blood on a log.

"Shit," Hayes muttered. "I wonder how much blood she lost."

"She was conscious when they took her away. That's a good sign." I scanned the trail ahead, my gaze catching on a bunch of dark spots in the dirt. "Hayes." I pointed.

He crouched, pressing his finger to the dirt. When he lifted it, the tip was a dark red—almost brown but not. "Blood."

I swallowed against the burn rising again. "That means they stayed on the path."

"For now, anyway."

Images assaulted my brain as we picked up our pace again. All the things that could make Hadley bleed. I shook my head and pushed my body harder, thankful for all the training I'd done in full gear.

Hayes slowed, holding up a hand to stop me. I strained to see or hear what he had. There was nothing at first, and then the soft sound of voices carried on the wind.

Hayes motioned me off the trail. We moved deeper into the forest to the point where we could barely see the trail and then began walking. As we moved, the voices got louder.

"What's the matter, Little Daredevil? Not in the mood for cliff jumping today?"

I stiffened at the use of my nickname for Hadley. I glanced at Hayes. "Are there cliffs near here?"

His eyes blazed. "About one hundred yards ahead."

"We need to move. Now," I whispered.

"We need a better lay of the land—"

With a single look, I cut him off. "We don't have time." I unholstered my weapon.

"You come in from the south. I'll come in from the west. I'll be loud, distracting. You're the ambush."

I gripped Hayes' shoulders. "We'll get her."

He nodded and took off running.

I dropped back, crossing over to the other side of the trail, hoping I could come up behind them.

"I said walk, you dumb bitch."

Hadley cried out in pain as she crumpled to the ground, holding her ribs. "I can't," she wheezed. "I need to catch my breath."

Calla pointed her gun at Hadley. "I really don't want to have to drag dead weight to the cliffs, but I will."

"I'll go. I just—I need a minute."

Hayes stepped out of the trees, his gun raised. "Don't move."

Calla's eyes flared as she took in Hayes.

"Now, slowly lower your weapon," he instructed.

She didn't move an inch. "I don't think you want me to do that. My finger could slip, and I could blow little Hadley's brains right out."

I tightened my grip on the gun as I moved through the trees, looking for a straight shot at Calla. A twig snapped under my boot, and I sent up a silent curse.

Calla hauled Hadley to her feet by her t-shirt, and Hadley cried out in pain. She dug her gun into the spot behind Hadley's heart. "You might want to tell your friend to stop trying to sneak up on us. That whole slippery finger business, you know."

My footsteps slowed as I stepped through the trees. "Let her go."

Calla turned and began backing towards the cliffs, pulling

Hadley with her. "Why? So you two can live happily ever after?" She snorted. "I don't think so."

"Calder," Hadley wheezed. "Birdie and Sage?"

My heart broke at her question. For all my girls' lives, they'd had a mother who never put them first. Now, they might lose their chance at having the person they'd deserved all along. "They're fine, and we got Addie to the hospital."

Her shoulders sagged in relief. "Good. Tell Birdie and Sage I love them, okay?"

Calla let out a laugh that sounded more like a cackle. "Isn't this just so sweet? Parting is such sweet sorrow and all that, right?"

"You're not going anywhere, Hads."

"Wrong," Calla shouted. "It's all for one and one for all now. No one gets their happy ending."

The cliff came into view, and my gaze darted to Hayes.

His gun was raised, searching for a shot. "Stop, Calla, or I *will* shoot."

I looked for my own shot, but all I could see was Hadley's beautiful face, bruised and bloodied.

Hadley's gaze met mine. "I love you, Calder."

"Don't you talk like that."

"Calla, stop!" Hayes shouted.

Tears streamed down Hadley's face. "Always have, always will."

One shot, then a second cracked the air. It was too late.

Chapter Fifty

Calder

THE DRONE OF FLUORESCENT HOSPITAL LIGHTS BUZZED IN my ears as I stared down at my hands. Blood. It seeped into the ridges and whorls of my fingertips, the beds of my nails. I didn't think I'd ever be able to get it out.

A hand curved around my biceps. "Let's get you cleaned up."

I focused on the owner of the directive. Everly's voice was as gentle as her face, full of concern and some sort of understanding.

"I can't." My voice broke on the second word. It was all I had left of Hadley in that moment. I couldn't wash her down the drain.

Everly pulled me into a hard hug, so much stronger than her slight frame alluded to. "You're not losing her. The doctors said she has a good chance. But we need you cleaned up so when Hadley wakes up, you're right there and don't scare her."

What Everly didn't say was that there was a bullet in Hadley's chest. Surgeons were working right now to get it out. To save her life. The woman who was everything to me.

I looked around the waiting room. Julia, pale as a ghost, wrapped in Gabe's arms. Shiloh, knees pulled up to her chest, rocking back and forth with controlled movements.

Everly released me but held on to my arms. "Once Hadley's

awake, Birdie and Sage will come to the hospital. You don't want them to see you like this."

I looked down at myself. So much blood. Too much. It hadn't just stained my hands. I could see it even on my dark uniform. "Okay."

"Good." Everly guided me down the hall to a bathroom. "A nurse told me you could use this, and here are some scrubs to change into."

"Thanks." My voice sounded rusty, as if I hadn't used it in weeks.

I stepped inside, locking the door behind me. My reflection in the mirror made me jolt. Blood smeared my face, down my neck. An image flashed in my mind. My hands pressed to Hadley's chest as blood seeped through my fingers. Voices shouting as a medivac landed in a meadow on the other side of the trees.

I squeezed my eyes closed, shaking my head. I'd never be able to get those images out of my brain. The panic in Hadley's eyes before they shut.

I tugged at my clothes, leaving them in a pile on the floor. I stepped into the shower, turning it as hot as possible. I scoured my skin as my body trembled. Shutting off the water, I grabbed a towel and dried off. I donned the scratchy scrubs and then bent to riffle through my clothes.

I picked up the pants, pulling out my wallet and phone and shoving them into the pockets of my scrubs. Then I threw everything else away. They'd never be clean again.

I opened the door and stepped into the hallway. Hayes had Everly wrapped in his arms. They fit together perfectly, whole on their own but making something even more extraordinary together. My throat burned. The idea that I might never hold Hadley like that again searing my skin.

Hayes looked up, meeting my gaze. He released Ev and strode to me, pulling me into a hard hug. "Thank you," he choked out.

"I didn't—it wasn't enough—"

He only hugged me harder. "You gave her a fighting chance."

I swallowed, trying to soothe the burn. It didn't help. "Calla?"

Hayes' jaw hardened. "Dead on the scene."

"I'm sorry." I wasn't sorry that she was dead, but I felt bad that Hayes would have to carry that weight.

"I can live with it. Just as long as Hadley's okay, I can live with it."

Everly rubbed a hand up and down his arm. "Did anyone get ahold of Beckett?"

Hayes sighed and ran a hand through his hair. "He's on a flight now. Hopefully, he'll be here by tonight. He's wrecked."

Beckett and Hadley had a special bond, an understanding, that need to fly so strong in both of them. To get this news in another country and not be able to be with his family...I wouldn't be surprised if he tore the plane apart by the time he arrived.

A man in scrubs strode down the hallway with the nurse who had updated us periodically throughout the surgery. I stiffened. "I think that's the surgeon."

The woman gave me a kind smile. "This is Dr. Addison."

He nodded at our group. "Would you like me to update everyone in the waiting room?"

Hayes shook his head. "Tell us first. I'll bring the rest of my family up to speed."

My gut tightened. I knew why Hayes had played it that way. In case there was bad news, he wanted to be the one to tell his parents.

Dr. Addison nodded. "Ms. Easton is doing remarkably well for her injuries. The damage was extensive. The bullet nicked an artery, and we lost her for a minute on the operating table."

My knees started to buckle, but I locked them in place.

"We got her back and were able to repair the hole. We gave her several blood transfusions during surgery, and she may need one or two more as she recovers. We'll have a better idea of prognosis after twenty-four hours."

"I need to see her," I croaked.

The nurse gave me that kind smile again, a pitying one. "They are moving her into ICU now. I can take you."

Hayes squeezed my shoulder. "I'll fill the family in and then come up."

I nodded, following the nurse down the hall. I couldn't tell you how many halls we walked down, how many floors the elevator rose, but soon, the nurse came to a stop in front of an open door. "Ms. Easton has several machines helping and monitoring her right now. Don't be alarmed. Just remember they're helping."

I nodded woodenly and stepped through the door. The sight sucked all the air from my lungs. Hadley looked so tiny, dwarfed by the bed and the machines. There were wires and tubes, something coming out of her mouth. The side of Hadley's face was already turning purple with a bruise. Blood caked her hair.

I turned just as the nurse was about to walk away. "I need some warm water and a washcloth." The nurse looked as if she were about to argue, but I cut her off. "I'm cleaning the blood out of her damn hair."

The nurse snapped her mouth closed and nodded.

I moved farther into the room, dragging a chair next to the bed and lowering myself into it. I reached out but didn't know where to touch Hadley, where it wouldn't hurt. Scrapes and bruises covered her skin. A huge gauze pad peeked out from her hospital gown.

Footsteps sounded, and the nurse set a pitcher of water, a washbasin, and a stack of washcloths on the side table. "Just take care not to go anywhere near her chest."

I nodded and picked up the washcloth. Dunking it into the water, I squeezed out most of the liquid. Ever so gently, I began wiping at the blood on Hadley's face, in her hair. I moved methodically, inch by inch until she was clean, and the water in the tub was a murky red.

"Hadley." I broke on her name, my shoulders shaking with silent sobs as tears tracked down my cheeks. "You can't leave me. I just got you back. We haven't had nearly enough time. I want to watch your hair get gray and laugh lines crease your face. I want to watch our girls grow up and make their own lives. I want to make babies with you."

I shifted in my seat, pulling out my wallet. I fumbled for that little compartment in the center, pulling out my grandmother's ring. I took Hadley's hand, careful not to dislodge the oxygen monitor. "I love you. I've been waiting for the perfect moment to ask you to be my wife. I waited too long. But there's no one else I could ever give this ring to."

I slid the gold metal onto her finger. "You're it for me, Hads. You, and you alone."

I leaned down, pressing my lips to the place where the ring rested. "Come back to me."

Chapter Fifty-One

Hadley

I COULD HEAR VOICES, BUT THEY ALL SEEMED SO FAR AWAY. As if they were on the other side of a long tunnel. I tried to shift, to move towards them, but I couldn't.

"Hadley?"

That was clearer now. And so familiar. That rough, sandpaper tone as comforting as coming home after a year away.

"Is she waking up? I'm going to get a nurse."

I knew that one, too. Something in me recognized it. *Mom*.

A hand slipped into mine. "I'm right here, Hads. Come back to me."

I strained to open my eyes, but I couldn't quite get there. The black started pulling at me again, and I slipped under.

I felt a light touch tracing my hand. Lips pressed to my palm. So warm.

Everything hurt. My head, my chest, even my legs ached. I tried to open my eyes. My lashes fluttered but didn't quite make it all the way to open.

"That's it. You can do it, Hadley. I need to see those ice-blues."

Light danced across my vision as I finally succeeded in cracking my lids. A face came into focus in front of me. Dark hair, dark eyes, his scruff the longest I'd ever seen it. "Calder."

His name came out more like a croak, and he instantly reached for a cup next to him. He placed the straw gently between my lips. "Nice and easy, just a small sip. You had a tube in your throat, so you're going to be sore."

The liquid felt like heaven as I drank. When Calder pulled the straw away, I blinked a few times, taking in the room. Hospital. "What happen—?"

I couldn't even finish the word before memories assaulted me. Calla grabbing Sage. Addie going down. The crack of a bullet. The hot, searing pain. My breaths came faster and faster.

"Hey, now." Calder's hands were on my face in an instant. "You're okay. You're safe."

"Birdie and Sage? Addie?" Oh, God, nothing could happen to them.

"They're all fine. Addie was a couple of floors down nursing a concussion, but she went home a few days ago. The bullet just grazed her."

My heart slowed a fraction. Safe. We were all safe. "Calla?"

Calder's expression blanked. "She didn't make it."

I went numb. I didn't know how to process the words that had slipped from his mouth. Relief, I realized. And, hot on its heels, shame for that relief.

"Baby." Calder leaned down, pressing his face against mine. "I'm so sorry. I didn't get there fast enough. I should've been with you."

I gripped his arms, holding on for dear life. "No. None of this is on you. It's on her." But I wasn't sure if that was even true. Calla was obviously sick, her mind twisted. "Toby," I whispered.

Calder straightened, taking my hands in his. "He and Jinx have been here every day. He's torn up."

"It's not his fault, either."

Calder traced a design on the back of my hand. "I think it'll help him to see you awake."

"How long was I out?"

A shadow passed over his eyes. "Almost a week. The last couple of days, you would wake up and were breathing on your own, but you weren't lucid. Hads, your heart stopped—" Calder's voice broke, tears slipping out of the corners of his eyes. "I almost lost you."

I lifted a hand and placed it over his heart. "I'm right here. I'm not going anywhere. You know how stubborn I am."

Calder slid a hand along my jaw to my neck. "I'm so damned glad for that stubborn streak."

"Me, too." I stared into eyes I knew almost as well as my own. "I love you."

"Always have, always will," he finished for me.

Something on my hand pressed against Calder's chest caught the light. I sucked in a sharp breath.

"What is it? Are you hurting? Should I get a nurse?"

Everything hurt, but I didn't give a damn about that at the moment. "What's on my finger?"

He lifted my hand off his chest, holding it up to the light. The diamond glittered in the sun. "It was my grandmother's. I've been waiting for the perfect moment to ask you, and then this happened. I needed it on your hand. Something to tether you to me…forever."

His gaze met mine. "Hadley, marry me."

Tears slipped from my eyes, falling down my cheeks. "Yes."

For the first time since my eyes opened, Calder smiled fully. "How about tomorrow?"

I laughed and immediately regretted the action, the wound on my chest sparking with pain.

"Shit, don't laugh." He pressed a button on my bed, and something beeped.

I laced my fingers through his. "One month. Enough time for me to get my sea legs back."

"One month." Calder brushed his mouth against mine in the barest of touches. It wasn't nearly enough, but we had forever for more.

My eyes fluttered against the light. It still felt like a battle at times to get them open again. The room came into focus, and I saw a figure sitting by my bed.

"Mom," I croaked.

"Here you go." She lifted the cup of water for me to take a sip. "How does that feel?"

"Better." Tears burned my eyes. What was it about being sick or hurt? The only person you wanted was your mom. I didn't think that would ever change. "Mom—"

She cut me off with a shake of her head. "I'm so sorry, sweet pea." She set the cup down on the table and took my hand. "I never dealt with it—your sister being taken. Not in the way I needed to. I'm seeing that more and more. Dr. Kensington is helping with that."

Tears glistened in my mother's eyes. "I love you more than breath. All my babies. I just want to keep you all safe, protected. Instead, I was the one who hurt you. God, Hadley. I've died a thousand deaths this past week. The thought that I might lose you, that our last encounters would have been ones of anger and frustration."

My chest burned, and it wasn't the stitches this time. I wanted to believe that we could make a fresh start. That I could have the mother I'd lost and missed like a limb since Shiloh was taken and everything changed. But there was so much hurt there. Piled up and left to fester.

She trailed her fingers over my hand the same way she'd always done when I wasn't feeling well. "We're going to get you healthy and home, and then you and I will have lots of long talks."

"I love you, Mom." That had never changed, even amidst the pain and strife.

"I love you more than life, sweet pea."

There was a commotion at the door.

"Don't give me a bunch of shit, Hayes. I wanted to make sure she had the flavor she wanted," a familiar voice griped.

"So, you bought twenty milkshakes?" Asked in an exasperated tone.

"It's only ten. So, sue me."

The tears fell now. "Beck?"

My oldest brother stepped into the room, a grin on his face. That grin fell as soon as he saw my face. "She's crying. Why is she crying? Are you hurting? Should I get your doctor?"

"Come here, you big oaf. I'm crying because I haven't seen my big brother in almost a year, and I missed him."

He handed the milkshakes to Hayes and strode over, sitting on the side of my bed. He leaned down and pressed a kiss to my temple. "Well, now you're going to be stuck with me."

I gripped his arms as if he might disappear again. "You're staying for a while?"

Hayes shook his head. "The prodigal son is moving back to Wolf Gap."

"Really?"

"Sure am. I'm taking over the practice for Doc."

The tears came faster. "You sure know how to give a girl a get-well gift."

He brushed the hair away from my face. "I'll be overseeing your recovery personally, so don't go trying to hide anything from me."

"Sir, yes, sir."

"Hads!" Birdie shouted.

Two tiny forms ran into the room, screeching to a halt on the other side of the bed.

Sage's eyes glittered with unshed tears. "You're okay? You're not gonna die?"

I reached out and squeezed her hand. "I'm going to be just

fine." I inclined my head towards Beckett. "I even have a personal doctor to make sure of it."

Birdie eyed Beckett carefully. "Do you know what you're doing?"

Hayes stifled a laugh, trying to turn it into a cough.

Beckett straightened on my bed. "I graduated at the top of my class."

"Okay, but I'll be watching you," Birdie warned.

I smiled, leaning over to kiss Birdie's head. "I missed you guys."

"We missed you, too," Birdie whispered.

The corners of Sage's mouth curved up. "Dad said you guys are gonna get married."

I looked up to see Calder leaning on the doorframe, so much love pouring off him, I swore I could feel it like a warm tide. "Would you guys like that?"

They both nodded. Birdie linked a finger with one of mine. "I don't like the mushy stuff, but I think I'd like it if you were my mom."

The tears began to fall as Calder moved in, taking Beckett's spot on my bed. He nodded encouragingly at me, and I turned back to Birdie and Sage. "If you want me, nothing would make me happier."

Sage smiled at me as her tears fell. "We always want you, Mom."

Sweeter words had never been spoken.

Epilogue

Hadley

ONE MONTH LATER

"**Y**OU LOOK BEAUTIFUL," MY MOM SAID AS SHE straightened the veil that hung down my back. But I also looked like *me*. Somehow, I'd kept wedding craziness in check and, surprisingly, my mother had only given me minimal pushback. The ceremony and party were small—just our families and a few close friends.

After the incident with Calla, I'd gained some notoriety for a while. Someone had made the connection between me and The Little Daredevil video channel, and the story had spun out of control from there. I had no desire for additional eyes on me anytime soon.

I might start the channel up again someday but for now, I simply wanted to live my life. To experience the freedom Calder had given me in so many ways. Most of all, to be myself and feel loved in all those incarnations.

I smoothed my hands down the dress. It was sort of boho chic with my brown cowboy boots peeking out from beneath the white. I turned, giving my mom a hug. "Love you."

"Love you, too."

"You're making me cry again," Everly said, dabbing at her eyes.

I shot my sister a look. "What about you, Shy? Any tears yet?"

She rolled her eyes. "I'm just glad you didn't stick us in some sort of pink taffeta."

Everly choked on a laugh. "That would've been epic."

"I'd never do that to you two."

Shy shifted, uncomfortable even in the more casual sundress she wore. "Thank God for small mercies."

"You know, it's not going to kill you to dress up for one danged day," Mom griped at Shiloh.

I covered my laugh with a cough. Shiloh sent me a dirty look. "I'm doing it, aren't I?"

Mom took a steadying breath. "You are, and today is going to be perfect."

It wouldn't be. Some sort of minor disaster would sideline some part of the ceremony or party. But that imperfection would only make today more meaningful, burning it into our memories a little bit more.

A knock sounded on the door.

"Who is it?" my mom asked.

"It's the father of the bride, ready to get this show on the road."

Everly opened the door. "Come on in, Gabe."

My dad stepped into the room and froze. "Hadley," he whispered.

I pointed a finger at him. "Don't you dare make me cry."

He sniffed but crossed to me, pulling me into his arms. "You're breathtaking. And you couldn't have picked a better man than Calder."

I held him tight for a few more seconds. "I know. I learned who the good ones were from my dad."

"Love you."

"Love you more." I straightened, looping my arm through his. "Let's do this."

Mom kissed my cheek and went downstairs with Shy and Everly. I didn't let go of my dad's arm as we followed.

Calder and I had decided to get married at the property that had once been mine and was now ours. The house had more life now with the four of us here. Shouting and laughter and love all seeping into its walls.

The music began, and Everly and Shiloh stepped out onto the back deck, making their way down a makeshift aisle lined with flowers.

Dad looked down at me. "Ready? I could always hide you in the back of my truck and make a getaway."

"I've wanted this for as long as I can remember."

He pressed a kiss to the top of my head. "I'm so glad you're getting your dream."

"Me, too."

With that, we stepped through the doors. I caught sight of the handful of guests. Hayes and Beckett standing next to Calder. Birdie and Sage in front of them in the dresses they'd picked out as honorary *groomsgirls* as they called themselves. But all of those sights were fleeting, my gaze yearning for Calder.

He took my breath away in his navy suit. His shirt was open at the collar, no tie, so perfectly Calder. But the eyes held me captive. Those dark depths that turned amber in the afternoon light.

It seemed as if a force born of the two of us carried me to him, a creation that would only ever be ours. My hands found his, and all felt right in the world.

"Hadley." My name was a gravelly whisper in his throat, both a ragged plea and an exaltation.

"I've loved you forever."

His eyes glistened with unshed tears. "Always have, always will."

We made vows that promised each other a lifetime of friendship and love and partnership. And when his lips met mine, that forever we'd almost lost began.

Acknowledgments

If you've read my books before you know I'm a big fan of gratitude and calling out the good in my life. It's honestly one of the most important things to my mental health and general happiness. From the big things to the small, marking them and counting them off reminds us of just how fortunate we are, even when things are hard. I'd like to start these acknowledgment gratitudes by thanking some of the amazing people who were so important to me as I wrote this book.

First, in my writerly world. Sam, your friendship has been such a gift. Your kindness and encouragement are such a balm to the soul. Thankful to share all the highs and lows of this crazy business and life! Willow and Laura, what would I do without you both? I truly don't know and never want to find out! #LoveChainForever. Emma, thank you for listening, empathizing, and encouraging. Forever grateful for the wormhole that brought us together. Grahame, for always being there to cheer me on or let me vent, and always keeping the best sense of humor through it all.

Second, in my non-writer world. My STS soul sisters: Hollis, Jael, and Paige, thank you for the gift of twenty years of your friendship and never-ending support. I love living life with you in every incarnation. My Charshie. My badass warrior. It is your strength that I want every single one of my heroines to have. You blow me away and I am forever grateful for your friendship.

And to all my family and friends near and far. Thank you for supporting me on this crazy journey, even if you don't read "kissing books." But you get extra special bonus points if you picked up one of mine, even if that makes me turn the shade of a tomato when you tell me.

To my fearless beta readers: Angela, Crystal, and Trisha, thank you for reading this book in its roughest form and helping me to make it the best it could possibly be!

The crew that helps bring my words to life and gets them out into the world is pretty darn epic. Thank you to Susan, Chelle, Janice, Julie, Hang, Stacey, Jenn, and the rest of my team at Social Butterfly. Your hard work is so appreciated!

To all the bloggers who have taken a chance on my words… THANK YOU! Your championing of my stories means more than I can say. And to my launch and ARC teams, thank you for your kindness, support, and sharing my books with the world. An extra special thank you to Crystal who sails that ship so I can focus on the words.

Ladies of Catherine Cowles Reader Group, you're my favorite place to hang out on the internet! Thank you for your support, encouragement, and willingness to always dish about your latest book boyfriends. You're the freaking best!

Lastly, thank YOU! Yes, YOU. I'm so grateful you're reading this book and making my author dreams come true. I love you for that. A whole lot!

Also Available from
CATHERINE COWLES

The Tattered & Torn Series
Tattered Stars
Falling Embers
Hidden Waters
Shattered Sea
Fractured Sky

The Wrecked Series
Reckless Memories
Perfect Wreckage
Wrecked Palace
Reckless Refuge
Beneath the Wreckage

The Sutter Lake Series
Beautifully Broken Pieces
Beautifully Broken Life
Beautifully Broken Spirit
Beautifully Broken Control
Beautifully Broken Redemption

Stand-alone Novels
Further To Fall

For a full list of up-to-date Catherine Cowles titles please visit
www.catherinecowles.com.

About

CATHERINE COWLES

Writer of words. Drinker of Diet Cokes. Lover of all things cute and furry, especially her dog. Catherine has had her nose in a book since the time she could read and finally decided to write down some of her own stories. When she's not writing, she can be found exploring her home state of Oregon, listening to true crime podcasts, or searching for her next book boyfriend.

Stay Connected

You can find Catherine in all the usual bookish places…

Website: catherinecowles.com

Facebook: facebook.com/catherinecowlesauthor

Catherine Cowles Facebook Reader Group: www.facebook.com/groups/CatherineCowlesReaderGroup

Instagram: instagram.com/catherinecowlesauthor

Goodreads: goodreads.com/catherinecowlesauthor

BookBub: bookbub.com/profile/catherine-cowles

Amazon: www.amazon.com/author/catherinecowles

Twitter: twitter.com/catherinecowles

Pinterest: pinterest.com/catherinecowlesauthor

Printed in Great Britain
by Amazon

46544795R00182